I0638992

Pentecostalism
Polyphonic Discourses

Pentecostalism
Polyphonic Discourses

Editors
Rajeevan Mathew Thomas
Josfin Raj S. B.

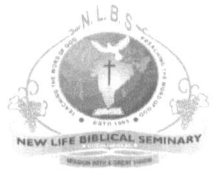

New Life Biblical Seminary (NLBS)
2019

Pentecostalism: Polyphonic Discourses- jointly published by the Rev. Dr. Ashish Amos of the Indian Society for Promoting Christian Knowledge (ISPCK), Post Box 1585, Kashmere Gate, Delhi-110006 and New Life Biblical Seminary (NLBS), Cheruvakkal, Ayoor, Kerala - 691533.

© NLBS, 2019

All rights reserved. No part of this book may be reproduced or transmitted in any form or by any means, electronic, mechanical, photocopying, recording, or by any information storage and retrieval system, without the prior permission in writing from the publisher.

The views expressed in the book are those of the contributors and the publisher takes no responsibility for any of the statements.

Online order: http://ispck.org.in/book.php

Also available on amazon.in

ISBN: 978-93-88945-04-02

Laser typeset by

ISPCK, Post Box 1585, 1654, Madarsa Road, Kashmere Gate, Delhi-110006 • *Tel:* 23866323

e-mail: ashish@ispck.org.in • ella@ispck.org.in
website: www.ispck.org.in

Contents

Preface

Indeed, it is a great privilege and joy to write a preface to our Silver Jubilee publication *Pentecostalism: Polyphonic Discourses*, an academic endeavor to contribute to the vast ocean of Pentecostal studies.

The New Life Biblical Seminary (NLBS), one of the leading Pentecostal seminaries in the global south, is the outcome of God's faithfulness to our parents. It is a historical manifestation of long cherished dream of my father (Late) Pastor C. K. Daniel, a traditional Pentecostal educator and one of the trailblazers of the Pentecostalism in Kerala. NLBS was founded in 1993 as an offshoot of the vision and burden of me and my wife Mrs. Lissy Johnson, for the land of India. As a fulfillment of the Great divine Commission, God in His abundant mercy has enabled us to launch this institution for the purpose of training young ones who have a definite call for the Lord's work and an aspiration to study the Word of God. For the last 25 years, we had the privilege to train and send 1500 full-time gospel workers to the different parts of the world. The major thrust of our mission comes from the Biblical vision of theological learning as it is found in II Tim. 2:15. It says: "Do your best to present yourself to God as one approved by Him, a worker who has no need to be ashamed, rightly explaining the word of truth" (NRSV). It is, thus, *A Mission with a Vision* which is precisely what we hold on as our motto. Our seminary is open to everyone who has a genuine commitment and dedication for Christian ministry. As an inter-denominational institution, we welcome students from all over India and abroad irrespective of the denominational and ecclesiastical confessions. It is our earnest prayer that the Almighty may continue to bestow His grace upon us as we seek to impart God's Word with wisdom, power and simplicity for the future generation.

I would really congratulate Rev. Dr. Rajeevan Mathew Thomas and Rev. Josfin Raj S.B for initiating this work and ISPCK for jointly publishing the work.

Your's in Christ,

Rev. Dr. Johnson Daniel
Founder & President
International New Life Ministries
New Life Biblical Seminary
IPC Vengoor District

Editorial

Pentecostal/Pentecostalism is a bamboozling term. It is being (mis)interpreted as a denomination, theology, ideology, empiricism, sect, a way of life, movement, and so on. Hence, it is a herculean task to apprehend this multifaceted aspect of Pentecostalism. To expound on this fact, we need profound readings rather than to stick on particular definition or interpretation. Therefore we deliberately choose the title – *Pentecostalism: Polyphonic Discourses*. Through this book, we anticipate to re-imagine holistic consensus on the theoretical and pragmatic framework of Pentecostalism from different perspectives like biblical, theological, historical, ministerial, missiological, sociological and so on. It would penetrate into global Pentecostalism and function as a guideline for further reflections to interface the challenges of the time.

This book comprises nine articles from various spheres of theological arenas to record the polyphony within the Pentecostal circle. David Shibley, in his article, proves Pentecostals have been faithfully following the unrepealed commission of Lord Jesus Christ. He argues that the vast majority of 'Great Commission Christians' have some identification as either Pentecostal or charismatic. He deliberately proposes the Pentecostalism is a

missiological praxis nexus with the sound moorings of Great
Commision. Hence, he emphatically persuades Pentecostal/
charismatic believers to stand obligatory for the evangelization
of the world.

M. Stephen and V. V. Thomas have looked at Pentecostalism
from a postmodern and post colonial perspectives.
M. Stephen has justified that Pentecostalism is a postmodern
and postcolonial movement. It examines the elements of
postmodernism and post colonialism found in Pentecostalism.
He discusses Pentecostalism is a vital movement characterized
with liberative, friendly nature and try to challenge anti-social
hegemonies and structures. He re-envisions Pentecostalism from
a theological and ethical perception. However, his writing is also
a prophetic warning to the institutionalization of contemporary
churches. V. V. Thomas shared the problems and challenges
that Pentecostalism as a thriving movement had to face in the
postmodern era. He understands the history of modern
Pentecostal movement over against the background of
people's quest for empowerment, particularly dalits. In
addition, he proposes valuable suggestions to the Indian
Pentecostal churches to redirect their mission and ministry
towards the empowerment of the downtrodden people.

Raju M. Thomas and Shaibu Abraham contribute Pentecostal
understanding of diabolism and exorcism respectively. Raju
M. Thomas derivates it from a New Testament perspective
where as Shaibu depicts Jesus as an exorcist to competent
enough to transform the integral life of the ordinary people
in India from a christological point of view.

John Thannickal articulates Pentecostal pneumatology
to face mundane human barriers. He explores his study
exclusively from a scriptural point of view. Josfin Raj argues that

Pentecostalism is a viable and alternative Christian philosophy or worldview embedded with spiritual and existential outlook.

Viju Wilson has tried to re-read and re-define the Pentecostal evangelism from a subaltern point of view. He argues that Pentecostal evangelism in India must be rooted in wholistic empowerment. From the department of history and culture, Rajeevan Mathew Thomas has taken a significant study to articulate the unique culture of south Indian Pentecostals. He has succeeded in drawing Pentecostal cultural contours for South Indian Pentecostalism.

New Life Biblical Seminary, being a premier theological academy in south India, took a serious challenge on the eve of her Silver Jubilee festive to listen and record multiple voices reverberated within the Pentecostal orbit. This book is a crystallization of such endeavor. We anticipate this book would regenerate further open-ended discourses and interactions.

We record our sincere thanks and appreciation to New Life community specially Rev. Dr. Johnson Daniel (founder president of NLBS) and Mr. Sam C. Daniel (Admin Officer) for their holistic support and encouragement. Further, we thank all the contributors who availed their valuable scholarship for this academic piece. Finally, we would like to thank ISPCK for publishing this work.

Editors
Rajeevan Mathew Thomas
Josfin Raj S. B.

Pentecostal Missiological Praxis and "The Great Unrepealed Commission"

David Shibley

God's Spirit is ever pointing in one direction - toward the preeminence of Jesus Christ. And He is ever pressing us toward one great goal – the fulfilling of the Great Commission.

Jesus left the Great Commission as His last words on earth to underscore, not diminish, its importance. He was echoing the heartbeat of His Father, an aggressive compassion that had always characterized God's dealing with humanity. The commission Jesus left His followers is not a nice suggestion; it is a mandate from our resurrected Lord. World evangelization is a supernatural enterprise that can only be accomplished by an enduring of supernatural power.

The Bible's integrating theme is the awesome story of how God Himself intervened to save His fallen creation, bent on self-destruction. There is a scarlet thread of redemption that runs throughout the Scriptures. God's eternal purpose is to call out a bride for His Son from fallen humanity. The composition of this bride will be redeemed people "from every tribe and language and people and nation" (Rev. 5:9).[1]

The Father-heart of God bleeds through all of Scripture. The apostle Paul, who said we were to "owe no one anything" (Rom. 13:8), in the same letter said that he had incurred a tremendous debt. "I am under obligation both to Greeks and to barbarians, both to the wise and to the foolish. So I am eager to preach the gospel to you also who are in Rome. For I am not ashamed of the gospel, for it is the power of God for salvation for everyone who believes, to the Jew first and also to the Greek" (Rom. 1:14-16).

Peter, as well, understood that God's great longing is to redeem humankind. In fact, the whole timetable for Christ's return is somehow tied to ensuring that the last person in the global family of faith is brought in. "The Lord is not slow to fulfill his promise as some count slowness, but is patient toward you; not wishing that any should perish but that all should reach repentance" (2 Pet. 3:9).

The writer of Hebrews says that because of Christ's sacrifice the potential of redemption reaches every person on Earth. "But we see him who for a little while was made lower than the angels, crowned with glory and honor because of the suffering of death, so that by the grace of God he might taste death for everyone" (Heb. 2:9).

The Bible is so abundantly laced with the missions mandate that it may not be fully accurate to speak of "the biblical rationale for missions." The Bible itself, the whole testimony of God's activity, is the rationale for missions. For the purposes of this article, I concur with the definitions suggested by missiologist Avery Willis: "*Mission* is the total redemptive purpose of God to establish His kingdom. *Missions*, on the other hand, is the activity of God's people, the church, to proclaim and to demonstrate the kingdom of God to the world."[2]

The explicit commitment of God the Father is to increase the rule and reach of His Son until Christ's benevolent kingdom encompasses the entire earth. "Of the increase of his government and of peace there will be no end." God the Father is passionately committed to see this consummation of all things in Christ. "The zeal of the Lord of hosts will do this" (Isa. 9:7). Any expression of the Christian faith that is devoid of a global context is not biblical Christianity. As Calvin Miller wrote, "Jesus loves widely, and if we have not seen the Savior in love with the whole world, we have not seen the whole Savior."[3]

For the kingdom of Christ to be fully revealed His followers must give His commission high priority. Our Lord's mandate to take the gospel to every person and make disciples of all peoples and nations remains in effect. As the venerated missionary Amy Carmichael observed, it is His "great, unrepealed commission."[4]

A primary thesis of this article is that the vast majority of "Great Commission Christians" have some identification as either Pentecostals or charismatics. It follows, then, that Pentecostal/charismatic believers stand most accountable for the evangelization of the world. This in no way diminishes the role that non-Pentecostal evangelicals have played and continue to play. Since the days of William Carey, they have been at the forefront of the world Christian movement. Pentecostals and charismatics must remember the immense debt we owe our traditional evangelical brothers and sisters. Yet, while we acknowledge with thanksgiving the pioneering work of other evangelicals, we must humbly yet honestly ask who is best suited to invade the final frontiers. Surely it will take supernatural spiritual dynamics to break through the obstacles preventing the final ingathering.

In the last few decades, the momentum for world evangelization has, in my opinion, shifted to those who would refer to themselves either as Pentecostals or charismatics. A large part of the reason for this is the sheer number of Pentecostals/ charismatics. According to the Global Status of Christianity there are now some 669 million Pentecostals/charismatics worldwide. The number of non-Pentecostal evangelicals is roughly 342 million.[5] The *Atlas of Global Christianity* reports that, of the world's two billion plus who embrace the name of Christian, some 700 million are "Great Commission Christians." As defined by the atlas, Great Commission Christians are "believers in Jesus Christ who are aware of the Great Commission, have accepted its personal challenge in their lives and ministries, and are seeking to influence the Body of Christ to implement it."[6]As I noted years ago in *A Force in the Earth*, "World evangelization can never be accomplished by charismatics alone. Neither can it be realized without us."[7]

However, Pentecostals/charismatics are not reaching their evangelistic potential. Nor are they as effective as they should be in making believers ardent disciples of Christ. A major reason for this is distraction and deception that allows something other than the gospel to be center stage. Millard Erickson states that the gospel is "the element which lies at the heart of all [the church's] functions"; it is the "heart of the ministry of the Church."[8]We must lamentably acknowledge that the gospel has not always been at the heart of all our functions over the last several years. As we celebrate the 500th anniversary of the Reformation, may God bring us back to the centrality of the gospel and our primary task of getting this Good News to the world. R. T. Kendall recently challenged us, "I believe we need a new Reformation today, a reawakening of the true gospel of God: the good news that you will go to heaven when you die – and not to hell – by transferring your trust in your good works to what Jesus Christ, the Son of God, did for you on the cross."[9] We are saved by grace alone, justified by faith alone, and redeemed by Christ alone. May this liberating message once again ring loud and clear from every Spirit-empowered church and ministry. As the Lausanne Covenant eloquently affirms, "We rejoice that, even when borne by earthen vessels, the gospel is still a precious treasure. To the task of making that treasure known in the power of the Holy Spirit we desire to dedicate ourselves anew."[10]

The Holy Spirit and the Gospel

The Reformation was not so much a discovery as it was a recovery. Luther recovered the gospel and again acknowledged the gospel as our greatest treasure and our supreme gift to the world. For Pentecostals/charismatics to rise to their God-ordained destiny in this hour, we too must recover the primacy of the gospel. Ed Stetzer, director of the Billy Graham Center, writes, "[A] missional response requires seeing the gospel not as merely the entry fee to Christianity but as the currency of the Christian life."[11] The natural response of a gospel-centric life is the desire for those who do not know Jesus to know Him.

I fully agree with Ed Silvoso's assessment that world missions must be at the core of how we view Scripture and life itself. "I believe the only way to adequately interpret the Scriptures is through the framework of the Great Commission," writes Silvoso. "Every promise, every command in the Bible will be misunderstood (by much or by little) when we fail to interpret it in the light of the Lord's command to win the world for Him. The Bible was written to demonstrate God's love for the lost and His provision for their salvation. Therefore, I contend, the Word can only be fully understood through a missiological grid. God so loved the world that He sent His Son to save it. In order to understand the Son, the Word Himself, we must view Him through His redemptive mission."[12]

God's Spirit is ever pointing people to Jesus. "But when the Helper comes, whom I will send to you from the Father, the Spirit of truth, who proceeds from the Father, he will bear witness about me" (Jn. 15:26). Missiologist Gary Tyra writes, "The Holy Spirit is all about the enablement of Christ's followers to glorify the Father, in the name of the Son, in such a way as to encourage lost and hurting human beings to accept the invitation to join the divine dance, experiencing justification, sanctification and empowerment for ministry themselves in the process."[13] That is why some writers refer to the Holy Spirit as "the go-between God." The power in the gospel is the Spirit's work in applying the work of Christ to us personally.

When we believed the gospel "he saved us, not because of the righteous things we had done, but because of his mercy. He washed away our sins, giving us a new birth and new life by the Holy Spirit" (Titus 3:5, NLT). The Spirit of God takes the message of God and drives it deep into hearts.

The apostle Paul prayed that believers might know "what is the immeasurable greatness of his power toward us to believe, according to the working of his great might that he worked in Christ when he raised him from the dead and seated him at his right hand in the heavenly places" (Eph. 1:19-20). The same meta-power that raised Jesus from the dead is now working in us to raise us to the destiny for which we were born – and born again.

The Holy Spirit is all over the proclaiming of the gospel and the applying of its benefits. It is the Holy Spirit who –

i.   *Convinces us of our need of a Savior.* "And when he comes, he will convict the world concerning sin and righteousness and judgment" (Jn. 16:8).

ii. *Anoints the preaching of the gospel.* "[O]ur gospel came to you not only in word, but also in power and in the Holy Spirit and with full conviction. You know what kind of men we proved to be among you for your sake" (1 Thess. 1:5).

iii. *Makes us new through the gospel.* "[H]e saved us, not because of works done by us in righteousness, but according to his own mercy, by the washing of regeneration and renewal of the Holy Spirit" (Titus 3:5).

iv. *Seals and protects our standing with God.* "In him you also, when you heard the word of truth, the gospel of your salvation, were sealed with the promised Holy Spirit" (Eph. 1:13).

v.   *Pours God's love into us and through us.* "God's love has been poured into our hearts through the Holy Spirit who has been given to us" (Rom. 5:5).

vi. *Empowers us as witnesses for Christ.* "But you will receive power when the Holy Spirit has come upon you, and you will be my witnesses in Jerusalem and in all Judea and Samaria, and to the end of the earth" (Acts. 1:8).

vii. *Produces Christ-like fruit in our lives.* "But the fruit of the Spirit is love, joy, peace, patience, kindness, goodness, faithfulness, gentleness, self-control; against such things there is no law" (Gal. 5:22-23).

viii. *Gifts us for effective service.* "Now there are varieties of gifts but the same Spirit . . . All these are empowered by one and the same Spirit, who apportions to each one individually as he wills" (1 Cor. 12:4, 11).

ix. Moves us toward maturity in Christ. "For all who are led by
the Spirit of God are the sons of God" (Rom. 8:14).

Why is this immense power made available to gospel believers?
For us to launch a global movement, not of terror but, on the
contrary, of compassion. Our weapons are entirely different
from those employed by other armies and militias. And no
effective counter has yet been found to our weapons! In our
arsenal of power we have the power of the Spirit Himself, who
then activates the power inherent in the gospel, the Scriptures,
the name of Jesus, the blood of Jesus, and the love of Jesus.

This is the reason that the Spirit empowers us. He desires
that we become, as esteemed evangelist T. L. Osborn said, "a
mighty army whose soldiers of love are to reach every land
and plant Christ's banner of salvation in every nation! As
ambassadors of the King of kings, the Christian's business is
to evangelize every land and 'take out of them a people for
His name' (Acts. 15:14). This is the purpose of Pentecost."[14]

Frankly, I believe all Christians who are truly Spirit-filled
are pre-set toward evangelism and missions. When the Holy
Spirit descended on the Day of Pentecost Peter's powerful
evangelistic message resulted in thousands of converts. When
believers prayed for boldness in Acts 4, God answered by filling
them with the Holy Spirit so that they boldly proclaimed the
good news. Robert Coleman notes, "People full of the Holy
Spirit are committed to God's work. They want to be where
laborers are needed most, and there is no more pressing need
than bringing the gospel to hell-bound men and women."[15]

As resistance to the gospel mounts there is an increased
need for what many refer to as power encounters. In Jesus'
ministry and in the ministries of the early Christian disciples,

some kind of power encounter often verified their Spirit-anointed announcement of the good news. These encounters are visible demonstrations that Jesus can overrule anything or anyone who tries to defy Him. John Wimber noted, "Any system or force that must be overcome for the gospel to be believed is cause for a power encounter."[16]

At a time of acute discouragement, John the Baptist requested reassurance that Jesus was indeed the Messiah. Jesus responded, "Go and tell John the things which you hear and see: The blind receive their sight and the lame walk; the lepers are cleansed and the deaf hear; the dead are raised up and the poor have the gospel preached to them" (Matt. 11:4-5). Jesus saw these miracles, or power encounters, as the verifying credentials of His ministry.

The only New Testament model we have for the ministry of the evangelist is Philip. The report of Philip's evangelistic event in Samaria is also a model for effective evangelism today. "Philip went down to the city of Samaria and proclaimed to them the Christ. And the crowds with one accord paid attention to what was being said by Philip, when they heard him and saw the signs that he did. For unclean spirits, crying out with a loud voice, came out of many who had them, and many who were paralyzed or lame were healed. So there was much joy in that city" (Acts 8:5-8).

Notice that Philip's audience did not just hear; they *heard and saw*. Philip's evangelistic ministry was first and foremost preaching the gospel of Jesus Christ. However, his preaching was augmented by a deliverance ministry and the working of miracles. The Scripture suggests that the people were not convinced of the veracity of Philip's message by his preaching alone. They "paid attention to what was being said by Philip, when they heard him and saw the signs that he did."

Paul said he brought the nations to obey the gospel "in word and deed . . . in mighty signs and wonders, by the power of the Spirit of God" (Rom. 15:18-19). Using this strategy of gospel proclamation, compassionate works done in Jesus' name, and miracles, Paul said, "I have fulfilled the ministry of the gospel of Christ" (Rom. 15:19). As Pentecostal theologian Gordon Fee observed, "Paul . . . frequently refers to his own effective ministry as a direct result of the work of the Spirit. This work included not only conviction concerning the truth of the gospel, but also signs and wonders, all of which resulted in changed lives."[17]Deeds of compassion generated by the gospel, along with miracles performed by the living Christ help authenticate the gospel of Christ, demonstrate the reality of the kingdom of Christ, and remove barriers to the reception of Christ.

The Gospel of Mark concludes by saying that the ascended Christ continued to empower His disciples as they shared the gospel, "validating the Message with indisputable evidence" (Mk. 16:20, MSG).[18] T. L. Osborn noted, "Whether it is Peter in traditional Jerusalem, Philip in immoral Samaria, or Paul on the pagan island of Melita, the same results always followed; they proclaimed the gospel, miracles were in evidence, and multitudes believed and were added to the church."[19]

Too often today we have softened the gospel's demands and replaced its glory with lesser agendas. The church (sadly including many Pentecostal/charismatic assemblies) frequently has been guilty of trading in a robust gospel for an anemic façade. We've capped the wells of living water with unbelief.

Let's get back to the gospel of Jesus Christ! When the gospel is preached we need to expect Jesus to show up in power. But when He shows up things can get uncomfortable, especially for those who "have a form of godliness, although they have denied its power" (2 Tim. 3:5, NASB). As believers in Jesus, let's open the tap and believe that living water can gush from us to thirsty seekers (Jn. 7:38). We have ample biblical and historical precedent for expecting just that.

May God raise up mighty gospel proclaimers for this hour! And may you be one of them. We are in need of preachers who will "preach the good news to you by the Holy Spirit sent down from heaven" (1 Pet. 1:12). We need marketplace missionaries who will bring the glory of Jesus into businesses and turn them into bases for evangelism and discipleship. We need hybrid healing evangelists who are also brilliant apologists. We need anointed media evangelists who have Holy Spirit savvy to leverage social media to give the gospel the largest possible audience and impact. We need steady, Spirit-filled witnesses for Christ in every arena of human interaction who will be salt and light in this decaying, dark culture.

The mighty work of the Spirit will keep changing us until we ultimately are conformed into the very image of Christ. "And we all, with unveiled face, beholding the glory of the Lord, are being transformed into the same image from one degree of glory to another. For this comes from the Lord who is the Spirit" (2 Cor. 3:18). Jerry Bridges noted, "As we behold the glory of the Lord as reflected in the gospel, the Holy Spirit uses the gospel as one of His transforming instruments."[20] No other message has such astounding power.

Supernatural Power for a Supernatural Commission

Charles Spurgeon was known as the Prince of Preachers. Part of his immense legacy was imparting wisdom to younger preachers. Spurgeon understood well the interplay between our Lord's commission to us and the attendant supernatural power necessary for its fulfillment. "Without Him our office is a mere name. . . If we have not the Spirit which Jesus promised, we cannot perform the commission which Jesus gave."[21]

Our job is to get the gospel to everyone everywhere. We may start with the friend next door, the person whose desk is next to ours, or perhaps a family member under the same roof. Every breathing human needs Jesus. "I am under obligation both to Greeks and to barbarians," Paul wrote, "both to the wise and to the foolish. So I am eager to preach the gospel to you also who are in Rome" (Rom. 1:14-15).

I am convinced that the gospel is not truncated. In the New Testament, I find no evidence for the "two gospels" theory often purported today; a "gospel of salvation" and a "gospel of the kingdom." I believe the New Testament presents one all-sufficient gospel of Jesus Christ. God's grace is its content and His kingdom is its context. Just as there is only one gospel, there is only one commission. Evangelism (bringing people to Christ) and discipleship (growing believers in Christ) are two parts of a single mandate.

Jesus issued what we term the Great Commission in some form in each of the Gospels and also in the Book of Acts. Each time there is an attending promise of supernatural power. In Matthew 28:18-19 before Jesus said, "Go therefore and make disciples of all nations," He affirmed, "All authority in heaven and on earth has been given to me." In Mark 16:15 Jesus commanded His disciples to preach the gospel to every person. Then He promised that signs confirming the gospel will attend those who believe. In Luke 24 He told His disciples they would be witnesses of the things they had seen. But stay in the city until you are clothed with power from on high" (v. 49). In John 20:21-22 Jesus commissioned His disciples, "As the Father has sent me, even so I am sending you." Then immediately He breathed on them and said, "Receive the Holy Spirit." In Acts 1:8 Jesus rebuked activism devoid of spiritual power. How motivated the disciples must have been when the resurrected Christ commanded them to evangelize the world! But then He cooled their heels saying, "Go, but not just yet." Before they became His witnesses, they needed to be empowered by His Spirit.

That same supernatural power to bear witness to the gospel is available to us in this present, throbbing moment. Even as threats against the gospel intensify we can carry the gospel with joyful confidence. This is a prayer God loves to answer because the results always bring glory to His Son: "And now, Lord, look on their threats and grant to your servants to continue to speak your word with all boldness, while you stretch out your hand to heal, and signs and wonders are performed through the name of your holy servant Jesus" (Acts. 4:29-30). In response, just as He filled those early disciples, He will fill us with His Spirit so we too can proclaim God's good news with boldness.

One day the Great Commission will be the Great Completion. Everything will find its consummation in Jesus Christ. His rule will be universal (Isa. 9:7). All kings and governments will bow to His rule (Rev. 11:15). This will be the Spirit's work throughout the earth. Then there will be new-born people from "all nations, tribes, peoples, and tongues, standing before the throne and before the Lamb" (Rev. 7:9). Between now and then we are God's delegated witnesses to reach every person on Earth with His message.

This will require the Spirit's power and the activation of all His gifts in His people. While the primary function of spiritual gifts is the edification of believers, there is often an evangelistic component, as well, in the use of these gifts. "The testimony of Jesus is the spirit of prophecy" (Rev.19:10). Cessationism as a dominant doctrine has seen its day. It seems an anomaly that some of those who most loudly support biblical inerrancy (which I too endorse) are also cessationists. When it comes to a rationale for cessationism, some otherwise conservative scholars can sound quite liberal. After all, the essence of liberal biblical interpretation is to either downplay or disregard the obvious intent of Scripture. This is what cessationism does.

Most cessationists will always consider Pentecostal/ charismatic doctrine and experience somehow "sub-biblical." But it is cessationists who have constructed a convoluted hermeneutic. While in seminary I was often reminded that we show respect to the Scriptures by careful exegesis. Yet to interpret Paul's 1 Corinthians 13 phrase, "when the perfect comes" to mean "when the Canon is closed," as many cessationists do, is to resort to weak, even embarrassing eisegesis.

We disagree with cessationists regarding present day manifestations of the Spirit. But this is an issue of interpretation, not authority. With conservative evangelicals who are cessationists we too affirm that the Bible is completely true, without any mixture of error, and the final arbiter in all matters of faith and practice.

We must rely on supernatural power, the power of the Holy Spirit, to complete the task of world evangelization. Avery Willis reminded us, "The Holy Spirit is the executor and the administrator of the Great Commission. He, rather than the Great Commission, is the motivator of missions."[22] At the same time, it is the Spirit who breathes God's passion for the global worship of His Son into us. He quickens us to be "Great Commission Christians." His anointing and power are dispensed to those who serve God's mission. Charismatic theologian Larry Hart writes, "Both Luke and John link closely commissioning and anointing, the mission and the Spirit. In Matthew's Great Commission the emphasis is on discipleship expressed through the baptizing and teaching ministries of the church (Matt. 28:18-20). Mark adds a note of condemnation for those who reject the gospel and mentions charismatic 'signs' that will accompany the mission (Mark 16:15-18). But John, briefly, and Luke, more extensively, highlight the Spirit's role in the Church's mission."[23]

We are to go to "every nation" (*ethnos*, Matt. 28:19), "to the ends of the earth" (*eschatos*, Acts 1:8). In John's vision recorded in Revelation 5:9, he describes redeemed men and women coming from "every tribe (*phule*), tongue (*glossa*), people (*laos*), and nation (*ethnos*). Concerning the inclusive nature of Christ's commission and the scope of these words in the original language, respected Pentecostal teacher Jack Hayford observes, "Here is scriptural evidence that the Holy Spirit has literally ransacked our language to confront us with adequate and specific terminology indicating the detailed nature of our assignment to evangelize *everyone*."[24]

What Drove the Early Pentecostals?

"The ultimate reason and goal for the Pentecostal gifting was world evangelization among the unreached," writes Pentecostal missiologist Grant McClung.[25] Aligning our thinking with God's heart, the Holy Spirit makes the Great Commission a holy imperative to us.

In the inception of the modern Pentecostal movement at the Azusa Street Mission in Los Angeles, the emphasis was first evangelism, not supernatural phenomena. William Seymour was the acknowledged leader of these meetings. His pastoral admonition to those attending these thrilling gatherings was, "Now, do not go from this meeting and talk about tongues, but try to get people saved."[26]

Remarkably, one of the earliest expressions of an emerging Pentecostal missiology was written by a young man only twenty years old. Even more remarkable was the fact that he had only been converted a year earlier. Yet in 1908 J. Roswell Flower would pen this incisive observation of the relationship of the baptism in the Holy Spirit to world evangelization: "The baptism of the Holy Ghost does not consist in simply speaking in tongues. No. It has much more grand and deeper meaning than that. It fills our souls with the love of God for lost humanity, and makes us much more willing to leave home, friends, and all to work in His vineyard, even if it be far away among the heathen. . . . 'Go ye into all the world and preach the gospel to every creature.' This command of Jesus can only be properly fulfilled when we have obeyed that other command, 'Tarry ye in the city of Jerusalem until ye be endued with power from on high.' When we have tarried and received that power, then, and only then are we fit to carry the gospel. When the Holy Spirit comes into our hearts, the missionary spirit comes with it; they are inseparable . . . Carrying the gospel to hungry souls in this and other lands is but a natural result of receiving the baptism of the Holy Ghost."[27]

There remains much discussion regarding the evidence of the baptism with the Holy Spirit. But all Bible-believing Christians should agree that an indisputable evidence of being filled with the Spirit is a holy boldness that expresses itself in evangelistic impetus. In response to early believers' petition for boldness, "they were all filled with the Holy Spirit and continued to speak the word of God with boldness" (Acts. 4:31). Referencing Pentecostal and charismatic churches, a friendly outside observer, theologian Arthur Glasser, wrote, "The achievements of their churches are . . . impressive, reflecting their settled conviction that the full experience of the Holy Spirit will not only move the Church closer to Jesus at its center, but at the same time, press the Church to move out into the world in missions."[28]

Having experienced the risen Christ ourselves, we long to bring His light and life to others. We are also more sensitized to the lost condition of those who do not know Him. The fruit of the Spirit enables us to see people as God sees them and respond with His love. "God's love has been poured into our hearts by the Holy Spirit who has been given to us" (Rom. 5:5).

We are fortified as gospel carriers by what Christ has bequeathed to us. Larry Hart writes, "The church has been given the two primary ingredients for success in her mission: authority (*exousia*, dominical authorization, Matt. 28:18) and power (*dynamis*, supernatural enablement, Acts 1:8). Culminating these provisions is the promise of our Lord's personal presence with us: 'And remember, I am with you always, to the end of the age' (Matt. 28:20). We are an *evangelistic* people. We are a

good news people. We come with a message that *lifts* people. . .
. Christians are simply purveyors of *abundant life* . . . in Jesus
Christ!"[29]

The gospel is the power of God for salvation – not for
everyone automatically – but for all who believe on the Lord
Jesus Christ (Rom. 1:16; 10:9). But the gospel must be *proclaimed*
in order to be *believed*. "How then will they call on him in
whom they have not believed? And how are they to believe
in him of whom they have not heard? And how are they to
hear without someone preaching?" (Rom. 10:14).

The story of Cornelius dramatically illustrates this. Cornelius
was devout, prayed often, was well respected, gave generously
to the poor, and even had an angelic visitation. These are
strong credentials. Yet God went to great lengths to get the
gospel to him so he could come to faith in Christ and be saved!
The biblical account clearly shows that Peter did not consider
Cornelius forgiven of his sins until he believed the message
of the gospel. In fact, the angel instructed Cornelius to send
for Peter, "he will declare to you a message by which you will
be saved" [future tense] (Acts. 11:14). The good works of
religious Cornelius did not and could not save him. He had
to hear and then believe the gospel.

All the gospel "invitations" in the New Testament are in
the imperative mood. The gospel is not a choice to consider,
it is a command either to obey or reject. You can forestall an
invitation with nebulous niceties. But you must either obey or
reject a command. The gospel doesn't merely invite belief. It
demands it. "Repent, and believe in the gospel" (Mk. 1:15).

Christianity by its very nature is evangelistic. Evangelism
is based on the assumption, massively supported by Scripture,

that people who are without Jesus Christ are lost. We are on a rescue mission with eternal consequences. If people are lost without Christ (and they are), and if faith in Christ is the only avenue of salvation (and it is), what could possibly be a higher priority than getting the gospel as far as we can as fast as we can?

Still, for many there seems to be a dark canopy over the truth of the gospel. They just don't get it; they just can't see it. Paul addressed this when he noted, "And even if our gospel is veiled, it is veiled to those who are perishing. In their case the god of this world has blinded the minds of unbelievers, to keep them from seeing the light of the gospel of the glory of Christ, who is the image of God" (2 Cor. 4:3-4).

Evangelism then involves not only the convincing of the mind but also the unshackling of the will. This is the Spirit's work. It is a spiritual eye surgery on those who have been blinded by unbelief. That is why intercessory prayer is so crucial to our gospel efforts. Through prayer we can wrench people out from the hold of the enemy, freeing their minds and wills to accept the gospel message. Antecedent to any great move of God, someone somewhere has been weeping instead of sleeping, agonizing before God for those who have not yet come to Jesus.

Until All Have Heard

Missiologist David Howard declared, "The largest manifestation of the presence of Christ is to those that are obedient to his missionary command. Have you ever reflected upon it that the baptism of the Holy Spirit is invariably associated with testimony and witness bearing? If we would have the Holy Spirit working with mighty power in all our communities – and is this not our greatest need? – we shall have this experience as we walk in the pathway of our missionary Leader in obedience to His command."[30]

Jesus prophesied, "And because lawlessness will be increased, the love of many will grow cold. But the one who endures to the end will be saved. And this gospel of the kingdom will be proclaimed throughout the whole world as a testimony to all nations, and then the end will come" (Matt. 24:12-14). He warned that the love impulse of many would be choked off in violent times. In other words, there is a natural tendency to "circle the wagons" and give our focus and energy to self-preservation. Tragically, many Christians today are in no mood to do anything redemptive for the rest of the world. Yet it should not be so, it must not be so, for those who claim to be filled with God's Spirit. Jesus prophesied that in the midst of a climate of global anger and recrimination the gospel would go to every nation and people. If we are to respond to the crisis of our times in a God-glorifying way we must recommit ourselves to fulfilling the Great Commission.

"But understand this," Paul counseled, "in the last days there will come times of difficulty" (2 Tim. 3:1, NASB). In a real sense these are both the best and worst of times. We cannot be reticent in our gospel witness. Jesus taught that those who are self-protective are actually the most at risk. "For whoever would save his life will lose it, but whoever loses his life for my sake and the gospel's will save it" (Mk. 8:34-35).

Anti-conversion laws are springing up in many countries as hostility to Christians mounts. Many places are beginning to experience the cost of following Christ in dimensions previously not experienced. For the first time the United States was listed as one of 12 countries to watch in regard to persecution by anti-persecution advocate International Christian Concern. Meanwhile, a similar ministry, Open Doors USA, noted that persecution against Christians worldwide increased in 2016. Christians in many parts of the Middle East and Asia are experiencing intensified opposition. The number one agent cited in that increase was religious extremism.[31]

Ours is the position of *The Millennial Manifesto* crafted by the AD 2000 and Beyond Movement: "We reject all forms of coercive proselytism and manipulative pressure, but uphold the right of persons to become followers of Jesus in response to the conviction of the Holy Spirit."[32]

Speaking the truth in love, as the Bible tells us to do, is not hate speech. It is mandated in Scripture, motivated by love, and part of what it means to have freedom of speech. Nor should earnest appeals, born out of love and concern, be considered manipulative. No one, no matter what his faith may be, should ever be prevented from urging others to embrace a conviction he firmly believes. Vishal and Ruth Mangalwadi remind us, "Freedom of conscience is incomplete without the freedom to change one's beliefs, to convert. A state that hinders conversion is uncivilized because it restricts the human quest for truth and reform."[33] Therefore, we contend that the most basic of all human rights is the right to hear the gospel and respond either positively or negatively without fear of reprisal.

Whether we speak freely or under threats, still we must speak. "For we cannot but speak the things which we have seen and heard" (Ac. 4:20). The most benevolent activity possible – the activity that undergirds all other ministry – is evangelism, telling the good news of salvation through Jesus Christ.

This is a call for all Spirit-empowered believers to recommit to "the great, unrepealed commission." We gladly join all true Christians "to pray for such a visitation of the sovereign Spirit of God that all his fruit may appear in all his people and that all his gifts may enrich the body of Christ. Only then will the whole Church become a fit instrument in his hands, that the whole earth may hear his voice."[34]

On the day Jesus walked up Calvary's hill the ultimate triumph of the gospel was irrevocably secured. A "kingdom beachhead" has been established that will ultimately blanket the entire earth. Victory is now inevitable. So lift up your head and "continue in the faith, grounded and steadfast . . . not moved away from the hope of the gospel" (Col. 1:23). The Father has sworn by His own name that He will bring global glory to His Son. When all the smoke finally clears, every knee will bow to Him. (Phil. 2:9-11). As William Carey wrote after he had suffered his greatest setback, "God's cause will triumph."[35]

"For the earth will be filled with the knowledge of the glory of the Lord as the waters cover the sea" (Hab. 2:14).

Endnotes

[1] Unless otherwise noted, Scripture quotations are from The English Standard Version of the Bible.

[2] Avery T. Willis, Jr., *The Biblical Basis of Missions* (Nashville, TN: Convention Press, 1984), 11.

[3] Calvin Miller, *The Taste of Joy* (Downers Grove, IL: InterVarsity Press, 1983), 120.

[4] See Elisabeth Elliot, *A Chance to Die: The Life and Legacy of Amy Carmichael* (Old Tappan, NJ: Fleming H. Revell, reprint 2005).

[5] See the details, http://www.gordonconwell.edu/ockenga/research/documents/StatusofGlobalChristianity2017.pdf, www.lausanne.org.

[6] Todd M. Johnson and Kenneth R. Ross, eds., *Atlas of Global Christianity*, 2009, 290-293.

[7] David Shibley, *A Force in the Earth: The Move of the Holy Spirit in World Evangelization* (Lake Mary, FL: Creation House, 1989, 1997), 18.

[8] Millard Erickson, *Introducing Christian Doctrine*, edited by L. Arnold Hustad, (Grand Rapids, MI: Baker, 1992), 340.

[9] R. T. Kendall, "Whatever Happened to the Gospel?" *Charisma* (October 2017), 24.

[10] John Stott, *For the Lord We Love: Your Study Guide to The Lausanne Covenant* (The Lausanne Movement, 2009), 12.

[11] Ed Stetzer, "Issues in the Future of Evangelicalism," June 29, 2016.

[12] Ed Silvoso, *Prayer Evangelism* (Ventura, CA: Regal Books, 2000), 127.

[13] Gary Tyra, *The Holy Spirit in Mission* (Downers Grove, IL: IVP Academic, 2011), 31.

[14] T. L. Osborn, *The Purpose of Pentecost* (Tulsa, OK: The Osborn Foundation, 1963), 105.

[15] Robert E. Coleman, *The Coming World Revival* (Wheaton, IL: Crossway Books, 1995), 155.

[16] John Wimber with Kevin Springer, *Power Evangelism* (San Francisco, CA: Harper and Row, 1986), 16.

[17] Gordon Fee, *God's Empowering Presence: The Holy Spirit in the Letters of Paul* (Peabody, MA: Hendrickson Publishers, 1994), 848.

[18] While the authenticity of the last several verses of the Gospel of Mark is debated by scholars, these verses are assumed to be trustworthy and authoritative by most Bible believers worldwide.

[19] T. L. Osborn, *The Harvest Call* (Tulsa, OK: The Voice of Faith, 1953), 143.

[20] Jerry Bridges, *The Transforming Power of the Gospel* (Colorado Springs, CO: NavPress, 2012), 127.

[21] Charles H. Spurgeon, *Lectures to My Students* (London: Marshall, Morgan and Scott, 1965), 186-187.

[22] Willis, *The Biblical Basis of Missions*, 60.

[23] Larry Hart, *Truth Aflame: Theology for the Church in Renewal* (Grand Rapids, MI: Zondervan, 1999), 375.

[24] Jack Hayford, "Hidden But Not Unreachable," *Foursquare World Advance* (October, 1981).

[25] Grant McClung, "Waiting on the Gift: An Insider Looks Back on One Hundred Years of Pentecostal Witness, *International Bulletin of Missionary Research* (April 2006), 65.

[26] Quoted in Stanley H. Frodsham, *With Signs Following: The Story of the Latter Day Pentecostal Revival* (Springfield, MO: Gospel Publishing House, 1946), 38.

[27] J. Roswell Flower, Editorial. *The Pentecost* (August, 1908), 4; quoted by Gary B. McGee, *This Gospel Shall Be Preached*, vol. 1 (Springfield, MO: Gospel Publishing House, 1986), 45-46.

[28] Arthur F. Glasser, quoted by Paul A. Pomerville, *The Third Force in Missions* (Peabody, Mass.: Hendrickson, 1985), vii.

[29] Hart, *Truth Aflame*, 557-558.

[30] David M. Howard, "Student Power in World Missions," *Perspectives on the World Christian Movement*, 3rd edition (Pasadena, CA: William Carey Library, 1999), 320.

[31] "New Ranking Warns of Expanding Persecution," *AFA Journal* (March 2017), 4.

[32] "The Millennial Manifesto."

[33] Vishal and Ruth Mangalwadi, *The Legacy of William Carey* (Wheaton, IL: Crossway Books, 1999), 85.

[34] Stott, *For the Lord We Love*, 52.

[35] Quoted in John Piper, "The Supremacy of God in Missions through Worship," *Into All the World*, 2001 edition, 8.

A Creative Discourse on Pentecostalism from a Post-Modern and Post Colonial Perspective

M. Stephen

The main topic that is chosen for the Silver Jubilee publication of New Life Biblical Seminary, Cheruvakkal, is 'Pentecostalism: Polyphonic Discourses' which provides room for a wider discussion on Pentecostalism. I have selected a subject on Pentecostalism from a postmodern and post colonial perspective. It is a creative discourse as so much of resources are not used, but it is based more on the observations and experiential dimensions. It examines the elements of postmodernism and post colonialism found in Pentecostalism. It is more a theological and ethical discourse.

The Pentecostal emergence in the modern era has crossed hundred years. It has made a tremendous impact in the spiritual and social life of the people. It has brought a radical transformation in the world. It is also important to remember that the Reformation has crossed 500 years and Serampore Mission had its impact in India for 200 years.

An Exploration into the Pentecostalism

The Pentecostals are usually regarded by the mainline churches as a sect or cult. They hardly accept the contribution of the Pentecostal churches. Though many of the theologians talk loudly about wider ecumenism, they do not want to include Pentecostals, as they look upon them as sectarians.

Whatever might be the allegations, the Pentecostals are Christians with some distinctive characteristics. They claim that their teachings are rooted in the Bible. Though all Pentecostals do not hold the same doctrines and practices, they have lot of commonalities. The speaking in tongues is one of the distinctive common elements for all Pentecostal denominations in India such as Indian Pentecostal Church of God, Church of God in India, Assemblies of God, Sharon Fellowship Church, The Pentecost Mission, World Missionary Evangelism Church and a wide variety of other Pentecostal denominations.

It is true that the Pentecostal churches have raised a tremendous amount of challenge today. It acts as a corrective and dynamic force in the Christian church. The faith, the practice and the very nature of the Pentecostal churches have a very special relevance and challenge for today.

Pentecostalism : Origin and Development

The attempt here is to provide a brief history of Pentecostal movement. The Pentecostals trace back their origin to the day of Pentecost (LK. 24:49; Acts 2). The *glossolalia* (speaking in tongues) is acknowledged by the Pentecostals as the distinctive experience along with the gift of prophecy, miracles, healing etc. and the visions. These phenomenon are also found all through centuries. Irenaeus (A.D 130 - 202) writes, "we have in the church many brethren who have the prophecy and speaking various kinds of tongues through the spirit".[1] Tertullian (3rd century) also testified that *glossolalia* was found in the Montanist church which he had joined.[2] The Pentecostal movement is also understood as an offshoot of the Holiness Movement.

The modern Pentecostal movement began from the Topeka, Kansas city in United States. According to Vinson Synan, "In January 1901, one of Parham's students, an eighteen year old girl named Agnes Ozman, was baptized in the Holy Spirit and began to speak in other tongues as the spirit gave utterance."[3] It is observed that Charles Parham holds the basic teachings of the holiness movement. They are justification by faith, sanctification and the divine healing and the pre-millennial second advent of Jesus Christ.[4] Parham was a former Methodist minister, and he had started a healing home in Topeka where he invited the students to study the scripture. This Bible School had the privilege to witness to the fire of the modern Pentecostal movement. But it took firm root from Azusa street experience (1906) and in India the Pentecost revival began in 1905 at Pandita Ramabai's Mukti Mission in Maharashtra. There were also few pioneers of Pentecostal revival in India. They are A.G. Gar (USA), Christian Schumacher (USA) and Thomas Barrett (Norway). In the state of Kerala also the Pentecostal movement spread like a violent storm and people from different faiths have joined this movement.

Today, Pentecostal movement is being recognized by the world Christian bodies, including the World Council of Churches as a significant movement. It was estimated in 1985 that over ten percent of all the Christians in the world were of Pentecostal or charistmatic type. David Barrett, a church growth scholar argues that at the end of this century the Pentecostals and charismatics would make fifteen percent of world Christians.[5] The Pentecostal churches are growing at a tremendous pace in South Korea and Latin America. According to Peter Wagner, three out of every four Protestants today in Latin America are Pentecostals.[6]

The Important Features, Faith And Practices of Pentecostal Churches

Now we will look at the salient features, the doctrinal statements and practices of the Pentecostal churches.

The Salient Features

The Pentecostals uphold the importance of unity, fraternity and holiness. The non-conformism is an important feature of Pentecostalism. They challenge the theology and practices of traditional churches. The Pentecostal church is a free church. They have a critical look at the other religious traditions. According to Steve Durasoff, "what makes them Pentecostal Christians is their earnest desire to recapture the early practices of the followers of Jesus of Nazareth."[7] They believe in the spiritual gifts (especially prophecy and healing).[8] While discussing about the theology and ethics of Pentecostalism Franklyn Balasundaram brings about the following things.

i.   A second Blessing to be taught and received after conversions,

ii.   Believers must seek the spirit's guidance in all of life,

iii. Believers ought to expect the imminent return of Christ.

iv.   Christians, should shun the world including things such as luxuries, cosmetics, jewellery, amusement, alcohol and tobacco.[9]

The aspect of sin and its consequences are given utmost emphasis by the Pentecostals in their preaching. They preach with enthusiasm. The eschatological emphasis is another feature of their preaching, Pentecostal churches entertain people from all castes and religious traditions. True repentance is demanded from those who would like to join the church. The Pentecostals advocate a simple life style.

The Faith and Practices

The following are the common beliefs and practices of the church.

The Scripture

The Pentecostals accept the sixty-six books (OT-39; NT-27) as the only authoritative book, It is inerrant and infallible. It is the inspired book. Pentecostals keep the place of the Bible above all other scriptures and traditions. The non-biblical scriptures (including Apocryphal books) are not authentic for Pentecostals. It is more closer to the view of reformers.

Trinity

Pentecostals believe in the Triune God-God, the father; God, the Son; and God, the Holy Spirit. They are one in essence, co-equal, and exists in three persons. Pentecostals believe in the virgin birth of Jesus Christ and the atonement through His vicarious death on the cross. They believe in the incarnation, death, resurrection, ascension and the second coming of Jesus Christ. Jesus is for them the only saviour (Acts 4:12) and the only mediator (1 Tim. 2:5). They reject the mediatership of Mary and other holy men. The immaculate idea that is attributed to Mary is also against Pentecostal theology.

Repentance / Salvation

Pentecostal theology accepts the fact that human was created in the image of God, but has violated God's commandment and now is under eternal condemnation. But the atoning sacrifice of Christ provides room for restoration. Pentecostals give utmost importance to repentance. The confessing of sins and acknowledging Christ as the personal saviour (Rom. 10:10) is understood as fundamental for anyone to achieve salvation. Christ is the eternal way, and the one who has faith only in him can attain salvation. For Pentecostal theology, neither the good works nor the rituals will help to achieve salvation.

Baptism in the Holy Spirit

The filling of the Holy Spirit and speaking in tongues is the distinctive mark of a Pentecostal. Speaking in tongues is the foremost sign of the baptism of the spirit (Acts. 2). The Pentecostals see it as a continuing experience. Quoting the Bible (1 Cor. 13), Pentecostals argue that one who speaks in tongues is speaking to God, and it edifies.

The Eschatology

Pentecostals believe in the second coming of Jesus Christ, the resurrection of the dead, the great tribulation, the final judgment, millennium and the new heaven and the new earth. They believe it as literal and not symbolic. The praying for the dead and the concept of purgatory are rejected by Pentecostals.

The Sacraments

Baptism and the eucharist are the most important sacraments for Pentecostals. The Pentecostals reject the infant baptism and sprinkling baptism. They found them as unbiblical. Baptism is given only to the believing adults by immersion. Baptism is received by Pentecostals in the name of the Father, Son and the Holy Spirit. Baptism is to unite with Christ, and to identify with the death and resurrection of Jesus Christ. The Lord's Supper is celebrated to commemorate the atoning death of Christ. They believe in consubstantiation and reject the theory of transubstantiation. Ordination is given to those who set apart for ministry. This is given by the leaders of the church by laying on of hands.

The Worship

The Pentecostal worship is not very ritualistic or liturgical. It is spontaneous in character. It is free worship. There would be clapping of hands, shouting Hallelujah, speaking tongues, prophecy and sharing of testimony in the Pentecostal worship. They also pray and sing aloud. Breaking the bread and the preaching of the word are given foremost importance in Pentecostal worship.

The Ministers / Ministry

The ministers of the church include the Apostles, prophets, pastors, teachers and evangelists (Eph. 4:11). The head of the church is usually called as the president. The terms like 'Bishop', 'episcope' 'metropolitan' are not used by Pentecostals. The Pentecostal churches do not accept the papal authority and his claim of infallibility.

The ministry is associated to the gifts of the spirit (1 cor. 12, 14). The preaching, teaching, prophecy, healing, pastoral care and evangelism are the main ministries among Pentecostals. Evangelization is recognized as the supreme task of the church (Acts. 1:8; Mt. 28:16-20) The salvation through Jesus Christ alone is the key theme of the evangelistic preaching. They try to prove that what they teach or preach from the Bible is the absolute truth. This claim may be criticized as fundamentalism by other churches and people of other faiths. It is, of course, an ideological encounter, and Pentecostals are pacifists. So they do not involve in any power encounter. So this attitude cannot be compared to fascism or Nazism.

One of the main strength of their ministry is their house visitation. The Pentecostals visit the houses and provide guidance to the problems of the people. They also pray for them and comfort them. They also share the message of good news to the people. This enables many to come to know Christ. The Pentecostals are zealous to organize evangelistic preaching and to distribute pamphlets.

Pentecostal Churches and their Challenges Today

This section would concentrate on the challenge of the Pentecostal churches today. It is easy to criticize, but difficult to study objectively any phenomenon. It is important for the episcopal churches to have an in-depth study of Pentecostalism, since it is not an insignificant movement today.

The Pentecostal churches have a message of transformation. This message is applied to Christians and non-Christians. Their message of repentance urges the drunkards, smokers, and those who involve in sin (sexual immorality, bribery, murder, exploitation etc) to change their attitude. Their life style enables the society to transform.

The Pentecostal churches are open to all. People from different religious, racial and social background could come to the church. It is a non-hierarchical, non-ritualistic and non-authoritarian, and a free church tradition. This kind of structure will enhance more freedom and participation for the laity and clergy in the worship and ministry of the church.

This kind of structure is a challenge to the hierarchical and authoritarian churches.

Pentecostal churches give utmost importance to the Bible. The preaching and teaching are rooted in the Bible. Their theological perspectives are crystal clear. They are taught with authority and certainty. Providing convincing Biblical proof is one of the main characteristics of Pentecostals. These factors are also a great challenge.

The preaching of the Pentecostals are very much linked with the problems of the people which are existential and social. It is very much contextual. The Pentecostal preachers use examples and symbols from the present context which have a great deal of appeal to the common people. The preaching always lead the people to renewal and commitment. The themes of the preaching such as cross, hope, peace and comfort also attracts many. The people finds the simple and enthusiastic preaching as attractive and meaningful for their life. It is a challenge to the monotonous preaching.

The pastoral care plays a very dominant role in the Pentecostal communities. The prayer, fellowshipping aspect, and the brotherhood are quite alive in the Pentecostal churches. The element of real *koinonia* helps the members to bind together in love. It is said that the pastoral care is lacking in many communities, especially in the mainline churches. The Pentecostal churches are comparatively small, and this helps the pastors to take care of the spiritual well being of the people more meaningfully.

The exercise of charismatic gifts is another dominant factor. They believe in faith healing. They also have visions, revelations and prophecy. The fasting and prayer for the sick and those who have severe problems are common among Pentecostal churches. It is a fact that deliverance through prayer is found even for the diseases like cancer. The extreme kind of confidence or faith in God is also a strength of Pentecostalism.

The Nature of Pentecostalism

The Pentecostals constitute more than 300 million people all over the world today. They are growing in tremendous pace in Latin America and in Asian countries. There may be around 20-25 lakh Pentecostals in India today. They have their own background and experiences. Among them, at least, two-third might come from the dalit background. They are the marginated ones.

Pentecostal theology is based on the experience of the people. It is also apostolic and biblical. Pentecostal theology is also Christ-centered. The Pentecostals give utmost importance to the role of Holy Spirit in the lives of the people. Pentecostalism was a movement in the initial stage, but later became institutionalized (Church). The Spirit of movement is still found in the Pentecostal community which accommodates people from all sections regardless of caste, colour, race, class or religion.

Those who have the Pentecostal experience are divided into three main groups. The classical Pentecostals have their Separate identity (they are not affiliated to any mainline churches), the neo-Pentecostals constitute the members of the traditional/ mainline churches, and the Catholic charismatics are the members of the Catholic church who are having Pentecostal experience. Now, we have a fourth group known as New Generation Pentecostals who are having no uniform doctrines or practices.

Pentecostal community is a restoration movement as it restores the apostolic elements such as holiness, baptism in the Holy Spirit, and charismatic gifts (prophecy, healing etc). It is a renewal movement as it upholds repentance, brotherhood, love, unity and faithfulness. It is a protest movement as it reclaims the biblical principles which accepts the inerrancy of the Bible, salvation through Christ, and challenges the historical episcopacy, infant baptism, mariolatry and papal infallibility. Many became members of Pentecostal community as a protest against indignity or because of problem with doctrines and practices of the community or religion or group they belonged. It is liberative movement since it promotes an open community in which people from any caste, class or religion could join this movement. It is interesting to note that a large number of oppressed groups became the members of the Pentecostal communities in different parts of the world. Large number of socially, racially, and economically oppressed groups found identity in the Pentecostal movement. Later the Pentecostal movement was domesticated by the elites and the dominant, so that the dalits and blacks (in America) found their separate identity and consciousness in the Pentecostal movement as their meaningful participation in leadership was denied and their dignity disregarded. However, the Pentecostal original vision has a spirit of socialism which would challenge the exploitation, oppression and dehumanization (Acts of the Apostles, chapters 2 and 10). Pentecostals today involve in the task of theologizing. They also give attention to the issues such as women, dalit, eco-concerns and religious pluralism.

Postmodern and Post Colonial Theology

It is important to know what is Postmodern and postcolonial theology and ethics in order to relate with the Pentecostal ideology.

Postmodern Theology

Nietzsche's philosophical ideas have influenced the secular or radical and even the post-modern theologies. One can find traces of post-modernity in death of God theology and process theology. Certain post-modern trends are found in theologies of the marginated like the liberation theology, dalit theology, black theology and feminist theology.

Post-modernism affirms the nihilism (Nietszche), chaos, uncertainty, absolute relativism, rapidity, localism and pluralism. It rejects any centre and also the fixity. Traditional understanding of structure and form (eg. arts, architecture and literature) are questioned and deconstructed (Jacques Derrida's deconstruction) The traditional understanding of God and faith are radically deconstructed in process thought and also in death of God theology. This post-modern trend is also found in the biblical hermeneutics. It affirms the 'death of the author' as what is meant by the author is not important, but the way in which the reader understands is important.

God is no more at the centre, as He is absent or eclipsed and faith and religion are not necessary for the present world. So the absolute relativistic understanding is found in secular theology like death of God and also in post-modern thought. The humanism is also challenged (man is no more at the centre) by post-modernism. The counter-culture (Sebastian Kappen) and non-legitimation of hegemonic or pyramidal structures (dalit theology - A.P. Nirmal) are closely related to post-modern thinking. The openness towards liberation, people (people oriented), pluralism and localism in theology are also having post-modern spirit. The critical and creative or positive use of post-modern elements in theologizing can be affirmed, and the extreme and negative aspects should be rejected.

A radical deconstruction is in process in theology. There is a movement from modern to post-modern in all aspects of life including philosophy, theology and culture. No theology can be, however, formulated by rejecting God, faith and the values, but the task can be a a re-conceiving to have the essence or original understanding.

According to Clayton Crockett, in the 1980's an initial post-modern theology developed around the work of Mark C. Taylor, Charles E. Winquist, Carl A. Raschke and other, which combined insights into the situation of the death of God with contemporary continental philosophy. An important collection appeared in 1982, called' Deconstruction and Theology', which include essays by Altizer, Taylor, Winquist, Raschke and Robert P. Scharlemann. In his influential book (1984) titled *Erring*, Taylor set forth four themes of postmodern all theological thinking, including the death of God, the disappearance of the self, the end of history and the closure of the book. Such works set an agenda for the radical theological inquiry.[10]

Charles E. Winquist explains the notion of postmodern theology as follows: "The notion of postmodern theology does not entail a specific agenda but is more importantly a thinking theology that accounts for the conditions under which we think that are themselves indexical marks of the postmodern condition. Post-modernity cannot be simply dated and the postmodern is not synonymous with the contemporary. There are instead distinctive traits of a postmodern sensibility that call for theological understanding and thereby characterize the meaning and possibilities for postmodern theological thinking."[11]

Winquist states again that, "the publication of the *Alchemy of the Word* (Raschke. 1979), *Deconstruction and Theology* (Altizer et al. 1982) and especially *Erring: A Postmodern Theology* (Taylor 1984) brought the deconstructive philosophy of Jacques Derrida into the arena of theological discourse."[12] Nietzsche, Marx and Freud did contribute to the postmodern environment. Marx, according to Winquist, emphasized the materiality of history; Freud, the materiality of the body; and Nietzsche, the materiality of language.[13] The influences of Jacques Lucan, Jean Francios Lyotard, Julia Kristeva, Giles Deleuze, Michel Foucault and Paul Ricoeur in post-modern thinking, hermeneutics, ethics and theology are to be recognized.[14]

In the early post-modern theology, 'Deconstruction' and 'Death of God' are celebrated as an influence for new thinking. Winquist observes that Taylor's publication of 'Erring' was a manifesto for a deconstructionist post-modern theology deeply influenced by radical theology and Derrida. Taylor claims that deconstruction is the 'hermeneutic' of the death of God. Raschke claims that deconstruction is in the final analysis, the death of God put into writing.[15] Post-modern theology moves against the totalization of thinking and it is commitment to an extraordinary discourse states Winquist. He points out that "A recent theme in post-modern philosophical and theological thinking has been the return of religion, but it is a religion can lead to a theology without religion"[16] states Winquist.

The process thought argues that everything is subject to change and is relative, so reality is a process. The concept of the absolute and immutable are not recognized by process thought. It stands for changeability and contingency. The evolutionary hypothesis is also found in process thought. These elements are found in post-modern theology also.

The Post-modern theology is a radical theology and its shape and nature are beyond any imagination. According to Victor E. Taylor, post-modern theology transforms shape into shapelessness, with shape refigured as "disbecoming".[17] Post modern theologians Raschke and Mark C. Taylor argue for a theology that is emancipated from the metaphysical discourse.[18] Post-modern theologians like Crockett understands God as a sign among other signs.[19] God is represented as power without (total) knowledge, as power is decentralized and "deconstructed", states Peter Canning.[20]

The meta or grand narratives are challenged by Lyotard and post-structuralism and so also post-modernism. The totalizing is rejected, so also foundationalism. There is also de-legitimation and decentering of power and knowledge. The heterogeneous aspects, pluralism and contexuality or localism are emphasized by post-modernism. It also stressed the particulars rather than the generalized and universal 'facts'. The hegemonic forces are also challenged.

So in post-modern theology there is room to do theology from the perspective of dalits, the tribals, blacks, women and other subaltern/marginalized people. Post-modernism has radically challenged the grand narratives found in the form of patriarchy, caste hierarchy, capitalism, western theology and Marxism. There is space for empowerment for the disempowered and to deconstruct and de-legitimize the discriminatory and enslaving systems and structures. There is possibility for a different and particular theology in post-modernism. It empowers and liberates the people of the margins. Hegemony like the Brahminic dominance, male-dominance or the dominance of the whites or west are not accepted by post-modernism, which is also providing a room for making a theology from the oppressive situation for the victimized people.

Post-modernism provides complete possibility to revise and deconstruct what is dehumanizing and oppressive. The formalistic and structuralist view of the divine power, knowledge, authority, narrations and frameworks are to be challenged in order to formulate a post-modern perspective of theology. The hierarchical and hegemonic understanding of power is also not emancipatory. But the elements such as disorder or chaos, nihilism and anarchy cannot be given importance as we critically use post-modern tools.

Postcolonial Theology

Homi K. Bhabha refers to postcolonial as the form of social criticism that bears witness to the unequal and uneven process of representation by which the historical experience of the once colonized third world come to be framed in the West, states Padmini Mongia.[21]

Postcolonialism points the effects of colonialism that impacted the structures and thought, and it look forward the deconstruction in the area of history, art, literature, philosophy and sociology. It challenges the colonial-imperialistic patterns of thought and actions and made a liberative attempt to redeem them from the distorted perspective of the West.

The colonizers (western countries) have been challenged politically, culturally and ideologically by de-colonized countries. The western notions of power, knowledge and methodology are questioned by the colonized as they organized themselves to struggle against the dominance of the West. Though it began early, the organized form of post-colonial thought was developed as freedom of power (political independence) and freedom of thought in the19th century. The people movements are also liberative movements as they affirm the dignity, identity and rights and they are also the vehicles of Post-colonial ideology. The emergence of liberation theology, women theology, Black theology, dalit theology, tribal theology and *minjung* theology which are known as subaltern theologies and the effort such as contextualization/inculturation have the influence of the post-Colonial ethos.

Post-colonial theory is emerged out of the new socio - historic pressure as it is found that the new social movements around the issues such as race, gender and ethnicity have revealed the limits of older conceptions about community, individuals and nation.[22] Post-colonial thought looks to what is 'native' and also looks forward as it challenges dominant, imperialistic world view. It is a re-reading or re-interpretation of history, methodology, theology and sources (e.g. scripture). As against the western, colonial, elitistic perspectives, the post-colonial theological and non-theological discourses argue for liberation from Patriarchy, slavery and challenges gender-injustice, human right violations, and different kinds of oppressions. In post-colonial theological discourses, the indigenous or native resources are critically and creatively used as methodology is more experiential, contextual and narrative, and also there is a 'deconstruction' and decolonizing in the whole perspectives. Post-colonialism explores the potentials of the Orient. The positive elements in the eastern or third world religions, cultures (in the from of myths, folklores, poetry, songs) and social life (historical consciousness) are explored by post-colonial ideology and theology.

According to Rey Chow, the post-colonialist affirms the resurrection of the native or challenging the dominant discourse by 'resurrecting' the victimized voice.[23] Nationalism, Sovereignty, Constitutionality, self-reliance, movements towards cultural and religious roots, resistance against gender and racial prejudices and emancipatory thrust are related to post-coloniality. The marginality, third world experience, feminity, Blackness, Asianness and Indianness, native or indigenous expressions in theology are holding the post-colonial character. The theology of the subaltern or the victimized groups is post-colonial in nature as they struggle against the imperial, colonial or oppressive powers.

According to Ruth Frankenberg and Lata Mani, for India post-colonialism means independence from Britain, birth of the nation- State, end of territorial colonialism, economic growth by the growth of indigenous capitalism, non-aligned either the First or Second world.[24] Post- colonialism means, for Britain the loss of most of their colonies, the appearance on British landscapes of a significant number of people from the former colonies which makes the predominantly white ethnic society into multi-racial society. It also refers to questioning western or white dominance by the movements of resistance and the emergence of struggles for collective determination which is articulated in nationalist terms, states Ruth Frankenberg and Lata Mani.[25]

According to Musa W Dube, "Postcolonial theories emanated from the rise of western empires in the eighteenth through the twentieth centuries, their scramble to divide the world among themselves, the strategies of subjugation and resistance engendered by colonialism, and the chain reactions that have been in motion ever since."[26]

According to Dube, postcolonial feminisms display a number of recognizable strategies and concerns in their decolonizing and depatriarchalizing practices. She continues to say that postcolonial feminist operates within the past and present international oppression which continues to exert its forms of oppressions in their lives. She also states that they indicate that international oppression of the former colonies have exerted a greatest influence on colonized women.[27]

Dube was very conscious of the colonial forces which subjugated and silenced the women. She argues that the postcolonial feminists in their reading and writing call for the decolonization of inherited colonial educational system, language, literary canons and reading methods. It is also stated that the decolonizing practices of two-thirds world feminists are accompanied by a willingness to embrace and confront indigenous religious and cultural worldview which include willingness to pronounce legitimate and adequate wherever possible, to interpret them where necessary, and to avoid the colonizing strategy of dismissing as negative all social systems of the colonized.[28]

Dube asserts that a decolonizing feminist practices also must show how international domination renders women of former colonies politically invisible, economically impoverished, and culturally suppressed while it highlights diverse way of resistance and liberation.[29] Muse W Dube insists also that post colonial feminist strategies must confront oppressive aspects in one's own indigenous systems of gender oppressive practices such as genital mutilation and sati. There are rooms for re-interpreting the old and promoting good as no culture is absolutely negative or wholly pure. In these decolonizing spaces, she states, postcolonial feminist analysis wrestles with the restoration of some aspects of the indigenous cultures and reinterprets others for the empowerment of women and all people.[30] Postcolonial ideology questions the colonization of women's bodies especially the black, and other marginated women which began in slavery; the brutalizing sexual assault on them is criticized.[31] The discrimination in the name of gender or race is questioned by post-colonialism.

According to R. S. Sugirtharajah, the western modes of scientific thinking whether it is liberal, rational or positivist only can enslave us, so we have to be freed from them. The indigenous or native expressions and thought patterns are to be upheld.[32] The central task of postcolonial biblical interpretation is described as recovery, reoccupation and reinscription of one's culture which has been degraded and affected from the colonial narratives and from mainstream Biblical scholarship, states Sugirtharajah.[33] According to him, "Vernacular hermeneutics tries to erase the painful memory of this degradation and effacement, and to make a fresh start by returning to one's roots. Impelled by a variety of cultural and political forces, it is an attempt to go 'home'. It is a call to self- awareness, aimed at creating an awakening among people to their indigenous literary, cultural and religious heritage."[34] Vernacular is understood as nativism, cultural nationalism, indigenous, struggle for the historical and political presences of groups suppressed or marginalized by colonization and modernization, an assertion and selfhood and self-respect instead of slavish conformity to received ideas, valuing the indigenous resources and deep distrust of the centralizing tendencies of Euro-American critical theories.[35]

The postcolonial intertexual reading is found in the biblical interpretation. According to Sugirtharajah, the postcolonial interpretation has the vocation to de-ideologizing dominant interpretation and the distrust of the totalizing,tendencies.[36] Sugirtharajah states again, postcolonial theory offers a space for the once colonized.It is an interpretative act of the descendants of those once subjected. In effect, it means a resurrection of the marginal, the indigene and subaltern."[37]

The task of the postcolonial criticism, according to Sugirtharajah, is to engage in reconstructive reading of Biblical texts. In his words, 'postcolonial reading will reread Biblical texts from the perspective of postcolonial concerns such as liberation struggles of the past and present; it will be sensitive to subaltern and feminine elements embedded in texts'.[38]

Postcolonial theology is narrative, liberative, nativistic and people-oriented. It upholds the struggle of the oppressed and goes against the elites or dominant class and the colonizers. There is a re-understanding of theology as postcolonial theology challenges the western thinking and methodology which is more individualistic, abstract, capital intensive and imperialistic. Postcolonial theology is concerned of the marginalized or subaltern such as poor, women, blacks, dalits and tribes. It re-reads the scripture in the light of the aspirations of the victimized and also give importance to the indigenous resources. It does value what is native.

The postcolonial theology is also having the elements of post-structuralism and postmodernism. The aspects such as orientalism, nationalism, indigeneity, and contextuality play vital roles in postcolonial theology. It also deconstructs the traditional, dominant and western forms of ideology and theology. Postcolonial theology challenges the authoritarian structures and it sides the oppressed or marginated. The subaltern experience and their consciousness is also very crucial in postcolonial Theology. Postcolonial theology is also liberative. It challenges patriarchy, caste hierarchy, racial discrimination and hegemony. The empowerment of dalits, tribes, victimized women, blacks and other suffering humanity is an essential concern of postcolonial theology.

Postmodern Ethics

In ethics and theology, changes are taking place because of the changes of the context. There is a movement from colonialism to postcolonialism. The postcolonial situation is now neo-colonial. Now the colonialism is almost come to an end, but we see the fierce emergence of neo-colonialism, which is a new way of exploiting or oppressing the third world by the first world. Now we are also concerned of the movement from modernism to post-modernism. The present era is described as post-modern.

The modernism was a challenge to the traditional ethos. The enlightenment played a crucial role in the emergence of the modern. The importance given to human reason, scientific worldview and the humanism have contributed to modernism. The critical spirit and the freedom of thought and human potentiality are hailed in modernism. The development of science and technology placed human beings very high. The scientific rationality is developed so the people looked for the autonomy and freedom from religious and social structures. It is critical of what is described as superstitious and irrational.

David Layon sums up the modernity as follows, "modernity is all about the massive changes that took place at many levels from the mid-sixteenth century onwards, changes signaled by the shifts that uprooted agricultural workers and transformed them into mobile industrial urbanities. Modernity questions all conventional ways to doing things substituting authorities of its own, based in science, economic growth democracy or law. And it unsettles the self; if identity is given in traditional society, in modernity it is constructed."[39] The meaningless and aloneness (the society of strangers) and ecological crises becomes the order of the day which contributes to crisis in modernism, and its name is post-modernity. According to Brian D. Ingraffia, "whereas modernism tried to elevate man into God's place, post-modern theory seeks to destroy or deconstruct the very place and attributes of God."[40] In post-modernism man is only a tiny being among the realities. Nietschze's transvaluation of values and elimination of God (God is dead) have influenced the post modernity.

Jurgen Habermas challenged the view that postmodernity is the end of modernity. For him, modernity is an unfinished project. In the view of Jean-Francois Lyotard, post-modern condition is characterized by incredulity (unwilling to believe) towards meta-narratives. Meta-narratives are those large narratives that undergirded and legitimated the knowledge enterprise in modernity. It is said that legitimation of knowledge always requires some narrative, but, in the post-modern context, such narratives are not credible. The grand narratives have lost its validity. The postmodernity challenged the possibility of the transcendent and the validity of the narratives are made local. There is no consensus, in Lyotard's view on true knowledge.[41]

Jacques Derrida is famous for his attempts on deconstruction. He tries to dismantle the Judaeo-Christian roots of metaphysics by his deconstruction. In his deconstruction of ontotheology, he considers Christian theology as a prime example of logo centric metaphysics. He also feels that Christian theology is unable to guard against foreign philosophical influences.[42]

According to Craig Bartholomew, as Thiselton points out, deconstruction in literary theory is often perceived as the strongest philosophical context of post-modernism and Derrida is one of the exponents.[43] For Derrida, language is the bottom line of reality and it is unable to represent the reality accurately. In his view, there is also textual instability. For him, writing is prior to speech. Writing is not mere inscription in his view. Writing is related to every system of communication-pictorial, musical and sculptural writing.[44]

Fragmentation and transience characterize postmodernity accompanied by thorough going pluralism, says Craig Bartholomew.[45] Derrida does not see any firm grounding of language which is not illusory. In Craig Bartholomew's observation, post modernity has raised all sorts of questions about our capacity to know and how we know and whether we can accurately represent reality, i.e., about epstemology. The possibility of universal knowledge is considered as impossible and it considers all knowledge to be local, communal and human construct. It also undermined the rationalistic, autonomous view of human which was dominant in modernity. In his view, postmodernity is characterized by pluralism, uncertainty, instability and fragmentation. The old certainties seem to have gone, with no unified vision to replace them.[46] Postmodernity leads to relativism.

In modernity, the factors like secularization, urbanization and the science and technology have contributed positively and negatively to the society. In the ethical reflection also these factors made greater impact. There was a wise and responsible use of science (knowledge) and also the abuse of science and technology. Man's potentiality and knowledge went even to the extreme to ruthlessly tap the resources and spoil the environment by their industrial enterprise and brought the ecological crises which become a severe threat to survival. At the same time, the irrationality and superstitions were questioned, and humanness was upheld. The traditional value system and religious authority have come under the attack. A new awareness of the reality was emerged which questioned the discrimination and argued for freedom. Modernism was a boon and a bane. If the responsibility is lost, any system or ideology can be a curse. Evaluating the crisis of modernism, Dr. K.C. Abraham has said that it is hazardous to life as it is destroying the basic fabric of human relationships.

The neo-colonial forces played a very crucial role to control the economic structure as they appeared in the form of IMF, MNCs and TNCs. It was also a bad effect of modernism. Modernism paved the way for different kinds of developments which were misused by the capitalistic forces. Man is only a spectator and he/she is a tiny being among several beings around. The pluralism supports the different experiences and realities and so also the relativism. The relativism is related to fragmentation and uncertainty which the post-modernism promotes. Homogenization and universalization are being challenged. The ethical norms also undergo radical threat. Ethics will be relativistic or ethics becomes absurd. There is no set standards as everything is uncertain or vague. It nihiliates God so also the ethical norms and value system. There can be misuse of freedom or absolute freedom where nobody is mutually responsible. Post-modernism provides a new culture, a new social structure, a new world-view and a new 'morality' as against the existing and traditional. It is after the new trends in all aspects of life.

Post-modern ethics has the following characteristics:

i. The post-modern ethics is people-oriented. It affirms decentralization. It is for openness and decision making is possible as it stands above traditional hierarchy and authority. It regards the 'other' or powerless or the marginated. It challenges the hegemonic forces or structures of domination. It stands for the empowerment of the disempowered. The subaltern groups like poor, dalits, tribals, blacks and victimized women and their emergence is a concern in post-modern ethical perspective.

ii. It is an ethics of deconstruction. Post-modern ethics goes beyond the dominant value and ideological system as it questions the systems and structures that are totalized. The anti-foundational and anti-hierarchical stance of post-modernism challenges the imposed values (e.g.: Marxism, patriarchy, caste system, deontology). It does not approve the superiority claim, dominance or impositions of any value system. It gives freedom to re-imagining as we deconstruct and re-construct the existing values.

iii. Post-modern ethics is contextual. It provides room for people to consider their experiences. Pluralism, contingency rapidity and fragmentation are recognized by post-modernism. The people and their context play vital roles in post-modernism. The context of the margins or the other (neglected persons and groups) are given importance by post-modern ethics.

iv. Post-modern ethics is liberative. Post-modern ethics has dealt with people of the margins. It challenges structures of domination or hegemonic forces that oppress them. The power, authority, the 'knowledge' (epistemology) of the dominant and hegemonic imposition of values are questioned by post-modern ethics. It looks for an epistemological shift as it considers the powerless. The liberative spirit is inherent in post-modern ethics. Disregarding the 'other' (marginated) is not approved by post-modern ethics. Post-modern ethics is other-regarding.

Post-Colonial Ethics

Post-colonialism challenges the colonialism and it resists the impositions and importation of any value system from the west or from the dominant groups. Neo-colonialism or globalization is the new form of colonization taking place all over the world. The powerless erstwhile colonized countries are badly affected by globalization. Globalization is an imposition of the culture, economic and political policies of the hegemonic forces (Western Countries) over the third world.

Following are the characteristic of postcolonial ethics:-

i.   Postcolonial ethics is anti-hegemonic: It is not compromising with the powerful or the dominant forces. It is concerned of the issues of the colonized. As we see in postmodernism, it is against the totalizing of the hegemonic forces and their structures. So it is post-structural in nature. The values of the dominant powers and the imposition of their ideologies are rejected by postcolonialism. It questions the oppressive and exploitative elements.

ii. Postcolonial ethics is contextual. Postcolonialism affirms the contextuality. The experience of the decolonized or the indigenous people are very significant for postcolonialism. The particular context, the pluralism, the persons and people are considered in contextual ethics. The struggles of the people of the third world and their socio-economic realities and the stark reality of poverty are responded in postcolonial ethics. Postcolonial ethics is praxis -oriented.

iii. Postcolonial ethics is liberative. Postcolonial ethics looks for deconstruction as we see in postmodernism. It challenges existing structures of domination (Western and Eastern) and look forward a radical re-restructuring of the society. Spivak was pointing the disregard towards the subaltern. Their identity and crisis are to be taken into account when we deal with postcolonial ethics. The victimized groups need empowerment and liberation. They include dalits, tribes, transgenders, blacks, other indigenous groups and victimized women. Postcolonial ethics is an ethics of the poor, powerless and victimized. It challenges the oppressing and exploitative structures. It is a decolonizing ethics.

The issue of land, nationalism, poverty, women, dalits, tribes, blacks and other marginalized groups and the struggle for equal distribution of resources and empowerment are major concerns in postcolonial theology and ethics. Postcolonial ethics is not rooted in what is classical, western or dominant, but radical as it is indigenous, people-oriented and anti-hegemonic.

Discourse on Pentecostalism in the Light of Post-Modernism and Post-Colonialism

The post-modern and post-colonial elements are found in Pentecostalism. It has deconstructive and decolonizing elements.

Pentecostalism and Post-modernism

There are anti-pyramidal, anti-hierarchical elements in post-modernism. Post-modernism is dynamic and it delegitimizes and deconstructive. It is also anti-hegemonic and empowering. Any kind of victimization is challenged by post-modernism. The authoritarian structures are questioned by post-modernism.

Any kind of fixity is rejected by both Derrida and Foucault. Foucault denies the value of punishment and discipline as they are against the freedom. The 'other' is given utmost importance in post-modernism. It sides the marginalized.

Pentecostalism challenges, like post-modernism, the hierarchical structures, as it was against the pyramidal structures which are Christian and non-Christian. Pentecostalism advocates an open community as against secluded and exclusive community. Pentecostalism did accept people from all communities in an integrated form as it challenges the concentration of power and authority. The marginated groups like the dalits, tribes, poor and other victimized groups are accommodated by Pentecostals. It does not mean that there is no discriminations against the marginalized in Pentecostalism.

The rigid forms of ecclesiastical structures are being challenged by Pentecostalism, but it is so happened that there are traditional elements that infiltrated into the Pentecostal churches as it becomes undynamic.

Pentecostalism and Post-colonialism

Pentecostalism is post-colonial in nature, as it is indigenous, people-oriented and liberative in nature. Pentecostalism accommodates the native elements in forms of structure, music, worship pattern and organization. It is a dissenting voice to the traditional mainline churches. It is postcolonial as it reacts to the colonial spirit of dominant structures and pyramidal framework which dehumanize others.

Pentecostalism is very experiential and narrative in its theology and it is contextual in ethical perspectives. It considers the emancipation and empowerment of the poor and marginalized as in post-colonialism. The imperial spirit is being challenged by Pentecostalism. It is more people friendly.

Some Pentecostal Challenges In Relation To Post-Modernism And Post-Colonialism

Following are some of the features of Pentecostalism in relation to post-modernism and post-colonialism.

i.   Pentecostalism advocates for the open church. It entertains the people from all classes, castes and races if they accept Jesus Christ as Lord and believe in/experience the spiritual gifts. The Pentecostal movement affirms the fact that the church is not meant for a particular group or class. It is meant for all including the marginalized. It is interesting to note that the Pentecostal Churches in Kerala have been very keen in giving membership to those who belong to the so called low castes, the Dalits. The Pentecostals did show willingness to accept their dignity to an extent.

ii.   Pentecostalism does emphasize the human dignity, equality and fraternity. The brotherhood is an important factor among them. Originally they had the feeling of oneness, the caring and the sharing. But it has to be noted that the Dalits are not given adequate representation in the leadership of the Pentecostal churches in Kerala. At the same time, it is important to make mention that the Pentecostalism has contributed so much to reduce caste feeling in our society.

iii.   Pentecostalism promotes free (non-liturgic) and spontaneous worship. The worship is so spontaneous that any one could exercise their gifts and to share their experience as testimony.

The worship services are so lively with singing and praising God, the preaching and the celebration of the Eucharist. There is freedom in the Spirit. The Pentecostal worship is not so ritualistic as in the episcopal churches. The worship also takes indigenous forms in India. Usually the church members sit on the floor. The vernacular is used in worship. The people could clap and express joy as they shout Hallelujah and praises to God. The worship services are not monotonous or dry, but live and refreshing. The traditional forms of liturgy/prayer books/worship orders are not used. The prayers are extemporary.

iv. Pentecostalism promotes lay participation. The laymen have an active role in the activities of the church. It does accept the reformed idea of the priesthood of all believers. Though ministers are recognized in the church, there is no much gulf between the ministers and the laymen.

v. Pentecostal churches do not give importance to ritualism, though it accepts the sacraments such as baptism and Eucharist. The hierarchical structure is not approved very much. It is more a democratic set up that we see in Pentecostalism. There is also decentralisation of power. The ecclesiastical structure of Pentecostals is not very rigid, but flexible. The different positions of the church is usually decided by election.

vi. The pastoral concern of Pentecostals are well appreciated. They give importance to each persons. Visiting the sick, praying for the sick and providing conselling and guidance to the persons are to be greatly acknowledged. There is a close relationship between the people and the pastor.

vii. Petecostalism promotes the women participation. The women have freedom to share their testimony, to preach, to sing and to exercise their spiritual gifts such as the gift of prophecy. The Pentecostals do accept the equal status between men and women, though some Pentecostal women are a great help for the church in the task of evangelization. They are very active in sharing the gospel with others. They are also given opportunity to train in the Bible Schools.

viii. There is anti-hierarchical and anti-hegemonic elements in Pentecostalism as in postmodernism and postcolonialism.

ix. The marginalized are integrated into Pentecostal community as postmodernism and postcolonialism empower the marginated or 'other' and liberate the powerless.

x. There is decolonizing and deconstruction in Pentecostalism as the ecclesiastical and social pyramidal structures are being challenged.

xi. Pentecostalism also challenges the postmodern understanding of chaos, indeterminacy and nihilism.

xii. It is found that the understanding of non-fixity (post structuralism) is found in Pentecostal hermeneutics as Pentecostal preachers are using the Biblical text without fixed meaning. It is used in a relative sense. The experiential and narrative elements are given importance in the Pentecostal use of Bible as in post-colonialism.

xiii. The people-orientation is formed in postmodern, postcolonial and Pentecostal ideologies. The people movements are greatly valued by postmodernism and postcolonialism. Pentecostalism is also a peoples' movement. It is also a movement of the marginalized. It is liberative in nature.

Conclusion

Postmodern and postcolonial elements are found in Pentecostalism. Postmodernism and post colonialism are for deconstruction and decolonizing. The pyramidal and hierarchical structures are questioned by them, which is also found in Pentecostalism. The marginalized are empowered by them and their ideologies. Their identity and dignity are recognized. The indigenous and local, the narrative and liberative elements are also found in Pentecostalism. There are also found the postmodern and postcolonial discourses. These three ideologies are people-friendly as they are concerned of people's struggle and issues.

The Post-modernism, post-colonialism and Pentecostalism are post-structural in nature as they are questioning any kind of set forms and structures. The hegemonic power, authority and set patterns are challenged by these ideologies. It is also important to note that certain traditional Pentecostal approaches are to be re-formulated by recognizing the values of post-modernism and post-colonialism. For example, the institutionalism is a great danger in Pentecostalism which leads to the imposition of hierarchy, power and authority.

Endnotes

[1] Quoted from *Ante-Nicene Fathers Vol.* (Charles Scribners Sons, 1885), 53 in Elmer Lewis Moon, *The Pentecostal Church: A History and popular Survey* (New York: Carton press. 1966), 6.

[2] Elmer Lewis Moon, *The Pentecostal Church: A History And Popular Survey* (New York : Carlton press, 1966), 7.

[3] In his introduction in the Book *Azusa Street* by Frank Bartleman (New Jersey : Logos International, 1980), x.

[4] Bartleman, *Azusa Street*, ix.

[5] Vinson Synan, *The Twentieth Century Pentecostal Explosion* (Florida: Creation House, 1987), 12.

[6] Peter Wagner, *Spiritual Power and Church Growth* (Florida: Strange Communications Company, 1986), 27.

[7] Steve Durasoff, *Bright Wind of the Spirit* (New Jersey: Logos International, 1972), 3.

[8] Durasoff, *Bright Wind of the Spirit*, 1-5.

[9] "The Voice and Voices," *Bangalore Theological Forum* (December 1989 - March 1990). 102-103.

[10] "Introduction," *Secular Theology: American Radical Theological Thought*, edited by Clayton Crockett (London : Routledge, 2001), 5.

[11] "Post Modern Secular Theology," *Secular Theology*, 26.

[12] "Post Modern Secular Theology," *Secular Theology*, 26.

[13] "Post Modern Secular Theology," *Secular Theology*, 26-27.

[14] "Post Modern Secular Theology," *Secular Theology*, 26.

[15] "Post Modern Secular Theology," *Secular Theology*, 27.

[16] "Post Modern Secular Theology," *Secular Theology*, 30.

[17] "Theography: Signs Of God In A Post-Modern Age," *Secular Theology*, 193.

[18] "Theography: Signs Of God In A Post-Modern Age," *Secular Theology*, 193.

[19] "Theography: Signs Of God In A Post-Modern Age," *Secular Theology*, 206.

[20] "God of Possibility," *Secular Theology*, 236.

[21] *Contemporary Post Colonial Theology: A Reader*, edited by Padmini Mongia (London : Arnold, 1997), 1.

[22] Ibid., 5

[23] "Where have all the Natives Gone?," *Contemporary Post Colonial Theory: A Reader*, edited by Padmini Mongia, 129.

[24] "Crosscurrents, Crosstalk: Race, 'Post-coloniality' and the Politics of Location," *Contemporary Post-Colonial Theory*, 347.

[25] "Crosscurrents, Crosstalk: Race, 'Post-coloniality' and the Politics of Location," *Contemporary Post-Colonial Theory*, 348.

[26] "Postcoloniality, Feminist spaces, and Religion," *Postcolonialism, Feminism and Religious Discourses*, edited by Laura E. Donaldon and Kwok pui-lan (New York : Rutledge, 2002), 100.

[27] "Postcoloniality, Feminist spaces, and Religion," 115.

[28] "Postcoloniality, Feminist spaces, and Religion," 115-16.

[29] "Postcoloniality, Feminist spaces, and Religion," 116.

[30] "Postcoloniality, Feminist spaces, and Religion," 116.

[31] M. Shawn Copeland, "Body, Representation and Black Religious Discourse," *Post Colonialism, Feminism and Religious Discourse*, 182.

[32] *The Bible and the Third World* (Cambridge: Cambridge University Press, 2001), 176.

[33] *The Bible and the Third World*, 177.

[34] *The Bible and the Third World*, 177.

[35] *The Bible and the Third World*, 177.

[36] *The Bible and the Third World*, 224.

[37] *The Bible and the Third World*, 250.

[38] *The Bible and the Third World*, 252.

[39] Quoted by Craig Bartholomew, from *Themelios* (January 1975), 27.

[40] *Post Modern Theory and Biblical Theology: Vanquishing God's Shadow*, 1.

[41] *Themelios* (January, 1997), 28.

[42] Brian D. Ingraffia, *Post-Modern Theory and Biblical Theology*, 13.

[43] Ingraffia, *Post-Modern Theory and Biblical Theology*, 29.

[44] Ingraffia, *Post-Modern Theory and Biblical Theology*, 30.

[45] Ingraffia, *Post-Modern Theory and Biblical Theology*, 30.

[46] Ingraffia, *Post-Modern Theory and Biblical Theology*, 32.

Pentecostalism in the Post Modern Era: Potentials/Possibilities, Problems and Challenges

V. V. Thomas

Jesus Christ came to the world with single purpose of redeeming the lost humanity and re-connecting them back to their creator and thereby restoring their lost status as dignified human beings. His famous utterance in the gospel of John "I have come so that you may have life and life in abundance" (10:10) was the motto of his life and ministry. That whole process of redemption of humanity by Jesus has been defined as the "Incarnation" process which had three major functions - namely the *Kenosis* (Self-emptying of Christ), the *Necrosis* (Cross –bearing of Christ) and the *Theosis* (Sharing the glory of God). As someone said "Incarnation is nothing but thinking about God in a worldly way so that we may think about the world in a godly way". So Christ came basically to transform the world and thereby create a new humanity. Therefore, at least, ideologically speaking, empowering people and changing them from "Oklos" (crowd) to "Lavos" (People) have been the motto of Christ and His Gospel. Thus, no doubt, this is also the mission that Christ has left with His disciples, who are called as Christians to carry on Christ's mission in the world. Therefore, Christianity can never stop thinking that they can ever survive in the world without the responsibility of empowering the subaltern (people of inferior rank), the Dalits, the tribal, the weaker ones in the society.

It is a matter of fact that people around the world, especially the weaker ones in the society are always in quest for someone to empower them; someone to play the role of a 'Messiah'; someone to play the role of a 'Mother Theresa'; someone to play the role of Babasaheb Ambedkar and others who can give them a helping hand towards their upward/ social mobility and growth. In our contemporary world, millions of people especially in developing countries like India are disillusioned with a materialistically oriented modernization, globalization and capitalistic kind of world economy. In such a world people are attracted to many forms of religion and religious sentiments, upsetting balances even in the socio-religious-economic-political lives of nations and peoples. The modern Pentecostal movement is one such form of the Christian religion to which many hundreds of people are attracted on a daily basis not only in India but in many different parts of the world.

I have been engaged in the study of the modern Pentecostal movement for the past many years although my concentration has been mainly on Pentecostalism among the Dalits. (Therefore, in this paper I will be often referring to the Dalits among the Pentecostal Churches in India). As a matter of fact the Pentecostal movement or 'Pentecostal-like movements' in the present day India has been growing in such a way even to the extent of upsetting balances even in the socio- religious –economic - political aspects of this country. Unlike the early years of the 20th century when Pentecostalism mainly appealed to the Dalits or the people of the lower strata of the society, it is now making inroads among the middle class notwithstanding the fact that its base is still among the poor, the down trodden, the lower middle class people. This vigorous revival of a fundamental form of religion like Pentecostalism in developing countries like India can only be explained with prudence when we try to understand the struggles of the people who are threatened with isolation, the evils of caste system, un-touchability (although banned by the law of the land, there are several places in India where it is still practiced unpronounced) and even death. In such situations, the downtrodden people develop their own moral and spiritual life potential to survive, resist, and build new alternatives like forming their own spirituality which answers their life questions and empower them to be dignified human beings. I am of the firm opinion that one of the ways to understand the modern Pentecostal movement of our time should be against this kind of a background of people's quest for empowerment.

Modern Pentecostal Movement: An Overview

The beginning of the modern Pentecostalism as a worldwide movement was started by a charismatic revival as early as 1901, in Topeka, Kansa. However it gained momentum and worldwide acceptance only after April 1906, with the "outpouring of the Holy Spirit" at the Azusa Street in Los Angeles. There are two personalities around whom the Azusa Street revival evolved, namely, Charles Fox Parham and William J.Seymour, a white and a black respectively. Charles F.Parham was a Methodist minister in the early part of the 20th century. According to Steve Durasoff, Parham left the Methodist Church because of certain ideological differences and became an independent evangelical preacher and remained a preacher for about thirty-five years. In 1898 he founded the Bethel Healing Home in Topeka, for lodging and faith training for individuals seeking a divine cure. In 1900, he opened an informal Bible school for Christian workers where about 40 students registered for the first batch. Miss. Agness N.Ozmen, one of the Bible school students, occupies a unique place in the modern Pentecostal movement. It is claimed by the Pentecostals that Miss Agness experienced the baptism in the Holy Spirit with evidence of speaking in other tongues. When one takes speaking in tongues as the major criterion for a Pentecostal experience, it can be said that Miss. Ozmen is the first known Pentecostal of the modern Pentecostal movement with the initial physical evidence of speaking in tongues. From Azusa Street Pentecostalism spread to other parts of the world by members who experienced the Pentecostal revival and formed Pentecostal Churches.[1] What is important here is to note that the very claim of the Pentecostals, namely that baptism in the Holy Spirit was first experienced by a woman is of extreme importance when one thinks of the contribution that women have given to the growth of the Pentecostal Church in particular and the Charismatic and other independent Churches in general.

Pentecostalism in India

We have observed that the Pentecostal movement emerged in the 20th century out of the revivals that took place in the United States of America. In India it was no different. Therefore it will be difficult to say when exactly the Pentecostal movement started in India. As noted above this is because it is closely associated with the Evangelical revival movements of the 19th century. If speaking in tongue which is the main symbol/

sign of the movement should be taken as the beginning of the Pentecostal movement then, it has already been seen in many of the revival movements that were taking place in the various parts of the country in the early part of the 20th century. According to one of the leading Assemblies historians, Garry B.McGee the first Pentecostal experience of speaking in tongues was manifested among the Christian and Alliance mission's missionaries at Akola, Maharashtra in 1906 but this was not documented. [2]. Another incident of speaking in tongues was witnessed among the girls at the Mukthi mission run by Panditha Ramabai, a Brahmin convert to Christianity. This was a result of the revival to which an eye witness, Minnie F. Abrams reported that, "there was weeping, long prayer, confession of sins, and visions."[3] However, classical Pentecostalism in India appeared through the efforts of the Western Missionaries who were part of the Azusa Street revival in 1906 in United States. The first Pentecostal missionary to come to India with the Pentecostal message that represents the Azusa Street was A.G Gar who came in the year 1907 to Calcutta. The others include Thomas Barrett (Norway), George Berg, Robert F. Cook and Mrs. Mary Chapman who was the first Assemblies Missionary to India who came to Madras (Chennai) in 1915.[4]

Over the past one century, Pentecostalism in India has grown far and wide. Right from the beginning the movement has shown a great trend towards growth. One often hears people asking as to what was the secret behind the growth of the Pentecostal Churches in India and elsewhere! While we can come up with many reasons, let me highlight a few major factors.

The first factor that I want to identify is what I call the "divine factor". The divine factor was the work of the Holy

Spirit. It is for this reason that Pentecostals are often known as 'Evangelicals with a plus'. Evangelical Christianity has emphasized upon seven major ingredients as their theological basis. They are:

1. The authority of the written word of God for life and conduct of human lives.

2. The orthodoxy of Biblical doctrines.

3. The importance of personal faith.

4. Commitment to the Lord Jesus Christ.

5. The importance of Evangelism and Mission.

6. The place given to fellowship.

7. The importance of social concerns

The Pentecostals are fully in agreement with all the above Evangelical doctrines. However they go one step further and give greater emphasis to the role of the Holy Spirit in the lives of every Christian. It is for this reason that they are known as 'Evangelicals with a plus'.

The early Pentecostal leaders in Kerala and elsewhere were not people with a lot of secular education or 'head knowledge'. But the fact that the Lord used them to build his Church in many parts of the state and in several other places can only be attributed to the working of the Holy Spirit in their lives. God used those ordinary people of the early days to accomplish extra ordinary things and the secret was the power of the Holy Spirit.

The second factor behind the growth of the movement is the 'human factor'. This has to do with the kind of life the early Pentecostals lived in Kerala. There was so much of fellowship and solidarity among the early believers. They were tied together by many factors. They carried the burdens of one another. There were many tarrying meetings in the Churches and people had living testimonies to share. There were prophetic ministries in Churches. The prophets of those days were able to discern the right from wrong. (Although today that sought of Pentecostalism is waning out). The Pentecostal movement has entered into their fourth generation. The fourth generation Pentecostals are unaware of the way Pentecostalism has traveled through. For the first generation of Pentecostals, Pentecostalism was an experience of the infilling of the Holy Spirit. For the second generation it was an experience with a kind of imitation of what their parents experienced. When it came to the third generation they began to lose the vitality because there were a number of changes that came into the movement. Today in the fourth generation, Pentecostals are trying to 'act' like the early Pentecostals but they are not really able to make an impact on their generation.

A third factor is one might call the 'push' and 'pull' factors. The 'push' factor has mainly to do with certain failures of other religious groups and denominations in meeting the spiritual needs of the people especially the Dalits. The 'pull' factor has to do with certain characteristics and particularities of Pentecostalism which in a real way respond to the spiritual / emotional needs of the people. These pull factors include gifts of the spirit, convincing teachings of the Pentecostals, and meaningful worship to name only a few.

In major Indian cities like Mumbai, Bangalore, and Chennai some of the fastest growing Christian Churches are the Pentecostal and Charismatic Churches. In fact some of the other main line traditional Churches are 'disturbed' by the tremendous growth that the Pentecostal Churches are showing. Many of their members are leaving these Churches and joining with the Pentecostal and Charismatic like Churches. For example the New Life Fellowship Churches which is very similar to any other classical Pentecostal Church is growing leaps and bounds in India. The fact is that the common people in these cities who long for God-experiences, hearing of God's word, close fellowship in community and true pastoral care were all fed up with dogmas and doctrines, formal and ritualistic worship services and rigid disciplines in their erstwhile Churches.

In fact the rigid institutional nature of some of the Main Line Churches frightens the poor and makes them uncomfortable. The poor feel excluded from these highly organized and elite institutional Churches where they have no role to play. The common people seek for a more emotional and indigenous form of worship. Miracles, dance, drums and traditional songs continue to give meaning to their empty and broken lives. The believing communities around them stand in support. This kind of Pentecostalism is welcomed by large number of people in North Indian states such as Orissa, Uttar Pradesh, Punjab and in several other places throughout India. Couple of years before, while on a ministry tour, I myself witnessed two consecutive worship services in the same Pentecostal Church, in the outskirts of New Delhi, attended by more than 4000 people, who were mostly from surrounding villages from the state of Uttar Pradesh. Some of them had to start their journey from their homes as early as 3:00 AM to reach the Church by 10: 00 AM. Most of them were from the Dalit background. I was thrilled to listen to their testimonies which narrate stories of their everyday life experiences. Stories like a child being bitten by a snake and the parents simply praying for the child and the child being miraculously saved.... and many other similar stories. In fact the pastor had a hard time in controlling people from sharing their weekly experiences due to the lack of time. These were all people from village background and some from towns. So the social location of the Pentecostal movement continues to be among the agrarian community who are mostly the Dalits. To a question as to where we can locate the real Pentecostal Church in India today, I would say that it is outside the so called 'official / Classical Pentecostal Churches', where she stands with the poor, the sick, the homeless, those suffering injustice and those looking for truth and justice, among those groups and communities where people enjoy the company of one another and long for fellowship. Therefore I am of the strong opinion that the powerful expressions of Pentecostalism are found outside the four walls of the 'official Church' than within it.

A careful study of most of the newly formed Christian groups in India will reveal the fact that most of them adhere to the 'Pentecostal kind of faith' although they may not be known as a Classical Pentecostal Church as such in the strict sense of the term. The above observation that many of these 'new generation' Churches may not be called purely as 'Classical Pentecostal Churches' sheds light on another reality and I would like to call it as "Post-Pentecostal movements". From a historical perspective, if the 20th century could be termed as the century of the growth of Classical Pentecostalism, what I perceive of the 21st century is a "Post – Classical Pentecostal Century" or simply as "Post- Pentecostal Century" which will be characterized by the growth of several 'Pentecostal like movements' and groups.

In fact those sociologists and theologians who predicted the collapse of traditional religion and the triumph of secularization have been proved wrong. As a matter of fact there is a resurgence of religiosity. What is happening in the Indian mission field is only a pointer to the reality that people still look for a way out of their everyday struggles not in a new political party or social organizations but in 'religion-based' forms of people groups where they can meet with God in real life situations. India is still a religious society unlike the West which has become a post religious society. In India they are still 'converting' people from one religion to other but in the West it is from 'no-religion' to a new faith.

I am excited by reports of what has been taking place in India in the mission fields where most of the new converts to Christianity prefer to join a Pentecostal or Charismatic like fellowship where their spiritual needs are met. Pentecostalism as a religion filled with both this-worldly and other-worldly concepts of spirituality appeals to the poor, and specially the Dalits. The Dalits on the other hand, complement Pentecostal spirituality with their emotional nature of worship, their longing for oneness and equality. The down trodden people in their search for dignity, freedom and recognition find the Pentecostal spirituality appealing to them. Of course this may seem like an assumption here and I do not deny the fact that it has to be verified and proved through empirical / field study. It is here that I would like to challenge some young scholars to do field research and bring out facts into the open space so that people know who belongs where and for what reason!

Of course there is another side to the whole story as to why there is a "Post-Pentecostal Movement". The answer to that question will open up another area of research into the already existing main line Pentecostal Churches in India such as the Assemblies of God, the Church of God, and the Indian Pentecostal Church. These Churches seem to have fallen into the 'trap' of their predecessors who gave precedence to institutions and structures over simple believing Christians. What once Pentecostals used to protest in their erstwhile Churches have now become part of their own Churches. In other words there is no 'protestant classical Pentecostal Church' today. What was considered once 'insignificant' has now become an acceptable practice in some of these main line Pentecostal Churches. Pentecostal movement in India and of course elsewhere has gone through several changes in its hundred years of existence. From being a movement, Classical Pentecostalism has moved into a structured, institutionalized and established organization/s (while I do not want to deny the need for proper administration of the Church) so much so that today there is a tendency among the Pentecostals to promote their 'Church' than promoting the founder of the Church and His Gospel who gave importance to empowering the poor and the downtrodden. There is a false understanding of evangelism among many Pentecostals who promote the church building or an organization over the people, without realizing the fact that the Church as a building or denomination has the poorest appeal of all to 'sinners'. Bishop F.D Washington of the Church of God in Christ says "… most of the sinners do not go to Church. Yet the fantastic fact remains that the person of Jesus Christ-when he is presented right- has the greatest single appeal to the human heart in this world".[5] I think this is the crux of the matter. The 'new generation' groups are not so much interested in building up denominations as they are in presenting Christ as the Lord to their listeners and bringing them into the saving knowledge of Jesus Christ. The main line

Pentecostal Church leaders are busy in "Pentecostalising" and fully incorporating their existing members into their Churches than adding new ones – a contention that I know many Pentecostal leaders in India may not agree with.

Potentials of Pentecostalism

The Pentecostal movement in India has challenged the Indian Church in many practical ways as an authentic mission. I would like to identify few of them in the following section.

Pentecostalism as a Movement of the 'Empowered Poor'

One of the interesting features of the Pentecostal movement from the very beginning was that Pentecostalism has been the religion of the lowly, poor, racial minorities, women, and "uneducated". The congregation of the Azusa Street Mission was composed of the lowly and "colored people and sprinkling of whites"[6] In America where Pentecostalism was born, its first adherents were the Blacks and the marginalized whites who were working in the sugar cane fields and factories and yet the movement shook the complacent and the optimistic mainline Christian Churches which had sidelined the needs of the poor and the marginalized.

This aspect of Pentecostalism being the religion of the poor is true mainly of Dalit Pentecostalism. While it is true that mainline Pentecostal Churches are becoming ever more sophisticated in their understanding and use of the media and of popular cultural styles,[7] Pentecostalism is still mostly among the poor around the world including India.

The Dalit Pentecostals stand as equals when they participate in conventions and when they worship in Church. There is no class difference when they worship. Therefore it can be said that

Dalit Pentecostal worship is an expression of true democracy and equality which is not the case with many other Churches including some Syrian Pentecostal Churches.

It is precisely for this reason that Pentecostalism has appealed to many of these rather unlettered Dalits than to the 'learned' people in the society. Along with several other reasons it can said that many Dalits who were caught up in the struggle for upward mobility at the turn of the twentieth century responded to the Pentecostal movement because they claimed to have witnessed its capacity to transform individual lives in the here and now for the immediate better. Among others things, it offered two valuable things to the people. It offered hope and practical ways to solve their problems arising out of structural conditions which were beyond the power of the people as individuals. Thus converting to Pentecostalism empowered people in ways that had tangible consequences for themselves and for society.

Cultural Adaptability and Pentecostalism

Pentecostals have been successful in differentiating religion from culture and generally have been successful in creating indigenous Churches, which incorporate unique local forms. According to Synan "Pentecostalism has appeared in cultural settings that range from high pontifical masses in St. Peters in Rome to African outdoor services that meet under trees where the faithful dance before the Lord, to the rhythmic throb of African drums."[8] Due to the belief that the Holy Spirit confers gifts and callings directly upon believers apart from their associations with the ecclesiastical institutions, Pentecostals have been able to contextualize their Church worship to a great extent. It has enabled them to produce indigenous and mission oriented Churches.

Pentecostals promoted an indigenous kind of worship because they were more at home with such patterns. People did not experience much of a cultural dislocation when they joined the Pentecostal movement because they saw a cultural continuity in many Pentecostal aspects of worship pattern. Of the many examples that can be looked into, one can cite the example of beating the drums and singing in ecstasy in Pentecostal Churches in their worship. The noise of the drum brings in a kind of atmosphere in the congregation to worship. This phenomenon has its parallels in other communities as well. Beating the drum is part of major functions/festivals among many Dalits communities whether they are Christian or Hindu. As someone who has been to many Pentecostal gatherings, I have personally witnessed some of these cultural realities within the Churches. I have witnessed how at the noise of the drum people can get into a 'mood' of worship. I have even heard Pentecostal believers saying after the Church that 'today the worship was not lively' because either the drum was under repair or the person who beats the drum had not turned up on that particular Sunday or even the sound of the drum was not sufficient. Therefore the drum plays an important role in the worship of Dalit Pentecostals.[9] One of the major reasons for many people mostly the Dalits to move into the Pentecostal movement was because they saw in Pentecostalism an ideal place to express the dynamics of their culture along with their newfound faith. In other words they did not have to be totally detached from their cultural setting when they accepted Pentecostalism. The Dalits saw in Pentecostalism powerful continuities with those folk elements which were part of their past culture. These included the Spirit-filled worship, which has strong emotional elements, the transmuted elements of Spirit-possession in worship centered on the third person of the Trinity, the whole aspect of faith healing and exorcism, which Pentecostalism offered. Religious activities and concepts were an integral part of their social existence. To put it in a different way, Pentecostalism made it possible for people who embrace the Pentecostal faith to re-live their religious experiences in their spirit, language and culture in song, dance, shouts, laments etc.

Pentecostals and Model Church Structure

Many Pentecostal Churches are built out of their own resources and efforts. Most of their pastors and evangelists are undergraduates who are trained for the work in the field without attaining a degree at the graduate level. (The pastors/ evangelists go through short-term courses, which do not last more than two or three years.) This seeks to break down the barrier between the so-called "qualified" pastoral workers and ordinary Christians. All believers are equipped to preach and evangelize by their experience of the baptism of the Holy Spirit. One of the interesting features is that the gift of the Spirit can fall as easily on the illiterate as on the educated, and *glossolalia* can bless an ordinary member of the Church as effortlessly as the gifted singer in the Church. The foregoing practices of priesthood of all believers and *glossolalia* for all points to the democratic spirit of the movement. Many individuals are rescued and incorporated into the community on an equal basis. Such democratic character of the Pentecostal movement has given itself a definite edge over other Churches where Church offices are held by the so called 'learned and able men'. On the other hand we see in many Pentecostal Churches that individuals are brought into the community of the Church, rescued from a life of abandonment and with a new hope, recovering their dignity opening up before them. One can observe in Pentecostal Churches, to a large extent, an egalitarian experience in different aspects of their day to day life especially in the context of ministry.

Many Pentecostals identify organized religions with modernism[10] as opposed to traditional ways of life and systems. According to them in the modern age dogmas and doctrines are carefully worked out for worship services. Many Pentecostals are not comfortable with this because they think the institutional nature of religion is always for the elite. The poor/Dalits cannot play a role in such an institutionalized religious setup. On the other hand they are more at home with primal forms of worship which are more emotional. Miracles, mysteries and myths still fill them with awe and wonder; dance, drums, and songs help in giving meaning to their empty and broken lives; and the community around them stands in support. Further there is a thirst for an experience of God among the Dalits, which is expressed in their own language. There is a longing among them for fellowship in community because they are still the underdogs in the society. This is one of the major reasons for the formation of many independent Pentecostal Churches in the recent years.

Pentecostalism and its way of life adopting 'puritan rules of life style' which rejects alcohol, drugs, and participation in the evil entertainments of postmodern media and certain contemporary culture such as going to a theatre for movies etc., are considered as some other factors for the success of the movement. Many Pentecostals still insist on chastity and modesty for both sexes and are not influenced by the postmodern life styles. This does not mean Pentecostals are still 'primitive' in their life style but just goes on to say that they are not caught

in the post modern life style. This is all the more true about
the Dalits among the Pentecostal Churches.

The Orality of Pentecostal Worship and 'Liturgy'

Pentecostals do not have a written liturgy in their church
worship. Their liturgy is more verbal. They are against an
established and organized form of worship and prefer an
oral form of liturgy because everyone can participate in it,
both the educated and the uneducated. Within the oral form
there is a lot of freedom that allows a person to worship God
using his/her own understanding of a personal God. Although
the liturgy is not written, everyone knows what he or she is
supposed to do. One is allowed to express oneself because
they are not bound by a hierarchical liturgy. It has facilitated
for many to be attracted to the movement.

The Narrative Nature of the Witness and Theology of Pentecostalism

Unlike the abstract theological elements that have dominated
the worship and witness in other churches, Pentecostals
prefer a narrative expression of their theology and witness.
For Pentecostals God is more than a concept. God is an
experience for them. There is a thirst among them for the
God-experience. They experience God when their children
are healed, when their financial needs are met and so on.
They would like to narrate their experiences of God and that
gives them a lot of satisfaction. I have witnessed this in many
Pentecostal Churches where one can observe people testifying,
praying spontaneously, preaching without written manuscripts
but with a lot of 'theology' that relates to the everyday lives
of the people, their struggles, their agonies and their burdens.
People find this kind of worship and preaching a satisfying
experience.

Pentecostals have been successful in creating indigenous Churches, which incorporate unique local cultural forms. The story telling form which is a popular Indian medium of communication and preservation of traditions is a common form through which Pentecostals have formulated their 'theology' and communicate it to others more clearly than through carefully written theology and dogmas.

Enthusiastic Participation by the People

There is a great emphasis upon group participation in prayer and singing. The sermons are generally simple with plenty of opportunities for men and women to respond not only verbally but with actions as well. The strength of the Pentecostal Churches is that they allow full participation of almost all the members. One's participation is not dependent on a gradation of their physical or academic qualifications but depends largely on the function of the Spirit in one's life. Therefore they participate fully in all the activities of the church like prayer, reflection, and decision making. Through all these they form a community that is reconciliatory. Everyone plays a part in the decision making process of the church. Again this is true mostly in the Dalit Pentecostal Churches.

The Place given to Dreams and Visions in Personal and Public Forms of Worship

Although the written Word of God is considered the fundamental revelation, this does not preclude God's direct communication through other means, such as visions, audible voices, dreams, tongues with interpretation, and other means. Dreams and visions form one of the most important parts of Pentecostal worship. These experiences of God do not just come from the theological books of great 'scholars' but from the everyday experiences of the people. Their dreams and visions include a future where God is on their side and there will be no more injustice done to them.

Pentecostals experienced a re-visioning of their Christian life by embracing the Pentecostal faith. This re-visioning of Christian life found a special place in the concept of community and its worship. Worship is at the heart of Pentecostal spirituality. In fact they function as a worshiping, witnessing, and reflecting community. They worship both verbally and non-verbally. The most important goal of the worship in a Pentecostal church is a personal encounter with the Spirit of God. They believe that God's personal presence is experienced among them when they worship. They claim to meet with God in their worship. They also emphasize an encounter with the Spirit of God in their worship and experience the transformational power of the Spirit of God. Singing in the Spirit is an important part of worship. Prayer is another important aspect of their worship. Through prayer they often 'unburden' themselves. It is quite often vocal and not silent prayer. Another part of the worship is sharing 'testimony'. It is telling one's story of how in the past the Lord led him/her through difficult times such as sickness, financial difficulties and other struggles of life. It is a kind of confession that they make before the congregation, of the ways God which brought them through. Often the community is shaped by the testimony of its members. Another important part is the sermon. While testimonies express the stories of God's people, the sermon declares the story of God. Sermons are usually preached in a narrative or story-telling form. It is a kind of dialogue with the congregation.

Community and Pentecostal Formation

Pentecostal spirituality is not devoid of social relationship. They do not see spirituality and their social relationship as two different things. They believe that in the Spirit 'there is no longer Jew or Greek, there is no longer slave or free, there is no longer male and female but we all are one in Christ'. Worship is the expression of real democracy and equality. There is a celebratory form of worship and communal life. This celebration and communal life is highly participatory.

Women play an equal role in Pentecostal worship. They stand as equals when they worship with their male counterpart. In fact in many Pentecostal churches women play a vital role in worship through their singing, prayer, and even pronouncing the word of God on certain occasions. Women play the role of prophetesses, inspired tongue speakers, healers and visionaries.

While the above are some positive observations of the results of Pentecostal praxis of mission, there are many negative aspects, which they need to rectify at the same time. Money and numbers play an important role in some 'powerful' Pentecostal ministries today. For many Pentecostals without these there can be no divine favor or blessing. There seems to be a tendency towards 'successful' ministries but most of it being 'stage-managed' ministries. According to Cheryl Bridges Jones, "Pentecostalism is an ethos which has more than its share of arrogant evangelists who use the masses for material gain. We have scandals of great proportion and witnessed unholy marriages between military dictators and Pentecostal congregations. Such things tamper any attempts to presume to have arrived at any plateau of spirituality."[11] There is very often a tendency among the Pentecostal leaders who are involved in what we call mission to enhance and build their own empire. Donald Gee, a Pentecostal theologian makes an eye-opening observation about modern day Pentecostalism. He says that 'Pentecostalism more often draws attention to the brilliance of the individual and glorifies man. However, true ministry on the line of 'spiritual gifts' leaves man in the background and glorifies God. Such was true apostolic ministry'[12]

Challenges Facing the Movement in the Present Era

Pentecostal-Charismatic Tensions

There were some interesting developments taking place within the classical Pentecostal denominations in the post-second World War period. From a separation that fed on rejection and its own early tendency toward isolation and intolerant exclusiveness, classical Pentecostalism has become interactive with Protestant evangelicalism and, in certain cases, even with the broader ecumenical Christian community. In many countries the result has been relatively higher level of acceptance and respectability- which Pentecostals now share with non-separatist charismatics who never suffered as high a level of rejection. Yet many Pentecostals, fearing compromise of basic convictions that might lead to a loss of distinctiveness, are not yet entirely comfortable with the entrance into the mainstream of other Christian denominations. The result has been that the movement tends to be divided between those who identify with the past and those who value their newfound identification with the larger church world.[13]

Growing pains became evident with the emergence of the charismatic movement. Pentecostals, who by the middle of the 20th century were identifying closely with mainstream evangelicals, initially applauded the movement. But when many charismatic remained in their own churches rather than shifting to classical Pentecostalism, more dogmatic Pentecostals became frustrated with them. However, the Charismatics aligned to their own church traditions and have tended to recognize the decline and flow of earnest spirituality in Christian history and have found their identity as part of the latest wave of renewal without moving out from their local affiliations. This is not to ignore the fact that there are many independent charismatic Churches comprising of many members who have come out of the traditional Churches.

During the 1980s and 1990s many Pentecostals recognized that the Holy Spirit was accomplishing a new work and sensed an affinity with it. The charismatic renewal brought pressure on the Pentecostals to broaden their identification within the universal church to groups previously considered apostate. In this regard, the untiring efforts of the late David J. du Plessis (1905-87), one-time secretary of the Pentecostal World Conference, proved to be particularly instrumental in building bridges between Pentecostals and charismatics.[14] Through such efforts, the early ideal of ecumenism among the Spirit-baptized has extended beyond the Pentecostal World Conference and so the recent North American Congresses on the Holy Spirit and World Evangelization (meeting annually since 1986), which have encompassed all stripes of classical Pentecostals, together with charismatic Baptists, Episcopalians Lutherans, Mennonites, Messianic Jews, Methodists, Presbyterians, Reformed, Greek Orthodox, and Roman Catholics. These events rank among the most important modern gatherings of Christians because of their size as well as their theological significance. Viewed with suspicion by both Pentecostals and charismatics as the new wave on the shore, neo-charismatic- by their very nature independent and resistant to ecclesiastical connection- have yet to be integrated in significant numbers into these ecumenical dialogues.

According to Hollenweger the famous Pentecostal theologian and historian, genuine Pentecostalism is distinguished by faithfulness to its roots both in its theology and in its outward manifestation. It began with a black ecumenist, by the name William J. Seymour, in the black, oral Afro-American culture; it integrated important elements of Catholic spirituality; it was inspired by the social and political interpretation of holiness developed in the American Holiness Movement.[15]

The Tension between Ministry as a "Call" and "Profession"

When Pentecostalism started in the early part of the 20th century, the movement was filled with people who had a sense of call from the Lord. However as time went by the "call" began to diminish and more of "professionalism" began to emerge. Today the question must be asked: Is it the call or the profession- which is the driving force behind the Pentecostal Churches or Pentecostal ministry? It must be said here that ministry is basically a calling and in that sense it is not a carrier or a profession that we do. There is a vast difference between a career and a calling. A career is something that I choose for myself where as a calling is something that I receive. A career is something that I do for myself but a calling is something that God does through me. A career promises status, power, money and positions and many other things whereas a calling involves difficulties, pain, suffering but at the same time it gives me an opportunity to be used by God. A career is all about upward mobility where as in calling you decrease and allow the *Guru* to increase in your life. Career is what you are trained for but calling is something that you receive from the Lord. Pentecostals should not look at ministry as something that they can perform but something that becomes part and parcel of their life, an extension of their life. Ministry should not be something that we do for God, but something God does through us.

It may be observed that the above struggle of ministry as career and calling is seen mostly among the younger generation of Pentecostal scholars. I fear that very often minor things have taken over our major concerns which are our life and relationship to God. The catch words in the movement today are 'faster, higher, and stronger, words which we have borrowed from the contemporary society.

Pentecostal Movement has gone through several changes. From being a movement, Pentecostalism has moved into a structured, institutionalized and established organization/s. So much so that today there is a tendency among the Pentecostals to promote their 'Church' than promoting the founder of the Church and His Gospel. There is a false understanding of evangelism because many Pentecostals today attempt to promote the Church building or an organization without realizing the fact that the Church as a building or denomination has the poorest appeal of all to 'sinners'. According to Bishop F.D Washington of the Church of God in Christ says that 'most of the sinners do not go to Church. Yet the fantastic fact remains that the person of Jesus Christ-when he is presented right- has the greatest single appeal to the human heart in this world'.[16]

The Danger of "Prosperity Theology"

Another serious concern is with regard to the so called 'prosperity theology' that many Pentecostal preachers' propagate today around the world. Prosperity theology has emerged from some quarters of the Pentecostal and charismatic movements. At the same time a few highly responsible Pentecostal leaders have been very critical of such newer developments within

Pentecostalism. Basically prosperity theology is a North American phenomenon. The socio-economic and political background of North America is the context of its development. Now it has been spread to different parts of the world especially among some Pentecostal and charismatic movements. It is basically a 'theology of success' It asserts that material prosperity is God's will for every Christian. Unfortunately some popular contemporary Pentecostal preachers are the proponents of such a theology. Many of these preachers advocate piety and prayer to be security against dangers and harms in life and criteria for material blessing. It is a kind of an 'insurance' theology. Yet the question that has to be answered is: how can success be at the center and prosperity be the goal of the Christian faith and mission whose central symbol is the cross and the son of God hanging on it, forsaken even by God? I am afraid that some of those proponents of the prosperity theology forget the fact that the distinguishable mark of the spirituality and ministry of the Church throughout the ages has been the crucifying Christ and His cross and not the success oriented Western theology and mind set. The Pentecostal Church and their leaders must learn to 'live simple so that others may simply live'.

In the present day context of our country where around 45% of the people are below the poverty line, where even after 66 years of independence the poor mass is still oppressed politically, economically, socially, and religiously, where the majority are deprived of drinking water, housing, health care, where in the name of development the poor tribal people and the farmers are dislocated in mass, where caste system continue to hold the Dalits and other marginalized groups under darkness, where women and children are treated in dehumanizing ways, what is the mission and ministry of the Church? I believe the ministry of the Church must be one of incarnating into the lives of people and their situations. Incarnation is identifying with the pains and sufferings of the people so that 'death is at work in us and life in the deprived ones of our country'. It should be life and life abundant. Therefore there is an urgent need for Pentecostal missiology to go back to its root when it was known as a 'religion of the empowered poor' where there was no discrimination based on any kind whether wealth/ class/ education etc.

The Tension between "Quantity" and "Quality"

Another aspect that needs serious re-thinking in Pentecostal missiology is its concept of quantity or the craziness for adding more members to the Church. Today there is a 'mega Church' concept that has crept into the Pentecostal Churches and its mission thinking. Very often this craziness for the number game is at the cost of quality and compromising many vital values. There is a big 'hue and cry' about souls being lost without Christ. According to Rene Padilla, a former Associate general secretary for the Latin America of the International Fellowship of Evangelical Students made the following significant statement "There is no place for statistics on how many souls die without Christ every minute if they do not take into account how many of those who die, die victims of hunger".[17]

No doubt there is a lot of influence of globalization that is influencing such above thinking. Globalization projects an ideal culture that is mostly the culture of the West. The basic value of this culture is consumerism and profit. The idea is that you have to make your product appealing. This kind of culture has begun to influence the way Christians/ Pentecostals do ministry. The Gospel is seen as a 'product' which the preacher must 'sell'. The more he sells, the more he becomes famous. According to Gerloff, "When Reinhard Bonnke[18] makes ten thousand people speak in tongues in half a minute or when he stages miracle after miracle in his services, then religion is marketed like a new shampoo or a disco song. That is neither the renewal of the Church nor of society."[19] Unfortunately some of the basic values of the Gospel like love, grace, mercy, relationship are now replaced under the influence of a marketing mentality with words like 'prosperity' and 'success'. In the urge to become famous some 'laborers' of the Gospel use whatever means that are available at their disposal. For many, the end justifies the means, not knowing (or intentionally ignoring) that in God's kingdom the means also matters. What we see here is a commoditation of the Gospel, human relationship and values. A lot of emphasis is laid on Church growth, not realizing the fact that all that grows is not the Church.

External Challenges

We are living in a historical moment, for it is a new millennium and a new age. We are faced with a number of challenges from the world around us and no responsible Christian and more so the Pentecostals can run away from the realities that they face. In the last three or four hundred years we have had several significant developments taking place in the world that have affected human relationships and values.

In the first place the whole concept of Modernism and then Post Modernism in the last few decades has challenged human thinking and values. (What I mean by modernism here is nothing but a scientific rationality or reasoning.) At the same time modernism also brought a crisis along with the challenges. As a result of modernism there began to emerge a critical spirit; this meant that people did not accept traditional thinking in its totality. They began to question the traditional way of thinking. Pentecostal tradition was not free from this challenge of modernism, which definitely influenced their concept of mission. There emerged a critical scholarship. It had both positive and negative impacts upon church and society.

The second issue is the change in the social systems in our society. In the past century a lot of development has taken place in the industrial world. Industrial development has given way to a large extent to the agricultural way of life. Therefore we have had structural changes taking place all around the world which pose a challenge to the mission of the Church. The market began to control our life in the society. Everything was affected through the market concept including the mission of the Church.

Thirdly the whole issue of globalization that we have today is another development which poses a great challenge to the mission. It is primarily an economic process, and unfortunately this whole economic process is now being controlled by a few international/ multinational powers. There is a global market, which is controlling us. As I said in the above paragraph in the traditional society we controlled the market, but now the market is controlling us. The market decides what product we need. Globalization has become a reality today.

There are also other realities in the Indian society like poverty, pluralism, castesism, political instability, environmental degradation, which have become great challenges to the mission. No responsible Christian can ignore such realities and do mission.

The consequence of the above developments has its own impact and implications for the mission in India. There is an ever widening gap between the rich and the poor. The poor are becoming poorer and the rich are becoming richer.

There is an ever-growing migration of people for security and economic reasons to 'other' places. There are ever growing internal conflicts and disintegration of communities. There is communalism, which is also a great challenge for mission. As a result of environmental degradation all sorts of disasters are taking place. People are turning to be militants and terrorists because their raised hopes and expectations are not being fulfilled. All these are great challenges to the mission of the Church in India today. Yet the fact remains that the Churches have not been able to provide adequate alternatives or answers to some of these burning issues in the society. Pentecostal Churches are not exempted from these failures.

What are some of the reasons for the above mentioned failures in the Pentecostal movement or in other Churches? I would like to identify a few and welcome other friends to identify other reasons.

In the first place as I mentioned already the whole issue of prosperity that has saturated the movement today. There was a time when the movement was known as a 'religion of the poor'. However that label is fast disappearing and there is a lot of emphasis laid on 'blessings' meaning mostly the material blessings. What has happened or is happening to the many Pentecostals today is similar to what had happened to the Israelites when they entered into the land of Canaan. Once they entered the land of Canaan they almost forgot the warning that was given to them through Moses while they were in the wilderness that there was every chance for them to forget the Lord when they get into the land of Canaan flowing with milk and honey. In fact what was feared has come true in the lives of the Israelites. They were no more in 'need' of the Lord because unlike in the wilderness where they had to wait for the water from the rock, they now had wells to draw their water from; now they had their own defense while in the wilderness the Lord fought the battle for them; I feel this is almost what has happened to the Pentecostals in India and especially in Kerala!. There was a time when they were very low in their economical status in the society. Like the Israelites in the wilderness, the Pentecostals had to depend fully on the Lord for their provision for each day. Now that situation is over and they are well paced in the society.

The second problem I see among the Pentecostals today is that they have found many substitutes for God. In the beginning of the movement they felt the immediacy of God. They felt the nearness of God but once they crossed certain hurdles on their journey, they began to distant themselves from God. For the third or fourth generation Pentecostals the concept God, Church, revival etc have become 'fussy'. There was a time when God was so near but where is that God today? Their so called "ministry" became their priority than the one who gave them the ministry. The approval of God is not the main aim in the lives of many Pentecostal leaders and members. I fear our 'busy work' for God has taken us away from reflecting his characteristics like holiness, integrity, justice, selfless love etc.

The third reason I find for the failure of Pentecostals is the kind of 'casual attitude' that crept into the Church. In the early years of the Pentecostal movement they felt the clear guidance of the Lord. They were 'on fire' for God. Like the Israelites saw the presence of God through the clouds that followed them, the Pentecostals literally experienced the presence of God (at least claimed to have experienced) in their lives. However now there is lot of nominalism. The original vision seems to have dimmed. Worship, preaching, and other ministries of the Church have become very superficial.

Another dangerous situation is that we have a lot 'satisfying symbols' in our Churches. Symbols are good but when it takes the place of the reality of God it is dangerous. Worshipping God from the heart should not take the place of making some noise or words like "Halleluiah" or "Praise the Lord". Such words should not become a symbol or it should not replace our love for God.

Another reason for the failure can be our 'give and take attitude' or going after the worldly pleasures. In the history of the Israelites, we see some of them seeking after the blessing of Baal. It is high time for the Pentecostals to see what are the areas that they have compromised with the world. Pentecostal ministers must always remember that like Disciples of Christ, they are primarily called to be with Him and then send by Him for the ministry. We must always remember that unless we continue to abide in Him we cannot bear fruit for Him. What is the level of our consistency of being with Him? Sometimes we are so close to Him but at other times we are far away from Him. What is the level of our nearness to Him? Are we improving upon our level of knowledge of Him? Apostle Paul writing to the Philippians says that "I want to know Him". All that I have known about Him is only little. I want to know more of Him. The closer we get to Him, we understand His demands better. However for many Pentecostals Christ is someone to follow at a distance because His demands are not in line with their agenda. Who is the real me or who is the real Pentecostal or more so who is the real disciple or Christian is an urgent question that each of us need to answer.

Conclusion

As I conclude this paper let me make some concrete suggestions for the Pentecostal Churches in India, whether it be classical Pentecostal Churches, Charasmatics, or Independent groups to give some consideration so that they can move forward.

In the *first* place I suggest that the Pentecostals go back to the earlier emphasis on purity of life and transparency in one's relationship with God and with one another. The life of the Apostolic Church was embodied by truth and purity. That was also true of the early Pentecostals.

Secondly there is a need to move from the concept of 'personal piety' to a Trinitarian community of discourse; let us learn to look at truth not as only a personal affair between God and me but a community based relationship. Let us learn to look at truth not as power but as love; let us learn to look at God as a communion and not as a power monger. Let us learn to look at the creation relationally and not as something that we can use to achieve our purpose. Let us not try to fix our problems by our own strength but listen to God so that He may instruct us as to what to do and how to go about resolving our problems. The people of God in Babylon under captivity could not fix their problem but had to listen to God who fixed their problem. Prophet Isaiah had to tell them that it is only those who wait upon the Lord shall renew their strength and not those who think that they can do it by themselves.

Thirdly I suggest that instead of looking at people as commodities, let us learn to look at people from the perspective of God. Today we see everything as commodities. Let us learn the fact that if we want people to know the love of God, it can only be done through the love that God has shown to us through the cross of Christ. What is evangelism? I believe it is making a bridge between our hearts and the other persons heart so that Jesus can walk into their hearts and take possession.

Fourthly I suggest that we move from individualism to covenant practices, practicing hospitality whereby we welcome the stranger. Today there is this fear of others. However let us learn the fact that welcoming the stranger is the biblical way. Hospitality is the practice of an established community. Let us learn that welcoming the stranger begins with our own conversion to the Gospel. Let us do away with such signs like 'beware of dogs' in front of our beautiful gates and begin to welcome people.

In the fifth place may I suggest that we take a journey from future to memory. In Deuteronomy chapter 8 we see God reminding the people of Israel through Moses to go back to their memory and see how the Lord led them through the wilderness through their forty years of journey. Israel only exists because of its memory. Without memory Israel becomes 'not my people'. Only by living in the memory of God's mercy do we become his people. Erasing the memory is to forget God and become no people of God.

The sixth area is that we must truly make every attempt to present an Indian Church that would reflect Indian cultural values and heritage. It was in this context that the Indian Church History Association came out with a new approach to the very writing of Indian Church history. The Church History Association of India (CHAI), especially through its publication *Indian Church History Review* encouraged Indian church historians to write their history from a nationalistic prospective. It was said that "History of Christianity in India is viewed as an integral part of the socio – cultural history of the

Indian people rather than as separate from it. The history will, therefore, focus attention upon the Christian people in India, upon who they were and how they understood themselves; upon their social, religious, cultural and political encounters, upon the changes which their encounters produced in them and in the appropriation of the Christian gospel, as well as in the Indian culture and society of which they themselves were a part."[20]

The seventh suggestion is that they come out of their superiority complex. Here I suggest that we see ourselves not 'over against other religions, other denominations, but in relation' to our friends from other faiths and traditions. The identity of the Church must be relational or else we can become like 'frogs in the well' whereby we do not see anything outside the 'well'. Pentecostal witness must avoid the language of 'you' and 'them' but must become a language of 'we' and 'us'. When we go to a new culture or community, let us leave our cultural baggages behind and should be willing to 'take off our shoes' for the ground we stand may be a 'holy' ground.

Last but not the least; Pentecostal mission must once again include a program to promote the poor, the unwanted, the rejected people of the society where the Church stand with the poor, the landless people, those suffering at the hands of the powerful land lords etc. No responsible Christian missionary can ignore the fact of such issues. Our mission in India today should also give emphasis to transforming human situations. Transformation of humanity and empowering the weak has to take priority over every other agenda because that was/is the main agenda of the Lord of mission during His earthly sojourn and should be continued through His followers. Amen.

Endnotes

[1] Walter J.Hollenweger, *Pentecostalism* (Massachusetts: Hendrickson Publishers, 1997), 184.

[2] Garry B.McGee, *Selected Documents on the Early History of the Assemblies of God in India*, spring field 1991.

[3] Minnie F. Abrams, "How Pentecost came to India," *Pentecostal Evangel*, May 1945, 4.

[4] J. Edwin Orr, *Evangelical Awakening* (New Delhi: CLS, 1970), 96

[5] Bisop F.D Washington at the 62nd convocation of the Church of God in Christ 1969 (Holy Convocation ,ed. J.O Patterson, n.p. 1969) as cited in Hollenweger, *Pentecostalism*,28.

[6] "Weird Babel of Tongues," *Los Angeles Daily Times* (Los Angeles), 18 April 1906, 2. Cited in Wonsuk Ma, "Toward an Asian Pentecostal Theology," in *Asian Journal of Pentecostal Studies*, 1/1, (1998), 33.

[7] The Main Line Pentecostal Churches like Assemblies of God, Indian Pentecostal Church of God, Church of God in India, Sharon Fellowship etc have changed to a large extent to modern ways of life. Their worship and Church structures are almost going back to the main line traditional Churches although these Pentecostal Churches do not have a written liturgy. They use all kinds of western musical instruments available in the market and pattern their worship after the Western model.

[8] Vinson Synan, "Pentecostalism, Varieties and Contributions," in *Pneuma: The Journal of the Society for Pentecostal Studies*, 9 (Fall, 1986), 41.

[9] This was also true of Syrian Pentecostals in their earlier years, but now with all other modern musical instruments, many Syrian Pentecostals have ceased using the drum. The other factor is that as the Syrians went up on their economic status especially in the recent years, some of the old practices of using the drum and sharing testimony, etc are giving way to a more 'programmed' kind of worship, where everything is controlled by the pastor. In other words what I see is a connection between one's economic status and spirituality. However that is another area that needs thorough research.

[10] With the rise of modernism there emerged a critical spirit. People began to question everything including religious faith. In this context people began to have more organized form of religion. Modernization is also a process whereby a society changes from a premodern, pre industrial economy to a modern industrial economy. It includes increased

urbanization, workers shifting from agriculture to industry, increased literacy, and increased opportunity for political participation. However the Dalits who hold tradition very high identifies organized religions with some of this modern thinking. They still follow their earlier patterns of worship and communal structure.

[11] Cheryl Bridges Jones, "Pentecostal Formation- A Pedagogy among the Oppressed," *Journal of Pentecostal Theology, Supplement Series*-2 (Sheffield: Sheffield Academic Press, 1998), 9.

[12] Donald Gee, *Concerning Spiritual Gifts* (Springfield: Gospel Publishing House, 1972), 52.

[13] Gee, *Concerning Spiritual Gifts.*

[14] Gee, *Concerning Spiritual Gifts.*

[15] Hollenweger, *Pentecostalism*, 397.

[16] Bishop F.D Washington at the 62nd convocation of the Church of God in Christ 1969 (Holy Convocation ,ed. J.O Patterson, n.p. 1969) as cited in Hollenweger, *Pentecostalism*, 28.

[17] Hollenweger, *Pentecostalism*, 305.

[18] Reinhard Bonnke is a popular itinerant German evangelist who attracts tens of thousands of people for his evangelistic crusades all around the world but mostly in African countries.

[19] Roswith I.H. Gerloff, "Afrikkanische Diaspora," as quoted by Hollenweger, *Pentecostalism*, 364.

[20] Mathias Mundadan, *History of Christianity in India Vol.1* (Bangalore, TPI, 198), 7.

Pentecostal Understanding
of Devil (Diabolos):
A New Testament Reading

Raju M. Thomas

The concept of Devil is very much prevalent among the Christians particularly among the Pentecostals. For everything that happens in an antagonistic way is always attributed to the devil as if he is the author of all mischief. Many are even fascinated by this mysterious personage. But many others are almost sceptical about the devil's existence and influence on the course of events. Meantime as a theological community though we may not question the actual existence of devil which would indeed be difficult, since it forms a part of revelation – we seem to have failed to put into practice the conclusion to be drawn from it. The devil actually exists. But there is a happy medium between saying this and seeing his influence everywhere. At this juncture I feel it proper to deal with this from the perspective of the Bible, particularly from the New Testament.

There are many scholars who have made extensive study about this topic from the biblical perspective and in relation to the contemporary situation. Some of those who deliberated in this area are Valery Faust, C. M. Magny, Water Farrell, Bernard Leening, Joseph de Tonquedec, Joseph Henninger, Calvin K. Katter, James Kallas and Trevor Ling. Some of them quoting the church fathers like Tertullian and Gregory of Nyssa argue that Lucifer, the bearer of light, is the one who became the Princes of darkness and named as Satan. Most of them claim that the devil is the fallen angel and he was also the creation of God.

In this paper I intend to do the study on the devil mainly on the basis of New Testament understanding. However, a survey of the understanding of the Old Testament, Deutero-canonical texts and the Rabbinical literature, I hope, would provide us more clarity about the New Testament understanding, particularly their influence on the New Testament.

The Term Diabolos

Basically *diaballw* and its derivatives *diabolh* and *diabolos* have sense of 'separating'. So the passive form, 'to be set in opposition to someone', 'to hate' or 'to be hated' by him etc., came into being as the meaning of this term. This was the understanding of Plato and Plutarch. However, the Greek usage leads us to the meanings like 'to repudiate', 'to misrepresent', 'to give false information' and 'to deceive'. Linguistically, *diabolh* and *diabolos* are almost commonly used in the sense of complaint and especially calumniation.[1] Meantime, the word *diabolos* is used for Satan in Septuagint, the meaning of which corresponds to the meaning of Satan in the Hebrew Text, that is, 'an accuser' or 'a slanderer'. The word *diaballw* also means to accuse, to malign etc. Josephus, however, is not seen using either *diabolos* or other names for Satan. He uses *diabollein* and *diabolh* in the sense of calumniation and accusation. The name Satan is a

judicious term referring to an accuser, slanderer, adversary etc.,
in a court. *Diabolos* is only one of those names of the Satan
in the New Testament. From *diabolos* only the English word
devil emerged and it seems to be applied to Satan as a proper
name (however, in certain places in the English translation the
term *diamoniov* also is translated as devil. But this is a wrong
translation. The real translation for *diamoniov* is demon).[2] The
New Testament, similarly, uses *Satanas* as a synonym for *diabolos*.
This is only a transliteration of the Old Testament word Satan
and a derivative of the Aramaic, which means an adversary.[3]
Meantime, there is no distinction that can be ascribed between
the two. Study of the Synoptic Gospels and Book of Acts
suggests that *Satanas* is closer to Palestinian usage. But in the
Gentile realm *diabolos* is more familiar.[4] However, the term
diabolos is rare outside LXX and the New Testament. It is also
found in Wis. 2:23-24 that identifies the serpent of Genesis 3
with devil.[5] The Septuagint uses *diabolh* mostly in the sense of
calumniation and this denotes 'enmity' in Sir. 28:9. In Numbers
22:32 *diabollein* is once used for 'to calumniate' and once for
'to accuse'. But the composite word *endiabollein* is used in the
Septuagint, which means to attack. In Ps. 108:6 *diabolos* is used
in the sense of accuser. Similarly, in Esther 7:4 and 8:1 *diabolos*
is used in the sense of 'opponent' or 'enemy'. In I Macc. 1:36
the 'acra' is called a *diabolos* in the sense of obstacle. Since the
term is used in the Septuagint in different context both for
celestial and terrestrial powers we can only deduce the meaning
from the rendering and from the context. Meantime, the most
acceptable meaning is the accuser or adversary and the most
acceptable translation is adversary. The work of the adversary
implies always an attempt on the part of the *diabolos* to separate
God and man.[6] But it is an open question whether the verb
diabollein influenced the usage.

Diabolos in the Old Testament

The Septuagint is seen translated three Hebrew words as *diabolos*. They are 1. *Tsar* or *Sair* (Lev. 17:7) 2. *Tsarar* 3. *śāṭan*. The first two are found in Es. 7:4 and 8:1 which mean adversary and showing hostility respectively. But all the others are Satan which means an adversary.[7] Whether Satan belong to the noun in *ôn* or whether it represents a simple construction. is a debated issue though in the case of *qāṭāl* it is based on the verb *śāṭan*. In the first instance the term denotes a quality rather than a function, and the basic meaning is 'enemy' or 'adversary'.[8] For the most part of the Old Testament usage does not follow this general meaning. The problem arises when one attempts to select the best English equivalent for Hebrew Satan. The choice usually appears to be between accuser, slanderer and adversary. Though there are a great deal of overlap between the meaning of an accuser and a slanderer, they are not synonymous. To accuse means to find fault and bring changes, falsely or accurately against another whereas slander is always a false statement of claim that is both inaccurate and damaging to the character and reputation of another. Meantime the question emerges whether Satan is or should always be translated as slanderer. Not necessarily, there are certain instances in which Satan is engaged in activities that are blatantly slanderous (Job. 1 and 2). However there are clearly non-slanderous (II Sam. 19:23{eng. 22}, Ps. 109:6). On the basis of the actual use of Satan, we may assume that Satan means "accuser" with the added nuance of either "adversary" or "slanderer", depending on the context.

Terrestrial Satan

In the OT human beings are sometimes called Satan. Nearly seven times out of a total of 26 times, the noun Satan is used in relation to human being. The first human being called a

satan is 'David' and the meaning is adversary (I Samuel 29:4).
The second instance is when Shimei comes to the scene as
the one who cursed David. When Abishai pushed for Shimei's
execution, David opted leniency and branded Abishai as an
adversary (II Samuel 19:23 {Eng. 22}). In Ps. 71:13 also we
find this. The third instance involves Solomon (I King 5:18).
Here Satan is designated as a military enemy with the meaning
of those who threaten the well being of others. In ps. 109:6
also we see human Satan. Here the Psalmist is asking God to
appoint a wicked man against his enemy. Only with the help of
such a prosecutor will culprit be brought to book. However, the
verb and the preposition used there are as same as those used
in association with activity of the celestial Satan against Israel
(I Chro. 21:1) and against Joshua, the High Priest (Zech. 3:1).[9]

Celestial Satans

There are four passeges in the OT that talk of a celestial Satan.
They are Num. 22:22, 23; Job. 1 and 2; Zech. 3:1-2 and Chro.
21:1. In all these passages nearly 19 times the noun Satan is
used. Out of which three are without the definite article where
as the rest (both in Job and Zehariah) are with definite article
hasatan which literally means the Satan. Leaving aside Num.
22:22-23 (where the angel of Yahweh is a Satan) we note that
16 of 17 references to the Celestial satan use the expression
'the Satan'. The lone exception is I Chron. 21:1. This would
seem to indicate that only in I Chro. 21:1, is Satan possibly
a proper name. In the remaining passages, with the definite
article, it is common noun, to be translated something like
"the accuser". It is argued that the use of definite article being
prefixed to a noun normally used in association to a whole
class when restricted to particular individuals. As such, the
definite article could be translated as 'a certain one of'. The

Satan is the enemy in a specific sense, i.e., the accuser at law. His place is on the right hand of the accused (Zech. 3:1). But the accuser may not be necessarily an evil. That is why in the places of Greek translation *diabolos* is used with an adjective *ponhron* (evil) to make it clear that the devil is wicked. The one instance where Satan is described as a celestial figure but not in any way hostile to God is in Num. 22:22, 23. The angel here is both adversary to and accuser of Balaam, and is dispatched on his mission by Yahweh.[10]

It is in the first two chapters of Job that *hasatan* most prominent. Here what we see is that when the divine council presents itself before Yahweh, the Satan is among them. But whether he is a legitimate member or an intruder is not clear here. However *Theological Dictionary of New Testament* says that in the court of Yahweh, Satan also is an official prosecutor. He goes around the world and considers man.[11] It is also interesting to see that this is the only instance where in the Old Testament we find both God and the Satan converse each other. However, the episode makes it clear that Satan may not act independently. Instead he works only with the permission of God.[12]

The second reference to an antagonistic celestial "satan" is found in Zech. 3:1-2. It is not clear exactly what the nature of accusation against Joshua, the High Priest, is. Unlike the Satan in Job, the Satan in Zechariah does not talk. But he is rebuked not by the angel but by Yahweh himself.[13]

The third and final appearance of a malevolent celestial Satan is found in the Chronicler's account of David's census of Israel. The version informs the reader that it was Satan who rose up against Israel and incited David to number his people (I Chro. 21:1). Two things are to be noticed here. Firstly, this is the only place in the OT where the Hebrew word Satan is used without a definite article. Most commentators say that here Satan has a personal name. Secondly, here we see a different version of the same story found in II Samu. 24:1, where it is Yahweh Himself who induces David to hold the census. Scholars make some explanations for this shift. Firstly, it was unbearable for the Chronicler to attribute morally questionable activities to Yahweh, i.e., insisting David to number the people of Israel and punish David as if it is an offence. So the Chronicler ascribed this to the Satan. Then naturally there raises the question why he did not change the other instances where the name of Yahweh is tarnished (For example II Chro. 10:15). But certain scholars argue that it is done by the Chronicler to explain the picture of relationship between Yahweh and David. Another explanation is that most of the OT literature explains evil in terms of primarily cause (Yahweh). But later OT literature expanded this by introducing the concept of a secondary cause (Satan) in its explanation of the evil.[14]

To summarize, so far we have seen that the Satan is a maligner of character, an accuser of God's servant and a seducer of Israel's royal leader. It seems that the OT Satan embodies a threat to man from the world of God. But we are not quite sure whether he appears as the mere prosecutor of ethical faults or as the demonic and destructive principle firmly anchored in the plan of salvation. Meantime, we may assume that in the OT Satan is not connected with some primordial realm, but with sin (of moral nature). Thus we may conclude that a positive and non-dualistic integration (of Satan) into the divine court and the divine government is the distinctive feature of the OT view. At this juncture what Kaufmann observed is pertinent. He stated that "Biblical religion was unstable to reconcile itself with the idea that there was a power in the universe that defiled the authority of God and that could serve as an anti-god, the symbol and source of evil. Hence, it strove to transfer evil from the metaphysical realm to the moral realm, to the realm of sin."[15]

In the Apocrypha and Pseudepigrapha

Setting aside I Chro. 21:1 and Ps. 109:6, one observes that the earliest evidences for 'Satan' as personal name appears in Ju. 23:29 and Assum. Mos 10:1. The majority of Deutero–canonical books produced by the pre-New Testament Judaism refer to a combination of Satan concept with different ideas. In most cases Satan is identified with evil principle or with angel of death. Those literatures, which attributed many features to such evil ones are derived from the independent sources particularly the story of fallen angels. However, it should be stressed that the idea of Satan originally had nothing whatever to do with human impulse or with fallen angel. Four points are to be considered here. A. We learn from Eth.En. 54:6 that there was a definite subjugation of Azazel and his hosts to Satan, and Jub.10:8ff says that Mastema has nothing to do with the fall of angels or the judgment of fallen angels, though he uses them as his instruments. B. The demons are really autonomous in relation to Satan. C. To Satan is attributed only the activity of prosecution and D. A fall of Satan from heaven would make his work impossible. This means that we are not to regard the stories of a fall of angels or of Satan as of first importance in depicting the Jewish conception of Satan.[16]

However, majority of these Deutero-canonical texts refers to variety demons by names and they seldom use the name 'Satan' in general. For example: in Tobit one Asmodeus is seen as archdemon. In the book of Jubilees the name of the devil is primarily Mastema, a Hebrew word that occurs in Hos. 9: 7,

8 with the meaning hatred, hostility and enmity. But the book of Jubilees identify him as the chief of evil spirits, who after the flood, received permission from God for one tenth of his spirits to expedite his will on humanity.[17]

In the Qumran literature Satan occurs only three times (IQH4:6; 45:3; IQSb 1:8) and never as a proper noun. Rather in this literature he is addressed as the leader of the forces of darkness with the name Beliar[18] or Belial, which means the 'worthless.' Similarly, in some pseudepigraphical books as well as in the Qumran 'Belial' is used as a proper noun.[19] However, regarding the understanding of the devil, two trends are visible during this period. One is the popular understanding and the other is the orthodox understanding. The popular Judaism was more concerned about the conception of demon. The principal effect of this was the conversion of many demons into Devils. That is to transform them from the anonymous gods into distinctive forces of evil whose function is not only to inflict misfortune and disaster but also deliberately seduce mankind from an ordered and profitable mode of life. Meantime, they believed that these malign spirits were subject to Satan or Belial. The idea of Mastmah found in Jubilees also is a part of popular religiosity and was understood like the archfiend beliar, but the orthodox tradition was a different one. They believed that the host of Satan (or Beliar) are a special order of angels of destruction and are emissaries of Yahweh, appointed by Him to condign punishment on sinners and heathens (Ecclus. 39:28-31).[20]

While summing up, it is clear that references to Satan either by that name or by a surrogate are much more extensive in apocryphal/pseudepigraphical literature than in the OT. But the reason for the change of understanding may be attributed to the exposure to Persian religion and its Zoroastrian-based dualism. These religious traditions might have provided some of the stimulus for the more pervasive demonology (or diabology) in the Jewish writings. Rather than viewing the world, as the canvas on which one God sketched his unique will for His world, the world now was viewed as a battlefield fought over by both benevolent and malevolent deities. It is difficult of course to trace how this borrowing or influencing worked and even why such a concept would have appealed to exiled Jewish in Mesopotamia. However, it is very clear that in the Deutero-canonical scriptures the Satan begins to emerge as a distinctive personality. We also find that the servant Satan of the OT has turned to be an enemy in the deuteron –canonical period. Similarly, the time honoured classic theory that disaster was divine retribution for apostasy had become increasingly insupportable, both emotionally and intellectually during the Deutero-canonical period.

In Rabbinic Sources

In the Rabbinic literature also we find the noun Satan being used as identical with many other figures. Although Satan does not appear in Gene. 3, Rabbinic sources identified satan with serpent in Eden (Sola. 9b; Sanh. 29a). He is identified in a more impersonal way with the evil inclination, which infects humanity (B. Bat. 16a). In a more personal way, he was the source behind God's testing of Abraham (Sanh. 89b). Additionally, Satan is responsible for many of the sins mentioned in the OT. For example: it was Satan who was responsible for the Israelites to worship the golden calf (Sabb. 89a) and he was the driving force behind David's sin with Bethsheba (Sanh. 107a). Only on the Day of Atonement, Satan is without power (Yoma. 20a).[21]

Satan in the New Testament

The New Testament makes frequent references to the Satan. He is mentioned by that name 35 times. The breakdown of these references is: a. 14 times in the synoptics, b. once in the Gospel of John, c. twice in Acts, d. 10 times in Epistles and e. 8 times in Revelations of which five are in the letters to Churches. As popular as the designation of Satan is the name *'o diabolos* that appears 32 times in the New Testament. There are also a number of other titles given to the devil (or Satan) in the New Testament. What John prefers is the 'Prince of this world' (12:31; 14:30; 16:11). This phrase parallels Matthew's 'the Prince of the demons' and Paul's 'the god of this world' (II Cor. 4:4), 'the prince of the power of the air' (Epha. 2:2) and 'rulers of the darkness[22] of this age' (Ephe. 6:12).[23] A Johannine parallel appears in I John 5:19, where the claim is made that the whole world is under the power of the Evil One. Actually these references correspond to the dualistic understanding of the Qumran and Rabbinical literature. Similarly, along with these titles that describe Satan's power, there are also other titles which describe him pejoratively. They are enemy (Matt.13:39), the Evil One (Matt. 13:18), a tempter (Matt. 4:3; I Thes. 3:5), Beelzebul, the prince of demons (Matt 12:24), Belial (Beliar) (II Corin. 6:15), an adversary (I Pet. 5:8), the father of lies (John 8:44), murderer (John 8:44), a liar (john 8:44), a deceiver (Rev. 10:9), an accuser (Rev. 10:10), Ancient Serpent (Rev. 12:9; 20:2) and one disguised as an angel of light (II Cor. 11:14).

Functions of Devil in the New Testament

All functions attributed to the Satan in the Judaism are found in the NT also. But in the New Testament, they culminate in a single, supernatural power and dominion of Satan to which, demons and the whole of this aeon are basically subjects.

The very meaning of the words used in the New Testament themselves is sufficient to highlight the activities of the devil. The devil in the New Testament is an adversary of God and Christ (Matt. 4:10; 12:26; Mk. 1:13; 3:26; 4:15; Luk. 4:8 [in some MSS]; 11:18; 22:3; John 13:27), an adversary to God's people (Luk. 22:37; Acts 5:3; Rom. 16:20; I Cor. 5:5; 7:5; II Cori. 2:11; 11:14; 12:7; I Thes. 2:18; I Tim. 1:20; 5:15; Rev. 2:9,13 [twice], 24; 3:9) and an adversary of Mankind (Luk. 13:16; Acts 26:18; II Thes. 2:9; Rev. 12:9; 20:7). Satan (or Devil) is not simply a personification of evil influences in the heart, for he tempted Christ, in whose heart no evil thought could ever have arisen (John 14:30; II Cori. 5:21; Heb. 4:15).[24] It is also said that being himself sinful (I John 3:8), he accuses man to God (Rev. 12:9-10) and God to Man. He afflicts men with physical suffering (Acts 10:38), instigates man to sin and do evil (Ephe. 4:27; 6:11) and encourages him by deception (Ephe.2:2) He holds power of death (But Christ through His death triumphed over him (Heb 2:14). His power over death is intimated in his struggle with Michael over the body of Moses (Jud.9).[25] He keeps the gospel from unbelievers (Luke 8:12; II Cor. 4:4) who are under his lordship. He also works to lure the Christians and trap them in sin (Ephe.4:27; I Tim 3:7; II Tim. 2:26 and I Pet. 5:8).[26]

The Relationship between the Devil and the Demons

The Greek word for demon is *daimonion*. In the Old Testament it is used with the meaning evil spirit, neutral anonymous gods or spirits. Meantime, it is a fact that OT lacks a coherent presentation of the demons. The generally accepted view is that the demons are the evil spirits who live in ruins and the desert and are responsible for illness and natural disaster. Sedim (Deut. 32:17; Ps. 106:37) and seirim (Lev. 17:7; II Chro. 11:15) are the two general classes of demons identified by scholars in the OT (in the two judgment oracle also we find this. Isa. 13:21; 34:14 – Seirim). Sedim means demons and seirim means hairy demons, satyrs. In addition, two specific demons are referred in the OT. They are Lilit and Azazel. Lilit is seen as a female demon associated with Isai. 34:14, with various unclean animals.[27] Additional clues to her character and activities are derived from references in ANE and rabbinic literature, which portray her as a 'child stealing demon' and as Adams's first rebellious wife.[28] Similarly, the natural phenomena are also seen as allusion to demons. The name Azezel occurs in Leviticus 16 in the atonement ritual. Almost all modern commentators accept the view that Azezel is a demon inhabiting in the desert. There was mention about Azezel in the book of Enoch where azezel appears as ringleader of the rebel angels who seduce mankind.[29]

Though Hebrew concept of Yahweh's sovereignty minimized the development of demonology in the canonical writings, Jewish literature in the Inter Testamental period elaborates a lot on the origin and activity of malevolent spirits. Thousands of demons were said to be at the side of every man, posing a threat to enter the personality and cause sickness and distress. Similarly, the pseudepigraphical Judaism was convinced that in the Gentile world and in its culture, there is at work an evil will, not of individual men but of demons.[30] It is believed that during the post exilic and Inter Testamental periods, the conception of demon, as of angels, was greatly influenced by the infiltration of the Iranian ideas and the demons were considered as spiritual legion and ministers of the deception according to their understanding.[31]

The New Testament document takes for granted the existence of demons, using the various terms of references from Inter Testamental literature.[32] The Textus Receptus has the word *daimon*, which occurs in Matt. 8:28; Mark 5:15; Luke 8:2 and Rev. 16:4; 18:2. The diminutive forms of *daimonion*, occurs more than 60 times in the NT mostly in the gospels. Paul uses this term in his speech in Acts 17 and I Cori. 10:20-21 with reference to pagan gods. In few instances the word pneuma without any modifier also is referred to demons (Matt. 8:16; Luk.9:39; 10:20). But the usual practice is to describe the character of spirit. Consequently, 'pneuma akatharton' occurs frequently in Mark and Luke. In the New Testament physical afflictions are mostly attributed to evil spirits. Jesus' ministry had a significant aspect of casting out demons.[33] However, it should be understood that in the Old Testament no connection is referred between the figure of Satan and the demons. The demons seem to work independently. But in the later Judaism there is no relative autonomy of demons. In the New Testament demons are completely subject to Satan (devil) who is called *archon thes exousias tou aeros* (Eph. 2:2). In the New Testament, there are two kingdoms, the kingdom of the prince of this world and the kingdom of God. Satan fights with all his might against the Kingdom of God. Therefore, there is no place of any special interest in the subordinate helpers in this conflict whether angels on the side of Christ and the demons on the side of Satan. In the New Testament the demons are angels and instruments of Satan. This unconditional subjection of demons to Satan may be seen from the Beelzebul story (Mark 3:20 ff). Here we see Jesus substitutes Satan with Beelzebul as the leader and says that it is impossible for the devil to have a divided kingdom. In virtue of this subjection, the activity of demons loses the occasioned and relatively innocuous character.[34]

The Satan at Present

Almost all NT understanding of Satan still remains within the Christian circle. But to understand the work of Satan at present is a bit difficult task. We must bear in mind that the power of the Satan continues even today. But we usually look up the picture of the Devil in the stories of gospel and think that it is for all times. We also look for the devil to act today precisely the way he did 2000 years ago. We assume that the devil does not change and his pattern and will be the same today. But the devil takes diverse forms, different disguises in every age. One of his tricks today is that he leads people to look for him in the same form that he took in the past. If we look for the literal reproduction of biblical devil we may fail. It does not mean that he may not appear in something ugly. He is subtle and attractive. He can lure, entice and give promise to people.[35] Satan, as Jesus has rightly pointed out, is the father of lies. Falsity, violence and pride are the three main features of satanic work in the present century. The lot of problems that dehumanize people in our society should be seen as the work of satanic powers. The widespread abuse of drugs, perpetuation of starvation and poverty, conflicts between ethnic, religious and linguistic groups should be understood as the work of the devil. The rise of religious fundamentalism, opposition to the gospel of the Kingdom of God, killings, bloodshed, genocide, homicide and all the vices that assault and threaten the very existence of humanity and nature should be seen as diabolic. Jesus says that the Devil is a liar and he comes to steal, to kill, and to destroy. Since the devil is the ruler of this world in contrast to the reign of God, he always works antagonistic to disrupt the work of God and to destroy God's cosmos to the extent of his power. The huge collective forces of modern societies with their bureaucratization of responsibility have produced the banality of evil. The very ideas of relativism, nihilism and cultural despair are weapons from the devils' arsenal. Similarly, the revival of the occult that began in the 60's of the last century as part of anti-establishment and counter cultural movements and also some of those 'New Age Movements' include an element of diabology. Whatever Jesus did in this world was to crush the rule of the enemy. Jesus' exorcisms were not merely isolated incidents. Instead, they were direct confrontation with the kingdom of the enemy. They were the demonstrations of God's power to establish the Kingdom of God. In that sense, whatever happens and exists against the kingdom values should be seen as devil's work. How the devil does his work in the world. Firstly, it is through individual psychology. He is a tempter, seducer, perfidious counsellor or the inspirer of evil actions. He also makes false true and makes the impression of evil being good by transferring himself into an angel of light. He plucks the divine seed from the human hearts. Similarly the devil's intervention in the material realm is always particular, occasioned and limited to special circumstances. Just as divine wonders, the devil also can perform miracles and wonders. In addition, just as the divine foreknowledge, certain events may be brought about by diablolical intervention.[36] Satan is the god of this present age and thus renders it evil. He manifests his malignant will through suffering and sickness, through hunger and deprivation and sets his final seal of the futility of human existence by capturing all children of human with weapon of death, of extinction.

However, it is an undeniable fact that as part of popular religiosity, there exists in the society so many beliefs. It is also found that certain set of people particularly in the rural area believes that there are certain demonic forces that work through and causes a lot of problems to them. On the basis of this many kinds of black art and other sacrifices have developed. This should be understood as part of diabology. It is also understood that there has emerged a church as Satan's church (Antony Azandor Cavay founded his church of Satan in 1966). The whole aim of that church is to disrupt the work of the Church of Christ and to bar the possibility of the spread of the gospel. This Satanism is an odd form of chio. Some satanic groups are merely frivolous with its breathless sexual hedonism in occult trappings. Some others practice cruelty. A third variety that pretends holiness is exemplified by the Jim Jones cult and that in the name of Christianity led hundreds to grotesque suicide in Guyana jungle. Recently, there has emerged a church with the name process Church. Their sole intention is to unify Jehovah, Christ, Lucifer and Satan. In addition, the heavy metal rock music with its occasional invocation of the Devil's name also has elements of diabology in it.[37]

The End of Satan

We read in the New Testament that Christ came to destroy the works of the devil (Heb. 2:14-15; I John 3:8; Ephe. 1:21-22). However, Satan still has a short time on earth (Rev. 12:12). Therefore, he will intensify his work against the humankind and God in the last days (II Thes. 2:9-10) as he did against Israel in the past. The epistles are full of warnings against Satan (I Cori. 7:5; II Cori. 2:11; I Thes. 2:18; Eph. 4:27; 6:11; I Tim 3:6f; II Tim. 2:26). Some argue that the story of Job makes an impression that the god of this story is not an absolutely omniscient God, because he was not sure of what the outcome would be when Job is smitten. It is not to limit God in any sense but this story forces us to think in such a way that God's knowledge does not encompass all possible hypothetical situations. But others argue that this is the worst way of interpretation. To them Yahweh is infinitely Omniscient and that the suffering scene of Job is only to prove that God is right in the eyes of one of his subordinates.[38]

Though in the story of Job we see a god who acknowledges the accuser and takes the challenge, in Zechariah 3:2 Yahweh rejects the accuser's indictment of the high priest and rebukes the accuser instead. However, in these two instances we see God as one who embodies and perfects the function of opposition and the Satan as one who accuses precisely those whom God is inclined to favour. But gradually, the ostensible defender of God subtly becomes God's Adversary and in the late centuries the figure of Satan develops more into the dualistic opponent of God. The New Testament also presumes this hostile image of Satan.[39]

The New Testament again assumes God as the good Lord, with whom Jesus Christ, the son and word of God, is identified. The devil is subordinate to Christ, but he fights against Jesus constantly and consistently. Meantime, the sense and degree of his subordination is unclear in the NT. The Devil in the New Testament is opposed to Jesus Christ and is the prime adversary to Christ.[40] The best literal reading of the New Testament seems to show Jesus struggling not only against individual sins but also against a power of evil. Kallas says that every facet of Jesus' life was dominated by his belief in the reality of demonic forces.[41] It is also interesting to see that Jesus spoke more about devil than he did about angels. From the gospels we find that much of Jesus' time was taken up by encounters with evil spirit. In the opening chapters of Mark Jesus encounters no less than five situations involving satan or evil spirit.[42] The work of Jesus casting out the demons was the manifestation of the greater work of casting out Satan. This is further illustrated by the Beelzebul controversy (Matt. 10:25; 12:24, 27; Mark 3:22; Luke 11:15; 18-19). From this controversy we assume that the devil has a kingdom with which Jesus is in close confrontation. What becomes clear here is that Jesus' work of exorcism was a sign of the coming of the kingdom of God. Similarly, we find a decisive confrontation of Jesus with the Satan in Luke 13:10 where Jesus relives one from the clutches of Satan. However, the best and tough confrontation between Jesus and Satan is the wilderness temptation. Mathew (4) and Luke (4) give an elaborate detail about this episode. Here we may perceive that the opening of Jesus ministry was marked by such satanic attack. Satan's role in this situation does not relate specifically to worship him. What is meant here is that Jesus was tempted to pursue Satan's task in the ways of the world, that is, to gain glory for himself. He wanted Jesus to compromise with the James 4:7 and I Pet. 5:8. It is said that in the last days Satan will summon Anti-Christ to serve him (Rev. 13:2; II Thes. 2:9f). Then the Anti-Christ will rise in the power of Satan and will prevail. Meantime, the fact that Anti-Christ can overcome the community brings sharply in to focus the tension running through. However, the Satan is not without limitation. In several ways the New Testament makes it very clear. First, the intercession of Jesus stalls the devil's design on Peter (Luke 22:23). Second, he is a fallen being (Luke 10:18). Third, he is judged (John 16:11). Fourth, his power over persons' life may be broken (Acts 26:18). Fifth, God may use Satan to chastise an apostate believer (I Cori. 5:5). Sixth, his temptations, however potent, may be overcome and his ruses exposed (Matt. 4:1-11). Seventh, he may be resisted, just as Jesus resisted him (Eph. 4:27). Eight, the NT never refers to Satan as simply the prince\ruler but as 'prince of devils' (Matt. 9:34) or prince of the world' (John 12:31). Ninth, at God's discretion he is bound (Rev. 20:2) and will finally be judged and thrown into the lake of fire (Rev. 20:10).

Reflection

Before conclusion, I would like to reflect on three things on the basis of certain selected passages from the Bible. 1. Relationship between God and Satan. 2. Relationship between Christ and Satan. 3. Relationship between the Church and Satan. First of all it is in the Book of Job that we see God and Satan face to face. Here, there is an ambivalence in the relation between Yahweh and the accusing angel. In Job Satan is rightly subordinated to God and all what he does seem to serve God's interests. The freedom with which Satan can address Yahweh, the influence he can have upon him and plenipotentiary power granted to him show that he was not in any way an intruder in the God's council. Instead he is supposed to be a member of the divine court to defend God's honour by exposing those who pose threat to it. In that sense he seems not to be God's adversary but the adversary of sinful and corrupt human beings. Scholars are of opinion that in Job the common royal practice (both in Egypt and Israel) is attributed to God, that is, god being pictured as king surrounded by his courtiers, receiving reports from them, taking counsel with them and giving directives to them. There are other clearest Old Testament analogies to support this view. In I Kings 22:19-22 we see Yahweh envisaged by Micaiah as sitting on a throne with his courtiers on his right hand and on his left. Similarly, in Daniel 7:9-11 'the ancient of days' is seen seated in a throne, thousands of courtiers attend him, and a court for judgment is constituted. Other allusion to the complex of ideas appear in Ps. 7:8 [Eng.7]; 29:9-10; 82; 103:19; Isai. 6:1-8; Job 15:8. In Job (1 and 2) it says that among the 'sons of God' (the Divine council) Satan also comes. The word 'among' gives the hint that he was also a member of God's council. Some scholars argue that the Sons of God or angels are manifestations of the divine personality and means of execution of divine decisions. Satan thus represents manifestation of divine doubt. Here the God who doubts himself and tests the loyalty of Job to test his own self-confidence is seen as interesting personality to be observed. They argue that this is more credible than to assume that God needs to allow 'Satan' to afflict Job to see whether Job's piety is disinterested or god of this story needs to wait for the infliction of the suffering to know Job's response. Since the God of this story appears to be more demonic forces that control it, He expected Jesus to be indebted to him as very successful man. But what Jesus sought was not his glory but of his father, God. Meantime, it is interesting to see that Jesus answering each one of the temptations in terms of right human piety. The stand taken by Jesus is proper to every human being.[43] However, the significance of Jesus' act and the final defeat of the devil are the sign of the coming reign of God and have become hope of the humanity.

Secondly, it is in the book of Revelation (12th Chapter) that we get the real picture of the confrontation between the church and Satan. Throughout the epistles we have the warnings given to the church against the Devil. But the book of Revelation was written at a time when the very existence of the Church was under serious threat. Therefore, in order to get a clear picture of the relationship between the Church and Satan we have to look into the book of Revelation.

Christian in Asia at the end of the first century had a lot of problems to face that the people at large did not. The Christians were a set widely suspected of being unpatriotic and irreligious. They were thus likely candidates to become scapegoats for disasters. They had the worst time under Nero and Domitian. They also had social and economic discriminations. They were also subjected to unofficial mob violence and plundering of property (Hebrew 10:34; 12:14; I Pet. 4:14, 16; 5:9). In such a situation, in order to empower the Christians in their faith, the apocalyptic literature started appearing. The book of Revelation is one among them. In the mythical story of revelation 12 we get a picture of the church. The woman in the story is compared with the Church. And the earthly throne of the Roman Empire is associated with the Devil (in Chap ii we see that at Pergamum, there was throne of the devil, which was actually a temple for the emperor worship). The Christians believed that the Roman imperial rulers were not their real enemy but the Satan who was the real power behind the earthly Roman Empire. Cullmann also accepts this view when he says that: "what ever our personal attitude towards this view may be, we must conclude from this fact that these powers, in the faith of the Primitive Christianity, did not belong merely to the framework 'conditioned by the contemporary situation'. It is these invisible beings who in some way... stand behind what occurs in the world."[44] In this story, the dragon[45] has been defeated (we do not know whether it was due to Jesus' work or due to the war in heaven between Michael and the Devil) and expelled from heavens. Therefore, he vents his last wrath and frustration on the woman. The dragon that represents the primeval anti- creation forces of the watery abyss, open his mouth to sweep the woman away with a flood. But, having failed in his attempt, the dragon summons an ally from the sea and gives him throne and authority. That is what is manifested in the Roman Imperialism. But 'the super personal forces of evil' are not speculative abstraction for John and his church but are met in their embodiments in the social structures of John's situation and in the institutionalized evil of Roman Empire. Early Christianity adopted this mythology as its way of expressing its conviction that evil was more than the accumulation of individual human sins. This super-individual power of evil, which has the world and the humanity in its grasp, was always in confrontation with the Church.[46]

Conclusion

In liberal Protestantism the tendency to wed theology and biblical criticism in an effort to 'demythologize' Christianity has continued to dominate in spite of the neo-orthodox revival of Karl Barth and his followers. Conservative Protestantism tends to reject the 'higher criticism' and continues to base its view upon Scripture. They literally believe in what the Bible says about the Devil, which is like that of the reformers, based upon patristic and scholastic exegesis and tradition. In the Catholic church, the traditionalists, aware of the virtually unanimous opinion of the Church throughout the ages on the existence of Satan, continue to affirm it where as the liberals discard the doctrine as old-fashioned and contrary to the discoveries of biblical criticism. To many it is a symbol rather than a real personality. For many others the idea of Devil is a post-exilic injection. Some say that even the Church Council's statements on the Devil's existence should be rejected as part of an outdated worldview. There are also claims that Jesus himself did not refer seriously to the Devil. All what he said were words put on the mouth of Jesus by the evangelist. But such a flat rejection of the teaching of Bible regarding the Devil as part of the primitive worldview poses serious dangers. Belief in the existence of Devil really permeates the NT. Therefore if the belief in the existence of Devil is rejected, any other belief expressed by the NT – including belief in the incarnation and resurrection – should be subjected to such treatment. Benaros says that without belief in the existence of Satan, one cannot fully believe in God.[47]

Satan language and mystery, like the language and imagery of apocalypticism generally, can be the vehicle of profound theological truths and may be the necessary vehicle for some essential Christian insights and affirmations. Therefore I feel that those who have deep social conscience should value the NT's imagery for the demonic power of evil and should take it seriously but not literally. Satan as a symbolic way of thinking of the super personal power of evil is a valuable dimension of Biblical theology. The power of evil is bigger than individual sins. Satan is not merely the individualistic tempter of pretty sins. He is the deceiver of the nations (Rev. 2:7-8). We might now label it more as "systematic evil" or picture it more in accord with our own times as vast impersonal computer-like network of evil in which our lives are enmeshed and which influences us quite apart from our wills. A valuable dimension of this imagery is that it pictures the vastness of the reservoir of evils by which we are threatened and from which we can not deliver ourselves. In the final analysis, the urgent and continuing task of Christians now is to affirm that there is evil in the word, and that evil can mount to such a pressure point for a person or a culture or a system, and that it may take on a personality of its own. Against that power we must stand with the assurance of the gospel that the redemptive power of Christ is greater than the evil present in the world.

Endnotes

[1] Gerhard Kittel, *Theological Dictionary of the New Testament Vol. 2* Trans. Geoffrey W. Bromily (Michigan: Wm. B Eerdmans Publishing Co., 1966), 71.

[2] W. E. Vine, *An Expository Dictionary of New Testament Words* (London: Oliphants, 1969), 306.

[3] Vine, *An Expository Dictionary of New Testament Words*, 320.

[4] Kittel, *Theological Dictionary of the New Testament Vol. 2*, 79.

[5] David Noel Freedman (Ed.), *Anchor Bible Dictionary* Vol. II (New York: ABD Doubleday, 1992), 183.

[6] Kittel, *Theological Dictionary of the New Testament Vol. 2*, 73.

[7] Edwin Hatch and Henry A. Redpath, *A Concordance of the Septuagint* (Oxford: The Clarenden Press, 1897), 299.

[8] Kittel, *Theological Dictionary of the New Testament Vol. 2*, 73.

[9] David Noel Freedman (Ed.), *Anchor Bible Dictionary* Vol. V (New York: ABD Doubleday, 1992), 985.

[10] Freedman (Ed.), *Anchor Bible Dictionary* Vol. V, 986.

[11] Kittel, *Theological Dictionary of the New Testament Vol. 2*, 73.

[12] Freedman (Ed.), *Anchor Bible Dictionary* Vol. V, 987.

[13] Freedman (Ed.), *Anchor Bible Dictionary* Vol. V, 987.

[14] Freedman (Ed.), *Anchor Bible Dictionary* Vol. V, 987.

[15] Kaufmann (KRI. P. 65) in David Noel Freedman (Ed.), *Anchor Bible Dictionary* Vol. V, 987.

[16] Kittel, *Theological Dictionary of the New Testament Vol. 2*, 75-76.

[17] Freedman (Ed.), *Anchor Bible Dictionary* Vol. V, 987-988.

[18] In II Cori. 6:15 Paul uses this word as antithetical to Christ.

[19] Freedman (Ed.), *Anchor Bible Dictionary* Vol. V, 988.

[20] George Arthur Buttrick (Ed). *Interpreter's Dictionary of the Bible* (New York: Abington Press, 1962), 821.

[21] Freedman (Ed.), *Anchor Bible Dictionary* Vol. V, 988.

[22] The ruler of the darkness concept also is seen very much prevalent in the New Testament. At the time of the arrest of Jesus, he said that this the time of darkness. It is also understood to some extent that during night the power of the devil in the increase. This is supposed to be the reason why Peter repents at the crow of the cock, which mark the beginning of dawn. This may the reason why the Roman law did not permit the trial of person during night, which really was violated in the case of Jesus, and some scholars say that this was why Jesus was denied justice.

[23] This is a special use of Paul. But elsewhere he speaks of *Arcontes tou kosmou toutou*, which carries the same meaning, that is something with cosmic emphasis. *Kosmokratores* is used in the Hellenistic mystical writing for supreme astral deities. It occurs in the rabbinical literature also. It is understood that Paul uses these terms also in connection with the astral powers. To him the 'reigns' means elemental spirits, which are astral powers, subjected to Satan. K. James Carl, *The Pauline View of Christian Freedom in terms of the Enigmatic Phrase stoicheia tou Kosmou* (Madras: The United Evangelical Lutheran Churches in India, 1983), 31 ff.

[24] Vine, *An Expository Dictionary of New Testament Words*, 320.

[25] Vine, *An Expository Dictionary of New Testament Words*, 306.

[26] Freedman (Ed.), *Anchor Bible Dictionary* Vol. II, 183-184.

[27] Freedman (Ed.), *Anchor Bible Dictionary* Vol. II, 139.

[28] Buttrick, *Interpreter's Dictionary of the Bible*, 819.

[29] Buttrick, *Interpreter's Dictionary of the Bible*, 326.

[30] Kittel, *Theological Dictionary of the New Testament Vol. 2*, 16.

[31] Buttrick, *Interpreter's Dictionary of the Bible*, 821.

[32] Kittel, *Theological Dictionary of the New Testament Vol. 2*, 16.

[33] Freedman (Ed.), *Anchor Bible Dictionary* Vol. II, 140.

[34] Kittel, *Theological Dictionary of the New Testament Vol. 2*, 18.

[35] James Kallas, *The Real Satan* (Minnesota: Augsburge Publishing House, 1975), 107-110.

[36] Bernard S. J, "The Adversary-Satan," in *Satan*, edited and published by Sheed and Ward (New York:1952), 48.

[37] Jeffry Burton Russel, *Mephistopheles – the Devil in the Modern World* (London: Cornell University Press, 1986), 251-256.

[38] David J. A. Clines, *Word Biblical Commentary Vol. 17* (Texas: Word Books Publisher, 1989), 17-28.

[39] Clines, *Word Biblical Commentary Vol. 17*.

[40] Jeffry Burton Russel, *Satan in the Early Christian Tradition* (London: Cornell University Press, 1981), 27.

[41] James Kallas, *Jesus and the Power of Satan* (Philadelphia, 1968), 202 in Russel, *Mephistopheles*, 1986.

[42] Lester Sumrall, *Demon: The Answer Book* (New York: Thomas Nelson Publishers, 1979), 37.

[43] John Nolland, *Word Biblical Commentary Vol. 35a* (Texas: Word Books Publisher, 1989), 177-182.

[44] Cullman, *Christ and Time*, 103 in G. H. Macgregor, "Principalities and Powers: The Cosmic Background of Paul's Thought," *New Testament Studies* Vol. 1 (1954-1955): 19.

[45] In this story John follows the Jewish tradition and indentifies Satan with the serpent of 'fall'. Similarly, he uses the term accuser (12:10) because that designation is powerfully appropriate in the situation of the Asian Christians who found themselves accused before the Roman Court.

[46] M. Eugene Boring, *Interpretation: Revelation* (Louisville: John Knox Press, 1989), 11, 158-164 and Robert H. Mouse, *The New International Commentary on the New Testament: the Book of Revelation* (Michigan: William B. Eerdmans Publishing Co., 1977), 236.

[47] Benaros quoted in Jeffry Burton Russel, *Mephistopheles*, 277.

Jesus the Exorcist:
The Emerging Pentecostal
Christology in India

Shaibu Abraham

Indian Christian theology can be termed as the conceptualisation and interaction of the person and work of Christ into the socio-economic and religio-cultural realities of Indian people. The history of Christological development in India is replete with various levels of pictures of Jesus Christ due to differing religious, cultural and social scenarios. The effort of Indian Christology, rather Indian Christologies, is to depict Christ in a way that is intelligible to diverse contexts has added shades and colours to Christological articulations. Moreover, by engaging in dialogue with various ideologies, philosophies, religious tenets and people movements, Indian Christologies as a whole have enriched the Christological articulations and contributed much to global Christological endeavours thus, eventually serve people better. A cursory glance reveals that these Christologies not only contextualised the person and message of Christ knowing the spiritual needs in Indian society but also presented Him as a transforming and empowering presence among the people. Among these Christologies, we will have a glimpse of an unexplored Christology, namely, Jesus the exorcist, that has emerged due to the spread of the Pentecostal Movement in India, which is relevant to the ordinary people. Before we do this, we will have an overview of various strands of Indian Christologies to see how they portrayed Christ.

Indian Christologies: An Overview

As we look back to the colonial period, the Indian churches and seminaries were widely used the imported western Christology with its philosophical categories and underpinnings, which was alien to Indian Christians. The theological scenario began to change by the end of the 19th century in which Indian theologians began to realise that Western Christologies were irrelevant to the Indian people. This was partially due to the socio-political and religio-cultural change which detonated the freedom struggle and rising patriotic feelings among Christians. This realisation facilitated the proliferation of diverse Christological articulations in the 20th century.

This evolution of the Indian Christologies, can be divide into various strands. This takes us back to the 19th and 20th centuries, when some social and political leaders, mainly of the Indian Freedom Movement, endeavoured to present Christ to educated Hindus. Their presentations of Christ primarily emerged as a reaction to the western mode of Christianity as well as due to the captivating power of the person and the message of Christ, which became an inspiration for their reform movement.[1] These groups belonged to Hinduism but had a secular outlook. After hearing the Gospel, they grappled with the person and teachings of Jesus and tried to appropriate what was feasible for them but rejected the western interpretation on Christ as well as what was incompatible with their own traditions.[2] They portrayed Jesus as a great moral teacher.

Prominent among them were Raja Ram Mohan Roy, Mahatma Gandhi and S. Radhakrishnan.[3]

A second strand of Christologies emerged in response to Hinduism and we can mainly divide them into two areas: the Christologies which emerged in response to the Hindu philosophical systems[4] and popular Hindu religious piety. The former mainly utilises the *vedantic* tradition of Upanishad, expounded by Sankara in which the ultimate or *Brahman*, in its timeless essence is beyond all predicates and qualities (*nirguna*) and identical with the self.[5] However, to overcome the difficulty of impersonal nature of Brahman, Brahman is also explained with attributes. This is *Saguna Brahman* and also called *Isvara*, so that people with a lower level of knowledge can approach him through devotion. Here, Jesus Christ is portrayed as *Isvara*. Some of the Indian theologians like Keshab Chandra Sen, Brahmabandhav Upadhyaya, Raimundo Panikkar and others re-interpreted and presented Christ in *vedanta* philosophical categories so that it would make sense to the philosophical Hindus.

The latter strand used popular devotional (*bhakti*) tradition especially Ramanuja's *Vishishta-advaita* - modified non-dualism. For Ramanuja, the impersonal *Nirguna Brahman* of Sankara was a useless God. God is related to the world as a human soul is related to the body, and since this is not a relation of identity, a personal relationship is possible between God and a devotee. In this relationship, Robin Boyd comments that, "… there is warmth and love and personal devotion; here there is experience of God's grace; here there is that utter self-abandonment to the love and the power of God…."[6] Thus, this strand depicted the person of Christ in devotional terms, as a favourite personal God, *avatar* or as a bridegroom, catering the need of popular Hindu religiosity. Theologians such as A. J. Appasamy, Narayan Vaman Tilak, H. A. Krishna Pillai, Vengal Chakkarai and others belong to this thought.

The third category of Christologies emerged in the Indian theology in response to the cultural situation of Indian society, attempted to present Christ in the categories of the common masses. These Christologies were indigenous in nature and reflected a mystical and popular religiosity understandable to the culture, language and concepts of the ordinary people. The people who were behind them were evangelists in the true sense of the word, who ministered among the common people. Their mystical experiences acted as the fountainhead of their theology while the cultural elements added shape and colour. Moreover, they were pioneers in contextualising the Gospel to make it understandable to the ordinary people. This strand presented Christ as great saviour, *guru* and *avatar*. Notable among them are Sandu Sundar Singh and Subha Rao.

The fourth category of Indian Christologies emerged in response to the socio-political and religious changes and advocates dialogue with secular and religious movements; it emphasised liberation from the socio-economic evils existing in Indian society. Religious conflicts, antagonism between communities and socio-political ideologies have threatened the integrity and safety of Indian society. Moreover, caste discrimination, religious oppression, and rampant economic exploitation also became sources for the development of Christologies. Therefore, dialogue and liberation are considered to be indispensable acts in the Indian context because they both reinforce and contribute efforts to address the struggles which exist in socio-economic and religious realms. Thus, some Indian Christians have felt the need of dialogues between different religions for peace and harmony among communities, while others have emphasised dialogue with socio-political and economic forces to bring liberation to the oppressed and the poor. Thus, Jesus is considered as the meeting point of various religious traditions for dialogue and also as a liberator for the oppressed. Prominent among the first group are P.D. Devanandan, Swami Abhishiktananda, and Stanley J. Samartha. The second group consists of persons as well as of theological movements; M. M. Thomas, Sebastian Kappen and K. C. Abraham are well-known among the people; Dalit theology, Tribal theology, and an Indian version of liberation theology are important among the movements.

Even though above description is not a neat categorization of Indian Christologies of more than 150 years, it is obvious that the existing religious, social and cultural needs have been well taken by these Christological presentations. They had taken strenuous efforts to tackle various important issues like religious pluralism, dialogue and other categories. They also attempted to address the plight of the ordinary people, Dalits, Tribals and vulnerable classes and presented the picture of a Christ who would liberate and lift them up. They also dealt with social, political and economic situations of the common people. The proliferation of these Christological articulations have brought a revolution in the Indian theological realm and the literature belong to them abound. Yet, knowingly or unknowingly, many of them were not able to acknowledge the ground realities, especially the spiritual realties of ordinary people. Some of these Christologies stand above the reach of the ordinary suffering people. Jesus as the liberator seems to be a good option to awaken the consciousness of the people, nevertheless, it was not fully successful in addressing the spiritual and cultural realities of the ordinary people. Besides, these Christologies did not have a provision to act upon the spiritual conditions of the common people which includes supernatural and miraculous dimensions of realities. The supernatural dimension needs to be addressed by a Christology as it is closely related to the liberation of the people, liberation from bondages of evil effects, that of cultural and religious systems.

Having said this, if we take a deep exploration into the life situation of the Dalit, Tribal and lower caste population of rural and urban areas of India, we see a different sort of social, cultural and spiritual circumstances that would give a shocking picture of Indian realities. They go through untold miseries such as lack of health care, sickness, draining of economic resources due to alcoholism and other evils. They face brutal attack of evil spiritual forces, evil effect of witchcraft, and exploitation of traditional healers. A research conducted among these people revealed that they have been oppressed by malevolent spirits and burdened under harmful religious and cultural practices, other than poverty, lack of health care, caste discrimination and communalism.[7]

As we look into the Indian church context, irrespective of denominational differences, it is a fact that the majority of the Christians come from such backgrounds especially in northern part of India. It is these suffering people who are responsive to Christian gospel and join the Indian churches. Besides, the rapid growth of Pentecostal churches among the Dalit, Tribals and lower strata of the Indian population has revealed the real plight of these people. The evangelistic and mission work among them have liberated many from the clutches of spiritual oppression, harmful religious and cultural practices which ruin their lives and drain their economic resources. The mission practices which emphasise miraculous healing and exorcism in the name of Jesus have highlighted the vital relevance of the power encounter and resultant Christological articulations. In addition, a research conducted among the Pentecostal believers from the Dalit, Tribal and the poor backgrounds shows that they understand 'Jesus as the exorcist' in such a context. This understanding is one of the basic Christological articulations of the ordinary believers.[8]

Therefore, here we shall look into this unexplored Christology or rather Christological theme of 'Jesus the exorcist' fully to understand its functioning in Indian context. Moreover, it is vital to identify its effectiveness in relation to the people undergoing oppression and suffering in spiritual, cultural and economic realms due to the peculiar situation of Indian villages. Here we shall first look into the contextual situation of ordinary people undergo and secondly, the Christological idea of 'Jesus the exorcist' which they cherish and thirdly, we will also have a glimpse of the Gospel testimony of Jesus as the exorcist to understand this Christology's validity.

Socio-Cultural and Religious Situation

Indian society is divided into different castes and sub-castes. The lower castes, Dalits and Tribals are being denied their right to live in mainstream society. The Dalits are not only discriminated, but their women are raped, their men are physically assaulted and their children are made to work as bonded labourers. They have no access to the land, are forced to work in degrading conditions and are often beaten up by the police and the dominant caste groups. Centuries of social conditioning and deprivation have seriously wounded the Tribal and Dalit psyche; they deeply long for recognition and respect. Very often they are reluctant to change, perhaps because of the terrible bitterness and indifference they developed through many years of suffering. The caste system and untouchability have pushed them into the peripheries of villages, deep into the jungles and mountainous locations.[9]

Spiritual Outlook

They have a three-tier worldview, based on a close relationship between nature, human beings and various spirits; their priority is in the order of material things, spirits and a high God. Proximity to the jungle, a primitive worldview and strong faith in supernatural elements made them fearful of spirits and ghosts.[10] A sick person is usually not taken to hospital, instead treated with *jadi-booti* (roots and leaves); they turn to traditional religious practices to ward off malevolent spirits, which are believed to be the cause of illness. They often consider *jadi-bootis* and traditional religious practices to be more powerful than allopathic medicines.[11] According to Saxena, their priority is for 'magico-medical and indigenous treatment' and therefore, it seems that they often seem to disregard sanitation and hygiene.[12] However, we should not forget the fact that it is their downtrodden condition and lack of resources which contributes such an outlook to a large extent.

Tribals and Dalits believe in a number of spirits, both benevolent and malevolent. Their whole social and religious life is intricately related to the spirit world.[13] The people consider these spirits as powerful enough to keep their children from sickness, make them fertile, provide rain, and the welfare of domestic animals. Various categories of spirits such as village spirits, clan spirits, and spirits of the ancestors are identified.[14] The fear of these spirits motivates the people to worship and offer sacrifices to the spirits. Every village worships a female spirit which is considered to be the guardian spirit and generally known as *mata*. These spirits are thought to protect people in distress and when the village pollute, it is thought that, they would withdraw protection. If these spirits are not placated or offered sacrifices, they are supposed to be angry and it is believed that they can cause harm to life and property.[15]

There are many malevolent spirits, which are to be dreaded and warded off by any means. Certain spirits create nuisance by playing tricks on people. There are dangerous spirits too; they cause illness, accidents and calamities. It is believed that the dead are a part of the community and have dealings with those who are still alive.[16] Images of dead men and women, riding on horseback with bows and arrows are found engraved on stone tablets in villages, to give protection to the people from malevolent spirits. Some spirits are thought to help those who engage in robbery, beating, killing and snatching others' property.[17]

If any benevolent spirit possesses anybody, it may show itself through various actions and signs and is not considered to be harmful. A message spoken by such a person is counted as prophetic, as coming from the spirit. Even though Tribals and Dalits believe in a benevolent high god, no offering or sacrifice is made for such a god, as he does not harm them. That God is known as *malik* or *ooparwala*, which means master or one who is transcendent. The belief in malevolent spirits has made them increasingly preoccupied with fear. Their material needs or physical problems are immediately attached to spirits, the benevolent high god is sought only as a last resort.[18]

Every village has a *devara* (shrine) and a *bhopa* or *bhua* who acts as the village priest.[19] People rush to village shrines whenever they face any natural calamity or epidemic to seek the protection of the guardian spirits of their village. It is believed that the spirit to whom they offer sacrifices and food has become angry and is, therefore, tormenting them. The *bhopa* wields great power and authority over the villagers and his words are obeyed with awe, as it is believed that the spirits possess him regularly. The priests usually ask for money, alcohol, cockerel, or goats for the ceremonies; some demand bigger amounts, unaffordable to the poor villagers, and even threaten the victims with consequences of spirit affliction, if they fail to give what they demand.[20] In the act of exorcism, the *bhopa* is either possessed by the spirit or acts as if controlled by it. The terrified family would bring the demanded items somehow, spending hard-earned money. He would declare that the spirit has descended on the sacrificed animal and left the house. Then gleefully, he would collect the money and other items and walk away. However, in most cases, after a few days, the patient would develop symptoms of possession or sickness. Then he would demand more money and materials to appease greater spirits. Having found no recovery, the family would look for a *bhopa* with greater powers, who would in turn demand more money and items; ultimately, the family becomes penniless and falls into irrevocable debt and poverty.[21]

In addition, according to the respondents of the research, magical practices are widespread among these people. Several of the interviewees acknowledge that many people are oppressed by the infestation of demonic spirits, as they claim. Some people even claim that using evil spirits (*dakan*) through magic and chants one can dry a plant or tree within a few hours. It is also believed that with the help of these spirits, witches can steal away the harvest produce or spoil the financial security of a person. Some claim that women are being sexually exploited using wicked spirits. More surprisingly, some people afflict their enemies with the help of witches to bring illness or even kill others. Evil spirits are also seen as causing illnesses such as paralysis, swelling all over the body, urinary problems and so on.[22] While exploring the religion of Dalits in Chhattisgarh, Bauman also portrays a similar picture:

> The religion of rural Chhattisgarh in the nineteenth and early twentieth centuries was (and in many ways still is) about power and control, about survival, protection and order. It was about the concerns of everyday, about diagnosing illness, interpreting omens and signs and about performing rituals intended to smooth one's path in this life and the next.[23]

There are many other beliefs concerning the spirit world. The people believe that the 'evil eye' causes diseases and ill-luck.[24] It can destroy family members, ruin the fortune of a person, and bring harm to domestic animals, crops and houses. To avert the evil eye, the villagers place skulls and monkey tails on poles outside their homes. Chickenpox is considered the blessing of *mata* and no treatment is undergone for it.[25] Moreover, they ascribe diseases like measles, typhoid and others to a spirit's attack. This attitude becomes a major reason for their ill-health and untimely deaths of many, along with overconsumption of alcohol.[26] They believe that gods drink alcohol and taught them to brew it and, hence, there are no ceremonies, whether it is worship, traditional hospitality, death or marriage, without serving alcohol. Some even say that 'my god is my alcohol'.[27]

Besides, by chasing the Tribals and Dalits into the jungles and the peripheries of villages, others have deprived them of their livelihood and 'caste Hindus look down upon them as backward and "jungali", i.e., uncivilised with bad customs and manners'.[28] Developmental plans of Government like industrialisation as well as onslaught of greedy contractors and middlemen have destroyed the natural resources and cures Tribals used, affected their life and health profiles. The forest dwellings, lack of education and natural resources, have made them very poor.[29] The complex worldview and lack of health care have a severe impact upon their psyche and health.[30] With this background information we shall look into the Christological understanding that 'Jesus as the exorcist' which has been come out of the research conducted among them.

Jesus the Exorcist

The Christological idea that 'Jesus the exorcist' is a prominent Christological element emerged in the research among ordinary Pentecostal believers who had been from the Dalit, Tribal and lower caste background. As we already have explained, these people in interior villages face the onslaught of malevolent spirits, superstitious practices and exploitation of traditional healers which in turn affect their health, life style and economic stability. Obviously, it is not surprising that people understand Jesus as the exorcist par excellence and greater than all the gods they know. Many of the interviewees testified that they had accepted Christ through receiving relief from demonic possessions and the attack of malevolent spirits. This is also a major reason why most of the people joined Pentecostal churches.

According to villagers, many diseases are caused by spirit attack or perpetuated by evil practices. An attack from wicked spirits can have severe repercussions and can be life-threatening.[31] Listen to the ordeal Yeshudas had gone through and how he was miraculously rescued from the attack of evil spirits:

> My father was the *bhopa* of my village ... Everything was fine until my father's death. After a month of my father's death, suddenly four of my sisters and mother fell ill in consecutive days. Their bodies were swollen and unable to pass urine. I realised that it was the attack of the spirits that were to be placated because no sacrifices had been offered after my father's death. In panic I began

to run pillar to post, consulting other *bhopas* and *tantriks* but to no avail. After few days my wife, who was pregnant then, also fell ill. It was a shock to me. I brought a powerful *bhopa* from a different village but he could not do anything. We spent lot of money... After a week I became ill with the same symptoms. All of my body was swollen and aching and I was unable to eat anything or pass urine. I was also bed-ridden and unconscious for some time.

One of my relatives, who was married off to a different village came to know about it; she was a believer. Knowing our condition, she came with her pastor. He prayed over me and in the name of Jesus rebuked the power of evil spirits. From that moment onward all of us began to feel better and within a few days we received complete release from the attack of the spirits. Now I know that Jesus is all powerful, greater than all other gods. He can do everything; he has power over every spirit. I will only worship him.[32]

In the focus groups conducted during the research, some people also shared their experiences of spirit attack and the deliverance they have received in the name of Jesus. Moreover, the discussion mostly revolved around the power of Jesus to rescue from the evil influence of wicked spirits as well as witch-doctors.[33] These people experienced the delivering power of Jesus in their life and now they do not fear any demonic spirits or traditional religious practices. For example, a participant narrates his testimony of freedom from an evil spell:

My first wife became ill and it turned out that she was infested with an evil spirit. I employed the services of the village *bhopa* and he had said that she was possessed by *hingotri mata*. I spent a large sum of money on sacrifices and other rituals; however, these could not save her. My wife and a four year old daughter died together. After a year I re-married. However, my wife was also attacked by evil spirits. Some people advised me that it was the work of some evil people, so I should go to the church and I would be delivered. Then I asked, 'what is church?' I did not know what church was. Then with my wife I came to the church. The pastor prayed for me and we got release from the torment of evil powers. Now it has been ten years and I have three children and we don't have any fear of spirits. Jesus is more powerful than all the spirits. I submit everything to God.[34]

In the focus groups, participants claimed that many people in the inner villages are either affected by the attack of spirits or live fearfully. Traditional healers first ask for a cockerel to sacrifice; if there is no relief, after seven days a goat is sacrificed. They also use alcohol, incense-sticks and other materials to either please the spirits or ward them off. A cockerel, even in the village will cost ₹ 250-300, and a goat more than ₹ 2000. Moreover, *bhopa* also may demand big amounts like ₹ 1,000-5,000. They claim that they can deliver the villagers from the spirits. When poor villagers fail to get any result through traditional religious practices, or dangerous events happen, as a last resort only they will approach Pentecostal pastors for their rescue. Many of the members who attend the churches share such incidents.[35] They often hand down their testimonies to the suffering people. This has resulted in a rapid growth of Pentecostalism among the poor villagers. The *Economic and Political Weekly*, for instance, undergirds this fact. Commenting on the reasons why Oraons, a group in Orissa, accept Christianity, Pati says:

> In a context of uncertainties and insecurities the Oraons, for example, felt that Christianity protected them from the witches and 'bhoots', who were powerless against this system.[36]

In another incident, the children fell prey to curse and attack from wicked spirits. Parsing Baria, an evangelist of the Filadelfia Church in the Panchmahal district in Gujarat speaks about the miraculous recovery of a family:

> ...the Lord told me to go to a family that was being tormented with sickness and consistent deaths. Four children in that family had died following which even the cattle began to fall prey. The entire household moved to another locality to escape the curse, but

the curse followed. Much prayer was done and the Lord through a miracle restored to them what they had lost over the years.[37]

Pastor Rajesh narrated an incident of miraculous recovery of a young man who was insane for some years, as a result of his ministry. According to Rajesh, the man used to wander in the forest and village with a sword. Due to his fear that his son would harm others, the father told the villagers that they might kill him if he harmed anybody. One evening people of the village came to kill him. However, his wife did not allow it.

The next day his sister, who was staying near Rajesh's house, approached and requested whether he could heal him. This woman had seen that people prayed for deliverance. Then the man was brought to his home, hands tied. Rajesh kept him in his home, providing food and everything for a month. Meanwhile he was constantly prayed by Rajesh and the church there. Now he is completely healed and has been undergoing Bible training and is involved in evangelism. According to Rajesh, due to this deliverance many people from the village joined the church.[38] It is remarkable that Pentecostal churches act as a refuge for tormented people. As Abraham has shown, even in Kerala (the state with 100% literacy rate), a good number of new adherents were delivered from evil spirits and joined Pentecostal churches.[39]

Another interesting fact came out in the research is that very often the attack of malevolent spirits results in paralysis. Hear the story of a married woman narrated by her husband:

> My wife was troubled by evil spirits from her childhood. Even after the marriage they used to torment her, make her fall down and wound her and sometimes make her unconscious. Later she was paralysed in one of her legs and became bed-ridden. We spent lot of money for traditional religious practices [He is a truck driver and earns good money]. All of my income would go

towards traditional religious practices and treatment but without any results. However, somebody introduced me to the pastor and he prayed for her; she got some relief. Then she continued to attend the church and now she is totally healed.[40]

People not only suffer from the direct attack of evil spirits, but there are many instances of the use of wicked spirits by witch-doctors to extract money and torment gullible people. Merchand Masih, an evangelist narrates:

A certain witch-doctor cast a spell on a simple villager and in the process, took nine hundred rupees from him. The man came seeking salvation in the church... When the people of God pray, something in the spirit realm happens. The villager got healed and the witch-doctor came and returned the money to him. This was an instant answer to prayer. This was enough to convince the man and several others to accept the Lord as their saviour.[41]

According to *Cross & Crown* magazine the influence of the person of Jesus is so powerful among the villagers that some powerful village-healers (*bhopa*) became pastors to deliver many from evil influences.[42] Moreover, it is also testified that a number of churches were being established due to instances of exorcisms in the name of Jesus and the poor people were rescued from evil spirit attacks.[43]

Jesus the Exorcist: A Liberative Christology

From the stories above, it is obvious that for ordinary villagers being freed from the fear of malevolent spirits as well as liberation from spirit possession is more than a life regained. They live in constant fear of the supernatural and this fear affects all their activities. The deliverance in the spirit realm positively affects the people's social, economic and spiritual domains; the spirit infestation breaks their financial security, their physical as well as their mental well-being.[44]

In the testimonies of the participants, deliverance brings a new awareness of the spiritual world. Earlier, the worldview was infested with dread of spirits and enslavement to them; always trying to appease them. However, deliverance removes their fear of demonic activities and fear is turned into safety and joy. It is the peace of mind and body which rules in them after they receive deliverance in the name of Jesus.[45] Earlier, even if they may get respite, nothing guarantees the uninterrupted security and protection from these evil powers, who can return and trouble them. Bauman's description also tallies with this understanding. These people are obsessed with 'performance of daily rituals, the *ad hoc* utilization of amulets and charms, and the protective repetition of *mantras*'.[46] Thus, deliverance in the name of Jesus assures them a long-lasting safeguard from the demonic powers.[47]

Further, exorcism enacted in the name of Jesus is totally free of cost and it does not impinge their financial security.[48] Pastors or members conduct exorcism without any rituals or chants. This raises a new consciousness: that satanic forces come to steal their financial resources (John 10:10).[49] "The power encounter with Christ, in which Tribals are healed, expelled the evil spirits that were blighting their lives, reformed their morals and ethics, broke the hold of the *bhagats*, and allowed them to stand up to the shopkeepers who exploited them," asserts Dasan.[50]

Later, believers are taught that they can also cast out demons in the name of Jesus. As one person explained, this understanding makes a huge shift in their worldview; they realise that they have control over evil spirits which have been tormenting them and proceed to rescue others from the clutches of tyranny.[51] The ordinary adherents come to know that through prayer and faith now they can counter the evil forces. Hardiman agrees with it, "There is a strong emphasis on the healing of all maladies and sicknesses through the power of faith alone. They consider that malign forces cause ill health, and that these forces can be countered through prayer and faith."[52] This brings spiritual empowerment and leads to what we call 'spiritual warfare' which is carried out as an everyday affair where no specialists are needed. Additionally, the act of exorcism is also carried out in the power of the Spirit. Here the work of the Spirit is paramount to obtain the desired outcome.[53]

This also results in a lofty understanding of the supremacy of Christ: He is more powerful than any other gods. Besides, unlike their old deities which may get angry now and then, He is kind enough to deliver them from suffering and ready to keep them safe forever. He does not ask for any sacrifices.[54] This perception leads them to the positive affirmation of the uniqueness of Christ over every other gods they know. Eventually, they are not hesitant to proclaim that Jesus is the only God. Nevertheless, what we need to emphasise here is that, this does not happen by the rational articulation of arguments and counter arguments. Even this understanding does not come from a thoroughly Bible-based divinity and greatness of Christ. But it emerges out of their life experiences of Jesus' pervasive power over all gods. For they have knocked on every door they are aware of but with no results. Therefore, they do not debate to prove the uniqueness and supremacy of Christ; rather, they relate this idea to their experiences and persuade listeners to accept the lordship of Christ. This method is often used in evangelism and mission. The believers would approach people who were sick and troubled by demonic spirits and then narrate their own testimony and stories from the Bible.

Then they would pray for the people in the name of Jesus.[55] Hence, the ordinary believer's past life struggles and their new experience in Christ undergird the Christological category of 'Jesus the exorcist'.

Jesus the Exorcist: The New Testament Testimony

As we turn to the New Testament testimony of the person and message of Christ, this aspect of Christology is not only prominent but also form the core of the Christological understanding, especially in the Gospels. "Nothing is more certain about Jesus than that he was viewed by his contemporaries as an exorcist and a healer," asserts John Meier.[56] Nearly one-fifth of the entire Gospel is devoted to Jesus' healing and the discussions occasioned by it.[57] Kelsey rightly observes, "The interest Jesus showed in the physical and mental health of human beings was greater than that of any other leader or religious system from Confucius through Hinduism and Buddhism to Islam."[58]

All three Synoptic Gospels agree that the casting out of demons was a significant element in the ministry of Jesus and He devoted a substantial portion of His ministry to perform healing and exorcisms for a wide variety of people. Mark devotes around thirty one percent of his Gospel to the miracles and healings of Jesus.[59] He focuses on the power of Jesus and on his dramatic confrontations with the forces of Satan (5:1-43).[60] Evangelist Matthew explains the exorcisms of Jesus as the sign and outworking of the kingdom of God which is enacted in the power of the Spirit (Matt 12:18). In Luke's Gospel, both disease and demon-possession are attributed to Satan, and the demons regularly recognize Jesus as the Son of God (4:41; 8:28) who is victorious over them. In fact, many writers, such as Achtemeier, believe that of the four Evangelists, it is Luke who himself a physician, makes most clear the possibility of miracles serving as a basis of faith.[61]

Blackburn contends that there is almost universal agreement among New Testament scholars that Jesus performed what is regarded as miraculous healings and exorcisms. The miracles of Jesus pass the dissimilarity test and satisfy the criterion of multiple attestations.[62] Gerd Theissen persuasively demonstrates that the accounts of the exorcisms and the healings in the Gospels are to be considered as independent genres with their own motifs.[63] Twelftree elucidates that the exorcism stories are the bedrock of reliable data about the historical Jesus and the most compelling evidence of Jesus being an exorcist.[64] The Beelzebul passages[65] clearly depict the power of Jesus over demons as the evidence that God's kingdom had broken into the present world order ruled by Satan.[66] Jesus' authority over the power of Satan was conveyed to His disciples as well.[67] Reese comments: "In fact, the only activity that runs consistently from the opening summary of Jesus' ministry through the accounts of his miracles and into the commission given to his disciples is the casting out of demons."[68] Thus, it is obvious that this Christological experience of the ordinary people of India is strongly anchored in the biblical tradition.

Conclusion

The Christological articulations in India present the picture of the person and message of Christ in the diverse socio-cultural and religious contexts. They are diverse in form and disposition, and have sprung up from divergent settings of theological thinking. However, the most vexing question is how far these Christologies are appreciated and comprehended by common people. Many a time their notions and explanations do not reach to ordinary folks. In the context of Indian realities of sickness, poverty, harmful rituals, spiritual oppression and witchcrafts, many of them do not address the needs of those who have been undergoing life and death situation. Here we need the Christological articulation of 'Jesus the exorcist' which delivers suffering people from the clutches of religious and cultural oppression. If Christ carried out his ministry in the power of the Spirit, touching the lives of the ordinary people and delivering them from perilous forces as the Gospels testify, the Indian Christologies ought to unearth this element of the biblical Christology in the Indian context.

Endnotes

[1] Jacob Parappally, *Emerging Trends in Indian Christology* (Bangalore: IIS Publications, 1995), 6.

[2] Anantanand Rambachan, "A Hindu Look at Jesus," *Vidhyajyoti Journal of Theological Reflection* 58/12 (Dec 1994): 773.

[3] Balwant A.M. Paradkar, "Hindu Interpretation of Christ from Vivekananda to Radhakrishnan," *Indian Journal of Theology* 18/1 (January-March 1969): 70-73 and 77-80; P. Fallon, "A Critical Evaluation of the Hindu Interpretation of Christ," *Indian Journal of Theology* 18/1 (January-March 1969): 81-87; Ronald Neufeldt, *Hindu-Christian Dialogue: Perspectives and Encounter,* edited by Harold Coward (Maryknoll: Orbis Books, 1989), 162-175.

[4] For a brief and lucid description of Indian philosophical systems, especially *advaita* philosophy, see Ramakrishna Puligandla, *Fundamentals of Indian Philosophy* (New Delhi: D.K. Printworld, 1997) and Aravind Sharma, *The Philosophy of Religion and Advaita Vedanta* (Delhi: Sri Satguru Publications, 1997).

[5] P. Nagaraja Rao, *Introduction to Vedanta,* 3rd ed. (Bombay: Bharatiya Vidya Bhavan, 1966), 113-133 and Eric Lott, *Vedantic Approaches to God* (London: The MacMillan Press, 1980), 20-26. Brahman is the inexpressible, invisible, inaudible and unthinkable ground of all existence. Brahman is neither a he nor a she but is the It. Brahman is neither to be identified with any God or gods men worship. Brahman can never be captured by the senses or intellect, but can only be examined in a flash of the highest mystical intuition. This is *nirguna Brahman*; see Puligandla, *Fundamentals of Indian Philosophy*.

[6] Robin Boyd, *An Introduction to Indian Christian Theology*, rev. ed. (Madras: The Christian Literature Service, 1975), 112.

[7] Shaibu Abraham, Ordinary Indian Pentecostal Christology (Unpublished PhD Thesis, The University of Birmingham, England, 2011). A research is carried out in 2009 in various parts of India using qualitative research methods such as personal interviews, focus groups, participant observation and also literature analysis to understand the Christological understanding of ordinary Pentecostals.

[8] See Abraham, Ordinary Indian Pentecostal Christology, chapter 6.

[9] James Massey, *Down Trodden: The Struggle of India's Dalits for Identity, Solidarity and Liberation* (Geneva: WCC Publications, 1997).

[10] Sathianathan Clarke, *Dalits and Christianity: Subaltern Religion and Liberation Theology in India* (New Delhi: Oxford University Press, 1999), 71; Chad M. Bauman, *Christian Identity and Dalit Religion in Hindu India, 1868-1947* (Michigan: Eerdmans, 2008), 40; Stephen Neill, *Out of Bondage: Christ and the Indian Villager* (London: Church of England Zenana Missionary Society, 1930), 21-34.

[11] Abraham T. Cherian, "Contribution of Churches and Missions to the Bhils of Rajasthan" (unpublished PhD Thesis, Asian Institute of Theology, Bangalore, India, 2005), 25-26; Interview by author, Rajasthan, 7 July 2009.

[12] L.L. Saxena, *The Bhils of Rajasthan – Their Habitat, Economy and Society* (Jodhpur, India: Books Treasure, 2000), 171-172.

[13] For a comprehensive understanding of the names of spirits worshipped by various Tribal groups in different states of India see, H. H. Risley and E. A. Gait, *Census of India 1921, Religion* (Calcutta: Superintendent Government Printing, India, 1923); also see http://www.archive.org/stream/cu31924014522746#page/n179/ mode/2up (accessed 11 July 2010). Paul G. Hiebert, "Spiritual Warfare and World View," in *Missiology for the 21st Century: South Asian Perspective*, edited by Roger E. Hedlund & Paul Joshua Bhakiaraj (Delhi: ISPCK, 2004), 472.

[14] Ghanshyam Shah, 'Conversion, Reconversion and the State: Recent Events in the Dangs," *Economic and Political Weekly* (6 February 1999): 315, http://epw.in/epw/uploads/articles/8620.pdf (accessed 2 May 2010); Cherian, "Contribution of Churches and Missions," 33; Abraham M. Ayrookhuziel, "Distinctive Characteristics of Folk Traditions," in *Religions of the Marginalised: Towards a Phenomenology and Methodology of Study*, edited by Gnana Robinson (Delhi: ISPCK, 1998), 2-4.

[15] Daniel Katapali, "Indigenous Missions and the Savara Tribal Church of Srikakulam," *Christianity is Indian: The Emergence of an Indigenous Community*, rev. ed, edited by Roger E. Hedlund (Delhi: ISPCK, 2004), 270; Clarke, *Dalits and Christianity*, 71-75; Bauman, *Christian Identity and Dalit Religion*, 40-41; Ayrookhuziel, "Distinctive Characteristics of Folk Traditions," 2-3; Kancha Ilaiah, *Why I am not a Hindu: A Sudra Critique of Hindutva Philosophy, Culture and Political Economy*, 2nd ed. (Calcutta: Samya, 2005), 91-96.

[16] Clarke, *Dalits and Christianity*, 73.

[17] Cherian, "Contribution of Churches and Missions," 33.

[18] Clarke, *Dalits and Christianity*, 76-77, 87-89; Cherian, "Contribution of Churches and Missions," 42.

[19] Ebenezer, Focus Group Interview, Tabor Church, Gujarat, 23 August 2009; Clarke, *Dalits and Christianity*, 76-77, 85; A female who has the power to heal is known as *bopi*.

[20] Focus Group Interview, Tabor Church, Gujarat, 23 August 2009; Interview, Rajasthan, 5 July 2009.

[21] Cherian, "Contribution of Churches and Missions," 27-28; Focus Group Interview, Hebron Church, Rajasthan, 9 August 2009.

[22] If a person needs protection from these witches, s/he has to get the help of the master witch, who gives some bangles to be worn over the shoulder, uttering certain *mantras*, which are believed to be powerful over all witchcraft. He is considered to be more powerful than a *bhopa*. Interview by author, Maharashtra, 2 September 2009; Focus Group Interview, Tabor Church, Gujarat, 23 August 2009.

[23] Bauman, *Christian Identity and Dalit Religion*, 40.

[24] The evil eye is a look that is believed by many cultures to be able to cause injury or bad luck to the person at whom it is directed for reasons of envy or dislike. It also refers to the power of certain persons of inflicting injury or bad luck by such an envious or ill-wishing look.

[25] Focus Group Interview, Hebron Church, Rajasthan, 2 August 2009.

[26] The drinking habit of the Tribals, even by borrowing money from unscrupulous money lenders, pushes them into debt and poverty. Mohender Singh Bedi, *Drinking Behaviour and Development in Tribal Areas* (Udaipur, India: Himanshu Publications, 1998).

[27] David Hardiman, "Healing, Medical Power and the Poor: Contests in Tribal India," *EPW* (21 April 2007): 1406.

[28] Shah Ghanshyam Shah, "Conversion, Reconversion and the State: Recent Events in the Dangs," *EPW* (6 February 1999): 315-316; http://epw.in/epw/uploads/articles/8620.pdf (accessed 2 May 2010).

[29] G.C. Manna, "On Calibrating the Poverty Line for Poverty Estimation in India," *EPW* (28 July 2007).

[30] Adam Wagstaff, "Poverty and Health Sector Inequalities," *Bulletin of the World Health Organisation* 80/2 (2002); http://www.scielosp.org/scielo.php?pid=S0042-96862002000200004&script=sci_arttext&tlng=en (accessed 3 January 2010); P. R. Sodani, "Determinants of Demand for Healthcare in Surveyed Tribal Households of Selected Three Districts of Rajasthan," *Demography India* 28/2 (1999): 257-271.

[31] Mani, Focus Group Interview, Hebron Church, Rajasthan, 2 August 2009.

[32] Yeshu Das, Interview, Hebron Church, Rajasthan, 5 August 2009.

[33] Focus Group, Hebron Church, Rajasthan, 9 August 2009.

[34] Yohannan, Focus Group Interview, Hebron Church, Rajasthan, 9 August 2009.

[35] Mathai, Focus Group Interview, Hebron Church, Rajasthan, 9 August 2009.

[36] Biswamoy, Pati, "Identity, Hegemony, Resistance: Conversions in Orissa, 1800-2000," *EPW* (3 November 2001), 4204.

[37] No Author, "Field News," *Cross & Crown* 26/6 (August-September 1996): 21.

[38] Rajesh, Focus Group Interview, Hebron Church, Rajasthan, 9 August 2009.

[39] P.G. Abraham, *Caste and Christianity: A Pentecostal Perspective* (Kumbhaza, Kerala: Crown Books, 2003), 116, 118.

[40] Reji, Focus Group Interview, Hebron Church, Rajasthan, 9 August 2009.

[41] "Field News," *Cross & Crown* 26/6 (August-September 1996): 20.

[42] C&C Reporter, "Field News: How do we Plant a Church in Remote Villages?," *Cross & Crown* 26/7 (January-February 1997): 2-5.

[43] C&C Reporter, "Field News," 2-5.

[44] Focus group, Tabor Church, Gujarat, 23 August 2009; Focus group, Hebron Church, Rajasthan, 9 August 2009.

[45] Joel, Interview, Maharashtra, 2 September 2009.

[46] Bauman, *Christian Identity and Dalit Religion*, 40.

[47] Yohannan, Focus Group Interview, Hebron Church, Rajasthan, 16 August 2009; Focus Group Interview, Hebron Church, Rajasthan, 9 August 2009.

[48] Mani, Focus Group Interview, Hebron Church, Rajasthan, 2 August 2009.

[49] Participant Observation, Tabor Church, Gujarat, 6 September 2009; Mathai, Focus Group Interview, Hebron Church, Rajasthan, 9 August 2009.

[50] Ebenezer D. Dasan, "Conversion and Persecution in South Gujarat," in *Conversion in a Pluralistic Context: Perspectives and Context*, edited by Krickwin C. Marak & Plamthodathil S. Jacob (Delhi: ISPCK, 2000), 161-164.

[51] For example, Pastor Mathew claims that he has a special anointing to cast out demons; Mathew, Focus Group Interview, Tabor Church, Gujarat, 23 August 2009.

[52] David Hardiman & Gauri Raje, 'Practices of Healing in Tribal Gujarat,' *EPW* (1 March 2008): 49.

[53] Mathew, Focus Group Interview, Tabor Church, Gujarat, 23 August 2009.

[54] Mani, Focus Group Interview, Hebron Church, Rajasthan, 2 August 2009.

[55] Mathew, Focus Group Interview, Tabor Church, Gujarat, 23 August 2009.

[56] John P. Meier, "Jesus," *The New Jerome Biblical Commentary*, rev. ed. (London: Geoffrey Chapman, 1989), 1321.

[57] The Gospels narrate no less than 34 specific miracles performed by Jesus out of which twenty-two are healings. In addition there are fifteen texts that refer to Jesus' miraculous activity in summary fashion; see Morton T. Kelsey, *Psychology, Medicine and Christian Healing* (San Francisco: Harper & Row, Publishers, 1988), 42. For a detailed classification and description of the healing and exorcism stories in the gospels; see John Wilkinson, *The Bible and Healing: A Medical and Theological Commentary* (Michigan: Eerdmans, 1998), 64-69; B. L. Blackburn, 'Miracles and Miracle Stories,' *Dictionary of Jesus and the Gospels*, edited by Joel G. Green, Scot McKnight, I. Howard Marshall (Illinois: IVP, 1992), CD Rom.

[58] Kelsey, *Psychology, Medicine*, 41-42.

[59] Blomberg, 'Healing', *Dictionary of Jesus and the Gospels*, edited by Joel G. Green, Scot McKnight & I. Howard Marshall (Illinois: IVP, 1992), CD

Rom; also see Andrew Daunton-Fear, *Healing in the Early Church: The Church's Ministry of Healing and Exorcism from the First to the Fifth Century* (Milton Keynes: Paternoster, 2009), 33; Wilkinson, *The Bible and Healing*, 64-69.

[60] Blomberg, 'Healing'; Daunton-Fear, *Healing in the Early Church,* 32-33.

[61] P. J. Achtemeier, 'The Lukan Perspective on the Miracles of Jesus: A Preliminary Sketch,' in *Perspectives in Luke-Acts,* edited by C. H. Talbert (Danville, IL: AABPR, 1978), 153–67.

[62] According to Blackburn, however, some like Burton Mack contend that Jesus was not a miracle worker. But Blackburn affirms that sober historical analysis will continue to affirm the high probability that Jesus performed healings and exorcisms. See Burton Mack, *A Myth of Innocence: Mark and Christian Origins* (Philadelphia: Fortress, 1988).

[63] Gerd Theissen, *The Miracle Stories of the Early Christian Tradition*, edited by J. Riches, translated by J. Bowden (Minneapolis: Fortress Press, 1983), 85-94.

[64] Graham H. Twelftree, *Jesus the Exorcist* (Peabody, Mass: Hendrickson Publishers, 1993); Graham H. Twelftree, *Jesus the Miracle Worker: a Historical & Theological study* (Illinois: IVP, 1999); Graham H. Twelftree, 'Demon, Devil, Satan,' *Dictionary of Jesus and the Gospels*, edited by Joel G. Green, Scot McKnight, I. Howard Marshall (Illinois: IVP, 1992), CD Rom.; Graham H. Twelftree, 'Miracles of Jesus Marginal or Mainstream?,' *Journal of the Study of the Historical Jesus* 1/1 (2003): 104-124.

[65] The Beelzebul passages deal with the charge that Jesus cast out demons by Beelzebul; see, Matt 12:25–29; Mark 3:23–27; Luke 11:17–22; Mk 3:22 [par. Mt 9:34 and 12:24; Lk 11:15].

[66] David George Reese, "Demons (New Testament)," *Anchor Bible Dictionary,* edited by David Noel Freedman (New York: Doubleday, 1997), CD Rom.; Twelftree, 'Demon, Devil, Satan'.

[67] Howard Clark Kee, "Medicine and Healing," *Anchor Bible Dictionary,* edited by David Noel Freedman (New York: Doubleday, 1997), CD Rom.; For example, Matt 10:8; Mark 3:13–19; 6:7–13; Luke 9:1–2; Graham H. Twelftree, *In the Name of Jesus: Exorcism among Early Christians* (Michigan: Baker Academic, 2007).

[68] Reese, "Demons (New Testament)."

Role of the Holy Spirit in Transcending Human Barriers: A Scriptural Exploration

John Thannickal

The Holy Spirit was promise by Jesus Christ as power to fulfill God's mission "You shall receive power after that the Holy Spirit is come upon you" (Acts 1:8). This is the power for witness and victorious holy living. The Holy Spirit's power is to enable us to overcome our human limitations of visions, understanding, motivation, energy, speech and action. This is supernatural, super-mundane power, yet not anti-natural. The Holy Spirit uses the human mind, spirit, and body and does not work against the natural function of our body and mind, but energizes them to fulfill the divine function.

The Holy Spirit and Our Mind

The natural mind is often weak, corrupt and rebellious against God and fellow humans. The human mind has the tendency to seek after vanity and pleasure, because it is unable to face the realities of life and choice matters of eternal and universal significance. The corrupt mind engages in destructive matters and is embedded with critical and negative thoughts. Satan even found fault with God's provision for human in the garden of Eden (Gen. 3:5). Human nature is in rebellion against God and holds the truth with injustice, motivated by selfishness and pride. The next step is to develop vain imagination, resulting in darkness of mind (Rom. 1:21). Paul outlines the degradation of human mind: (1) Rejection of truth (2) Rejection of the God of creation (3) Vain imagination (4) Professing themselves to be wise (5) They become fools (6) Demeaning God by idolatry (7) Dishonouring their bodies (8) Developing vile affections (9) Depraved mind (Romans 1:18-32)

Even at the end of the 20th Century, in spite of the scientific advancement, technological progress, and space-age discoveries, the human mind is depraved, selfish, destructive, distorted, immoral and alienated from God. But Paul sees healing and restoration to the mind as he states them clearly in Romans Chapter 8.

The Renewal of the Mind by the Spirit of God - Romans 8

The feeling of condemnation is removed by the spirit v.1

A sense of freedom to think right emerges v.2

Moral satisfaction and strength through Jesus v.3,4

Mind moves from the mundane sphere to the spiritual v.5

The mundane realm is death and the spiritual is life v.6

The hostile attitude towards God is changed v.7

The spirit of Christ now dwells in the Christian v.9

The Holy Spirit who raised Jesus from the dead lives

in us and quickens our body v.11

The Spirit gives new life v.13

The Spirit gives the sense of divine sonship v.14

No spirit of slavery, but the spirit of divine sonship v.15

Therefore, we are co-heirs with Christ and share in

His glory v.17

Therefore, the present sufferings will be replaced by

the future glory vs. 18-25

The Holy Spirit helps us in our weakness v.26

The spirit intercedes for us when our words fail v.26

All things move towards fulfilling God's purpose of

conforming us to the likeness of Jesus v.29

No hardship shall separate us from the love of Christ v.35

We are more than conquerors through Christ who loved us v.37

Conflicts of life, death, demons, time or space cannot separate us from God's love and care v.38, 39

Therefore, a Believer in Christ Can Have a Strong, Confident Mind

The Apostle Paul presents the character of the Holy Spirit in his letter to Timothy; "For God has not given us the Spirit of fear but of power and love, and of sound mind (2 Tim. 1:7). A sound mind is a mind that thinks right, relates to people and things properly, analyses and judges what it sees and hears in the light of eternal truth. A right mind remembers, organizes and harmonizes ideas and enables us to make right choices. Jesus had the perfect mind. He remembered things well and judged properly. His choices were always in harmony with the Father's will (Jn. 14-17). Jesus used His mind to meet the demands of the human mind (Mt. 22:35-37). The sinful and defiled mind thinks unreal things (Tit. 1:15)

Renewal and recreation of our personality take place in our mind, not merely in our emotions (Eph. 4:23; Rom. 12.2).

Peter, though he was not as educated as Paul, gave importance to the mind and advised the believers to gird up the loins of their mind (1 Pet. 1:13). Paul's prayer for the Ephesian Christians was that, "The eyes of your understanding being enlightened; that ye may know what is the hope of his calling, and what the riches of His inheritance in the saints," (Eph. 1:8). Enlightenment of heart and knowing (*eidenai*) are the results of the Holy Spirit. The Holy Spirit removes the evil effect of sin and recreates and sanctifies us to think and work in harmony with God's eternal plan. The restoration and reorientation of our mind is the fruit of our salvation in Christ Jesus. We are transformed by renewing of our mind (nous), said Paul. "And be not conformed to this world: but be ye transformed by the renewing of your mind, that ye may prove what is that good, and acceptable, and perfect will of God. "(Rom. 12:2). The Christian mind is not worldly or contra-world, but Christ-like. "Let this mind be in you, which was also in Christ Jesus" (Phil. 2:5). Jesus made the right choice of the cross, rather than forsaking the Father's will, by boldly teaching divine justice and love for the whole world. Christ's mind was fully humble, not self-asserting or self- advertising, but self-sacrificing for the benefit of others.

The Holy Spirit illumines the human mind to grasp the divine truth. He unfolds the hidden mysteries of the past, present and future to human understanding so that men may be enlightened. The Apostle John was in the spirit when he saw the throne (Rev. 4:1-4). The future events were unfolded to him through visions. The inspiration of scripture is the work of the Holy Spirit. The Holy Spirit is the holy wind which breathes on the human mind to write down or prophesy the truth of God. What the Spirit revealed is designed for teaching instruction which involves the exercise of the mind (2 Tim. 3:16). Christian spirituality is not disengaging or neutralizing of mind, but proper use of mind to grasp the things of God and be conformed unto Christ's image.

Some Christians think that when the Holy Spirit fills us, He disengages and paralyses our human mind. They believe that spirituality is an expression of joy and exuberance in worship without the participation of the mind. A leader of a Pentecostal group in USA writes: "Praise is a spontaneous expression that comes from your heart, not your head, and gives glory to God for what He has done for you." (63/5). Separating the head from the heart is not a design of the New Testament Worship. Jesus emphasized the co-operation of the mind and heart that is, the thinking and the emotional spheres of our personality in the service of God when he said "Love the Lord your God with all your heart and with all your soul and with all your strength" (Mk 12:30). Joy of the heart must be controlled and directed by the head. It is dangerous to let the emotions go uncontrolled. Joy and wisdom go together in Christian worship.

Certainly, joy is better than sadness in worship. Many denominational Churches avoid joyful singing or preaching in worship. Instead, they follow a ritualistic order of worship. The Holy Spirit wants to engage our total being of spirit, soul and body in worship. Paul admonishes the Ephesian Christians to use the mind and holy emotions in worship.

Wherefore be ye not unwise, but understanding what the will of the Lord is. And be not drunk with wine, wherein is excess; but be filled with the spirit; Speaking to yourselves in Psalms and hymns and spiritual songs, singing and making melody in your heart to the Lord; (Eph. 5:17-19).

According to Paul, a Spirit-filled man is wise, knowing the resources of God and a capable of making right choices by preferring the spiritual to the material and finding avenues to joyfully relate to people and to the Lord. "Be filled" (*plerusthe*) is an imperative verb showing that we need to desire the fullness of the spirit and ask God to keep us filled daily to meet the challenges facing us. The Holy Spirit strengthens and straightens our mind.

A certain Pentecostal group which originated in the former Ceylon insists on the separation of the family, rejection of formal education, avoidance of medical treatment and denial of social involvement as a mark of spirituality. This group which has above 850 local churches in India and Sri Lanka emphasizes extensive use of babbling and emotional ecstasy in worship. Their emphasis on vibrant singing and emotional expressions of Holy Spirit fullness appeal to common people. Although their sincerity and dedication to Christ are commendable., their extreme views of exclusivism, anti-intellectual, and isolationism cannot be attributed to the Holy Spirit. This group which is now called 'The Pentecostal Mission' (T.P.M) is opposed to Bible schools or Theological study centers where, they fear that, the reading of the books written by others may result in unspiritual intellectualism. They have good minds, but they believe that the Holy Spirit is not pleased with the mental exercise of understanding, comprehending, analysing and choosing, but pleased by revelations.

The anti-intellectual spirituality undermines the very foundation Of Christianity, because it deprives man of the image of God in which he was created (Col. 3:10). We are doing a great harm to the Church of Jesus Christ and to our future generations when we promote emotionalism at the expense of intellect. It is like enjoying a meal served to us without questioning what is it made of and where was it cooked. However, a person who knows what he eats will be healthy. God has created man with a mind to know and to make the right choices. He who does not exercise his mind is rejecting God's plan of creation.

The Holy Spirit Breaks Physical Barriers

We live in a body that has many limitations and often many defects. But God has given us the gift of the Holy spirit to overcome physical barriers. The Spirit who raised Jesus from the dead and who lives in us quickens our bodies and heals all our limitations (Ro. 8:11). This power is available to those who believe in the resurrection power granted to us and appropriate it to fulfil God's mission.

Miracles were done in Jesus' Name by the power of the Holy Spirit and in the ministries of the Apostles. Miracles can take place even today, because the Spirit is with us. We as human face challenges of physical healing as Peter and John faced at the temple gate in Jerusalem. Then Peter said, "Silver and gold have I none: but such as I have give I Thee; in the name of Jesus Christ of Nazareth rise up and walk." (Ac. 3:6). Every Christian can appropriate this healing power without a Peter or John present. The Holy Spirit indwells in every believer in Christ and is ready to act.

The Holy Spirit Crosses Medium

Some people think that healing can take place only through the mediums of Priests, Evangelists, Oil, handkerchiefs or laying on of hands. The wonderful privilege Jesus extended to us in the New Testament is direct worship, direct communion, and direct access to God's presence to claim our blessings of power and healing. Evangelists and Pastors can remind and encourage individuals to seek God's power, but they should not serve as mediums. Medium construction and perpetuation has been the greatest evil of all religions. Temples, priesthood, pilgrim centers, holy mountains, holy rivers and holy ashes can become obstructing mediums. It is unfortunate that some evangelists try to sell holy keys and cups and water from Jerusalem to receive healing and special blessings. This is medium-building, which is idolatrous.

Jesus came to abolish the material and physical barriers that existed between God and man and to establish direct relationship. We have only one mediator, who is the risen Christ. He is not a picture or physical person but the name. Jesus prompted directness in worship and prayer. Therefore, He said, "True worshippers shall worship God in Spirit and truth" (Jn. 4:23). Jesus de-centralized and personalised worship. Where two or three are gathered in Jesus Name, there is God's presence and therefore, that is the holy place. No land, mount, river, or building is holier than any other. In a Christian sense, we cannot call Palestine the holy land or a Church building a sanctuary. God and the Holy Spirit came down to dwell in man, not in mediums.

The Holy Spirit Crosses Natural Barriers

Miracles are God's way of breaking natural barriers to meet a spiritual need. A miracle is not a natural or anti-natural happening, but a super-natural event. God, who is the creator of nature has the right and the power to supersede the course of nature in order to fulfil His purpose in the world. God does not do miracles to show His power or to impress man, but to meet a specific need of His people. The objective of a miracle is to show God's love and concern for suffering humanity.

Other religions also believe in miracles, yet not as acts of a loving God, but of manipulating mysterious powers. The animists expect miracles to happen through magic. The Hindus believe *pooja* (ritual offering to god) or through *darshan* (seeing a particular god in a temple) and satisfying the demands of that god as prescribed by the priest. Muslim also believe in miracles through their prayers to Allah as prescribed by the prophet Mohammed.

In the Old Testament

The old testament religion believed in miracles by the mighty hands of God. The birth of Isaac to old Abraham and Sarah was a miracle. The parting of the dead sea was a miracle. The supply of manna in the desert and water from the rock were miracles during the journey to promised land, Canaan. Raising from the dead, the Shunamite – woman's son and the healing of the Naaman's leprosy took place in the ministry of Elisha.

In the Ministry of Jesus

The life and ministry of Jesus was a miracle, witnessed by ordinary people and recorded as eye-witness reports. Jesus was God in flesh. His miracles were not a mere display of power but of divine love to meet a human need and bring reformation to the society.

When a leper approached and knelt before Him, pleading for healing, Jesus touched him (Mk. 1:41), contrary to the law of Moses (Lev. 13) and healed him.The healing of the Roman centurion's servant (Mt. 8:1-13) was an occasion to showthat non-Jewish people do come under the blessings of God. Thus, He defended the mission of love to the whole world (Jn. 3:16). Similarly, the deliverance of the man possessed of demons in the Gentile territory of Gadara, on the east side of the lake of Galilee, is another occasion that demonstrates Jesus' love for the Gentiles (Mt. 8:28-34).

The healing of the paralyzed man in the Jewish territory of Capernaum (Mk. 2:1-12) was an occasion to teach the Jews that Jesus was interested in both spiritual and physical healing. The healing of the woman who was suffering with the issue of blood for twelve years (Mk. 5:25-30), was an occasion to show that Jesus cared for women, in spite of the prohibition of Mosaic law that such women should not be touched (Lev. 15:27).

After opening the eyes of the two blind men, Jesus told them not to publish the news (Mt. 9:28-31). The purpose of His healing was not to get any fame for Himself. The healing ministry of Jesus was not a self-publishing scheme. However, the people who were healed testified about Jesus anyway.

The healing of the man with a shrivelled hand in the synagogue on the Sabbath day (Lk 6:6-10) and the paralyzed man at the pool of Bethesda (Jn. 5:1-9) was to show that Jesus cared more for the physical needs of individuals rather than the observance of religious rituals.

Thus, the miracles of Jesus imparted love to humanity and prompted the cause of God's kingdom. Jesus viewed man as a wholly integrated being. He was interested in physical healing and in spiritual restoration. Healing of the body was an occasion to be thankful to God and know His love. Faith in Jesus was the only requirement to be healed. The proof of God's direct involvement in human affairs through miracles is further established by the resurrection of Jesus. His resurrection became the good news for His disciples to publish (Mt. 28:19,

20). The decent of the Holy Spirit on the day of Pentecost was a further proof of His ascension to the father (Ac. 2:1:1-4).

In the Ministry of the Apostles

After the ascension, the holy spirit took charge of the ministry of Jesus in the world. Jesus promised that the disciples would do greater miracles because of the gift of the Holy Spirit from the Father (Jn 14:12). Let us look at the miracles recorded in the Acts of the Apostles;

1. Signs and wonders by the Apostles (2:43)

2. Healing of the lame man at the temple gate (3:8)

3. Prayer for signs and wonders in the name of Jesus. (4:30)

4. Signs and wonders by the Apostles (5:12)

5. Philip did miraculous signs in Samaria (6:8)

We can expect the Holy Spirit to enable us to overcome the natural and physical barriers today. If we do not believe in the presence and power of the Holy Spirit in us, miracles will not take place. Faith in the promise of the Lord Jesus who is risen from the dead and is seated at the right hand of the Father in heaven open the door of miracles.

The possibility of miracles does not cancel our natural limitations and make us supernatural beings. We will still be living in our body of sickness and death. Jesus himself was subject to human limitations of pain, hunger and death. He died as a man. But, God raised Him from the dead by the spirit of holiness (Rom.1:4).

Christians must live in expectation of the supernatural, but cannot escape the realities of this earthly life. We have to face sickness, hunger and death. The Apostle Paul confesses the reality of living in a body of death and decay.

"What a wretched man I am! Who will rescue me from this body of death?" (Rom. 7:24). "I am torn between the two: I desire to depart and be with Christ, which is better by far; but it is more necessary for you that I remain in the body" (Phil. 1:23,24).

It is normal for us to expect miracles in our lives, but we cannot escape from our mundane realities. What makes an event a miracle is that it is a supernatural event in the midst of natural events. A miracle is an unusual event, not the usual. We can always expect God to do miracles, knowing that God is at the helm of all affairs and we are the recipients of the benefit of miracles.

Men are not miracle workers; God is. He knows when to act and when to leave us in the state of expectancy and dependency. As long as we are in the body, we have fleshy limitations. We are not supernatural beings, but we have supernatural faith and hope.

The possibility of new power of healing and new energy for our tasks, make life worth living. We live in hope of the power of resurrection. It is better to live in hope than in despair. Our hope is not based on speculation, wild imaginations or false rumours, but on historical reality of the resurrection of Jesus and His continued presence with us through the ministry of the Holy Spirit. Our faith is historical faith and our hope is living hope.

Pentecostal- 'ism':
An Alternative Christian Worldview

Josfin Raj S. B.

Rarely people notice the suffix 'ism' behind 'Pentecostal*ism*'. Perhaps, Pentecostals are hardly having a sophisticated or stereotyped philosophical articulation of their faith and practice. I would argue Pentecostal'ism' must be seen as another/alternative Christian way of looking at things – i.e., worldview, if one considers 'Marx'ism', modern'ism' etc as world views, since all of these nomenclatures end with 'ism'(philosophy). Human thought-pattern and our experience reciprocally interact in creating or modifying our worldview. It is true with Pentecostals as well. Douglas Jacobsen says "Pentecostal experience has been circumscribed by theology, and pentecostal theology has been grounded in experience."[1] Experience being one side of the coin, Pentecostals has a unique way of looking at the history, spirituality, word, world and everything else around them.

I am aware that there can be a strict censure for this articulation within my own flock by saying that Pentecostalism is nothing to do with philosophical jargons or activities.[2] Interestingly, I am not alone in this endeavour. There were few recognized spokesperson talked about Pentecostal philosophy and its distinctive natures.[3] In addition, a person cannot bypass Pentecostal's worldview or vision of life, since Pentecostalism is one of the mounting movements in the 21st century.[4] This trend is stated in the well acclaimed *International Dictionary of Pentecostal and Charismatic Movements* which raised a query, "What is new in 20th century Pentecostalism is its spectacular growth and its impact on the larger Christian world?"[5] In the words of Grant Wacker "Pentecostals' distinctive understanding of the human encounter with the divine"[6] is the base for the formulation of Pentecostal worldview.

As an insider, I am always wonder why Pentecostals (we) think and act in such a way as an emotional, experiential and sometime anti-rational(?) in thought pattern! This distinct or sometimes weird (for others) nature of Pentecostalism must be translated. We must agree with Martin E. Marly who writes "Forward" to *Signs and Wonders* that "their [Pentecostals] word and world and workings need translation… if that audience [non-Pentecostals] is to make some sense of Pentecostalism."[7] Here I do agree with Anand Amaladass who states, "for it appears that there is probably no human being who does not philosophize."[8] And for a Pentecostal philosophy, according to James K.A Smith, "will be a philosophy informed and nourished by a Pentecostal spirituality."[9] Here I attempt to *philosophize* the Pentecostal movement or spirituality and its worldview.

Being Spiritual in Telling (Hi)stories: Seeking the Root to Unearth the Route

It is alleged against Pentecostals that they do not have a legitimate historical identity as other traditions in Christianity. Perhaps, this is not a correct observation. The root of the Pentecostal identity goes back to the experience-oriented first century Christian community and later sidelined such experience oriented spirituality and its history by designating as 'heresy' or 'sect'. The attempt to rewrite Pentecostal history from this perspective is numerous.[10] For instance, Eddie L. Hyatt takes two approaches such as restorationist approach, and traditionalist approach to rewrite Pentecostal/charismatic history of the Christian church. Restorationist approach argues that Pentecostal movement is simply a replica of the first century Christian faith or a latter rain movement, where as traditionalist approach tries to unearth or re-read the history of Christianity from Charismatic perspective and find continuity with the past along with other traditional churches.[11] Both approaches, though in different directions, point towards the first century experience of the apostolic church. Therefore it is not a risk to say that every Pentecostal movements can trace its origin from its first century root.

Eddie L. Hyatt also shares the concern of the isolation of Pentecostal history or identity in the main stream of Christianity.[12] However, the history of Pentecostal-like movements are sidelined or undermined by so-called dominant or orthodox traditions of Christian faith. It was in the periphery. Hyatt urges to find the root of Pentecostal movements with its "legitimate history". "Because these were often condemned or marginalized by the institutional church, their history has been submerged or misconstrued. It is, therefore, a history in need of discovery and full recovery."[13] His work attempted to recover the misconstructed history of Pentecostal like movements into the wide academic arena. Having the first century origin at hand, we must ponder upon the after effect of such vision in Pentecostal community.

I would like to highlight two perspectives to dig the root of Pentecostal history that reciprocally nurtured Pentecostal-charismatic Christianity. First perspective Pentecostal faith is originated and nurtured due to the Pentecostal orientation available to them. It is true with contemporary or modern Pentecostal movements. This perspective must be maintained for the study on the current developments of Pentecostalism since the modern Pentecostalism was a revival of old Pentecostal experiences of the church and people. The philosophy of modern Pentecostals is simply an adaptation of the early church pattern. It implies that current Pentecostals already have a written, experienced or other form of what is an ideal form of Pentecostalism from apostolic teachings and they strive to/ for achieve it. Peter Hocken narrates this identification lucidly as follows:

> Pentecostals believe that the Holy Spirit is restoring to the Church to the original power enjoyed by the first generation church from the day of Pentecost. The term 'Pentecostal' was also appropriate because the Pentecostal believers spoke in other tongues, thereby claiming a direct link between the twentieth-century experience and the first-century experience described in Acts 2.[14]

The second perspective is that Pentecostal philosophy is developed after the Pentecostal experience of the people. This perspective is apt for the study the early church since after the experience of Pentecost, their (apostles or believers) outlook towards the world, human and God changed. Therefore, one can argue/claim, as a Pentecostal, that the philosophy of Pentecostalism is not a personal, but was an experience of the early first century communities of faith. Thus, Pentecostalism has a legitimate lineage within the wider Christian community. The apostolic origin of Pentecostalism is well stated by Simon Samuel, an expert on Christian Origin and New Testament, and he writes that "the modern Pentecostal and Charismatic Christians trace their origin from the earliest tradition, teaching and the kerygmatic and other spiritual experiences and practices of the first followers of Jesus in Jerusalem and Palestine."[15] This historical vision of the past makes Pentecostal worldview a concrete Christian philosophy in the contemporary historical realities. It affects their worldview on society, marginalized people, and will reflect in their spirituality, worship and reading the Scripture.

Being Spiritual to 'See' the World: Differentiating Spirituality and Religiosity

We find a spiritual perspective with strong imaginative power among Pentecostals to 'see' the world.[16] Pentecostals 'see' the world from a spiritual category and not "in intellectual categories".[17] 'Seeing', for Pentecostals, refers to a spiritual act of discerning the work of God and work of evil in the world. That is to say, world is dualistic (i.e., spiritual and material world) in nature and constituted with the spiritual forces. The material world always is battlefield between divine spirit and evil spirit. The spiritual war affects every aspect of existence including "public spaces, institutions, or even whole countries."[18] Therefore, 'physical eyes' is not sufficient to see the movements of the spirit(s). For that 'the spirit of discernment' or extraordinary vision power is required. Nevertheless, their joy is that, at the end, the divine Spirit will gain the victory. That confidence leads them to have a high view about the life in this world. In a way, it can be argued that Pentecostal view on the world is built upon the first century worldview.

However, the 'world', for Pentecostals, denotes a negative connotation. It is the place you find all kinds of turmoil. The 'pattern of the world' is just opposite to the 'pattern of the other world'. Therefore, the believer is not supposed to be confirming with this world. Once you are saved, you must reject this 'world' so that you are received well in the 'world yet to come'. The technical term is used here is 'rupture', a break. It is visible in all aspects of the life of the believer. Csordas says that "Pentecostals work to maintain a break between themselves and profane life such that they never participate in contexts they define as wholly profane."[19] You are liberated from the past. Birgit Meyer defines what is past: "'the past' may well concern coeval beliefs and practices that are however dismissed as 'backward' or even 'satanic'."[20] Though they live in the turmoil world, their vision is for getting ready for the world yet to come. Theologically, it is an eschatological vision! It does not matter for them whatever may happen to this world. As Robbins put it, "Pentecostalism expands via a simultaneous process of "world-making" and "world-breaking."[21]

I think, it is Pentecostals who distinguish between being religious and spiritual. To say vividly, they give a negative connotation to the religiosity and glorified spirituality. They differentiate religion and spirituality based on following criteria exposed by Douglas Jacobsen

> ..."religion" is associated with organized institutionalized faith while "spirituality" focuses on personal values and practices. Religion is seen as promoting norms of belief and behavior that are codified and standardized for an entire group. By contrast, spirituality is more individualistic, discovered from within rather than learned from the outside. Religion is embodied in doctrines, creeds, and formal liturgies, while spirituality finds better outlet in poetry, song, and dramatic performance.[22]

In this division of being religious and spiritual to see the world, Pentecostals select 'spiritual'.[23] That means, Pentecostals departs from anything that is religious and poignant towards spirituality.

With this wide perception only, one must understand all other thoughts of Pentecostals.

Being Spiritual in the Society: Methodology for Societal Transformation

In a world of much division and turmoil, how do Pentecostals act in the society? What is their expectation of societal change? The Pentecostals are known for their rupture from the past and leading a 'transformed life' after baptism of the Holy Spirit. In the words of Joel Robbins "Pentecostalism is a powerful driver of radical cultural change."[24] The nature of their change is not a gradual process of evolution, though sometimes, it seems so. It is with certainty they repent of the past and transformed. Rupture is the technical word is used to denote such a change as elsewhere shared. Joel Robbins shares the transformation happens in a new Pentecostal believers life as follow: "Pentecostal converts do not imagine that what is required of them is some kind of gradual transformation or development…. Instead, they focus on reforming their lives by effecting a series of ruptures with the ways in which they have lived up to the time of their conversion."[25] The method of societal transformation begins with this individual transformation. For instance, Walter J. Hollenweger observes the transformation of William James Seymour to the Pentecostal experiences as "love in the face of hate, to overcome the hatred of a whole nation by demonstrating that Pentecost is something very different from the success-oriented American way of life."[26] Another instance Kimberley Snider, an anthropologist narrates different individual cases of Philippiano women's transformation. He finds four areas of change that Snider notes are: (1) spiritual disciplines, (2) God's activity, (3) the individual's desire to change, and (4) the individual's relationships with others.[27] Further Robbins talk about Ghanaian Pentecostal films which focus on moralizing messages with a motif of personal change in viewers' life.[28] These illustrate us that the process of social transformation begins from individual transformation that spontaneously affects social renovation.[29] The world for Pentecostals is also a place for "action and transformation, even though this is full of difficulties and dangers. In this sense, Pentecostal cosmology is strongly oriented toward world-making."[30] We find a spiritual struggle in these social actions as Brigit Meyer writes, "A born-again Christian can in principle use the "weapon of prayer" and invoke the power of the Holy Spirit in any setting, from the personal to the political."[31]

In relation to personal to social transformation J. Kwabena Asamoah-Gyadu's work *African Charismatics…* is important. His major concerns are: 'Salvation as Transformation and Empowerment,' 'salvation as healing and deliverance' and 'salvation as prosperity'.[32] To rent the words of Birgit Meyer, "In this sense, Pentecostalism is always in the process of becoming, a matter of movement and performance rather than a fixed religious system backed up by frozen structures of authority."[33] Pentecostalism gives all freedom to change oneself in the maximum for a better life and envisioning a healthier society ahead within the scriptural boundaries.

Being Spiritual with People: Taking Side with the Sidelined

Pentecostal's spirit motivated life exemplifies in Pentecostal social deliberations and their attitude towards marginalised people groups. As elsewhere shared, the growth of Pentecostal-charismatic movements happened, throughout the centuries, at the margins. 'All are welcome!' is the motto for the Pentecostals.[34] The modern manifestation of Pentecostal-charismatic movements is also not different from it. J. W. Shepperd shares the same notion when he writes, "Pentecostalism has attracted poor and marginalized people since its modern inception."[35] Douglas Jacobsen also describes the first participants of the modern Pentecostalism in the USA were "solid working-class folks.... But virtually none came from the ranks of the blue-blooded East Coast intellectual elite."[36] On geographical and social origins of Pentecostalism, A. Cerillo Jr. and G. Wacker also point to stress its lower-class character. He writes many people weight that the revival had started among the poor people.[37]

There are quite number of reasons that can be said to be this phenomenon of sidelined people, mostly embraced this movement. Joel Robbins, from an anthropological perspective, shares a weird idea that Pentecostalism is one among the sect that encourages discontinuity and tension, therefore "...the people who find Pentecostalism appealing tend to be those whose lives have already been subject to a good deal of discontinuity and tension."[38] An example for this narrated by Joel Robbins on the women who had to "equally disobey their husbands and other men who push them to behave in sinful ways. Furthermore, they are authorized to directly and publicly criticize men who themselves engage in sinful behavior" in the Philippiano context.[39]

In short, the Pentecostal movement has been consistently characterized by a central commitment to social justice, with a preferential option for the marginalized by transforming social structures.

Being Spiritual to Read the Scripture

How do Pentecostals lead such high moral life? Perhaps, one can observe that Pentecostals want to lead a holy life according to the Word of God. Bible has pertinent place in the Pentecostals' individual and communitarian life. Grant Wacker observes that the Bible "served as the final authority on all questions of daily living as well as human salvation" among the Pentecostal pioneers which solved their life's mundane problems.[40]

Pentecostals emphatically stressed the need to active involvement of the Holy Spirit in the process of interpreting and applying the scripture. In other words, the uncritical yielding to the work of the Spirit is visible in various spheres of Pentecostal's life including interpreting the Word. In the words of Douglas Jacobsen about the early Pentecostal pioneers that "[t]his was not abstract speculation; it was theological reflection grounded in real life."[41] It justifies why the traditional Pentecostals literally follow the Bible. They are critic towards the liberal trends in reading the Scripture.[42] Over against liberal interpretation, Pentecostals hold the stories of their daily experience and activity to derivate spiritual wisdom. Robeck says about this situation as he writes, "In pentecostal circles it[wisdom] has been commonly understood to be a word of revelation given by the Holy Spirit to provide wisdom to the Christian community at a particular time of need, often applying scriptural wisdom to the situation."[43] It is the high view of the scripture. Therefore, the words of Kenneth J. Archer worth to quote: "Pentecostals, both laity and academicians, actively invite the Holy Spirit to inspire the community and reveal meaningful understanding of Scripture."[44]

Kenneth J. Archer answers to the question that "How does the Spirit speak in and through the Scripture? The community must discern the Holy Spirit's voice, and the Holy Spirit must be granted an opportunity to be actively involved in the hermeneutical process."[45] The prayer of David Wesley Myland was "Oh God make our heads soft . . . give us softness of the brain!"[46] And he continue to admonish that hard-headed fellows cannot get the meaning of the text- Pentecostals hold.[47] It means spiritualization is another significant tool of interpretation to generate meanings from the text. Perhaps, Pentecostals prefer to rupture from the world with this experiential view on the Word.

Being Spiritual in Life and Worship

Along with spiritual interpretation to the scripture, Pentecostalism tries to experience the Spirit in their day-to-day life. After analyzing New Testament teachings of the Holy Spirit in relation to current Pentecostalism, James D. G. Dunn concludes his study as follows:

> Against the mechanical sacramentalism of extreme Catholicism and the dead Biblicist orthodoxy of extreme Protestantism they [Pentecostals] have shifted the focus of attention to the *experience* [original] of the Spirit. Our examination of the NT evidence has shown that they were wholly justified in this. That the Spirit, and particularly the gift of the Spirit, was a *fact of experience* [original] in the lives of the earliest Christians has been too obvious to require elaboration.[48]

Generally, Pentecostals do not find a distinction between their life in the world and in the worship. It has something to offer to their practical living. Exuberant worship, subjective religious experience and spiritual gifts, supernatural miracles, signs and wonders are the major characteristics of Pentecostal spirituality.[49] Joel Robbins argues, "Placing a high value on spontaneity and authenticity, Pentecostals condemn ritual as too routine, mechanical...."[50] Modern time, Pentecostalism emerged as a reaction against traditional theology. Since traditional "theology had lost touch with the Spirit and become dry and brittle, incapable of conveying the living truth of God's love to anyone."[51] It has nothing to do with the real life of the people. Then what is the antidote for that? After analyzing the historical documents of Pentecostal pioneers, A. Cerillo Jr. and G. Wacker comes to the following conclusion: "They [Pentecostal pioneers in modern time] presented a version of the past that was congruent with the theological and institutional needs of the movement at the time that they were written."[52] It was spontaneous movement of the Spirit.

However, Pentecostal worship is distinct from other traditional churches. They give importance to experience. Their worship is concentrated on "song, prayer, sermon, and testimony, [and] not in the format of lengthy treatises laced with philosophical concern."[53] Walter J. Hollenweger also shares that the reason for the development of Pentecostalism, which is not because of Pentecostal distinctive doctrine but the following reasons:

> The reason for its growth lies in its black roots, which can be summarized: orality of liturgy; narrativity of theology and witness; maximum participation at the levels of reflection, prayer and decision making and therefore a form of community that is reconciliatory; inclusion of dreams and visions into personal and public forms of worship; they function as a kind of icon for the individual and the community; an understanding of the body/mind relationship that is informed by experiences of correspondence between body and mind; the most striking application of this insight is the ministry of healing by prayer.[54]

Further, the involvement by the leader and congregation makes Pentecostal worship more alive and vibrant. In the words of Walter J. Hollenweger: "in principle everybody has access to the total information of the community."[55] In this way, Pentecostal worship becomes more democratic and people oriented.

One cannot simply snub Pentecostalism as merely an exuberant worship. But it is a qualitative Christianity. Some of the allegations that outsiders say about Pentecostalism are they only care about outward expression. They do not bother about social values or virtues. An authentic researcher Grant Wacker apprehends when has studying on early Pentecostalism. He writes his experience of research as follows:

> Almost immediately I began to hear—off in the distance—other words, other sounds, not anticipated. I heard about mundane realities like budgets and schedules and financial accountability. I heard about adjusting doctrine to the needs of the moment, the value of a carefully trained leadership, the importance of working hard and getting ahead. I heard respected leaders calling for good common sense in the conduct of the revival. I even heard heated arguments about power of the human kind, who had it and who did not (or should not). Before long it became clear that pentecostals, though primitivists, were never purely so. For all of their declarations about living solely in the realm of the supernatural, with the Holy Spirit guiding every step of their lives, they nonetheless displayed a *remarkably clear-eyed vision of the way things worked here on earth.*[56]

This shows that Pentecostal worship is lead by a concrete living reality outside of the Church which try to please God.

Conclusion

Pentecostalism, the main component in Global Christianity, needs to be philosophized, since its popularity and influence reaches to wide arena. It is neither an emotional outburst of some particular people groups nor a sectarian movement. It has something to say concretely, something needs to adapt in the postmodern and postcolonial era. Pentecostalism seems to be metaphysical externally, but concretized with the realities of the people and their struggles internally. It has a bold voice against the social concerns that pertaining to human society.

Its discontent voice is the need of the hour to transform individual and the societies. The worldview of Pentecostals will help us to be native and contextual to the so-called third world countries. This document would supplement and challenge both Pentecostals and outsiders to boldly engage in dialogue with the polyphonic Christian philosophies. It would wrestle and interact with the mainstream thought pattern to be radically reexamined or rechecked. It would also serve as a catalyst for social change and mobility and leading to a social empowerment. It would create a responsible and relevant community in their given context. Further, it would help us to reveal our identity in more comprehensible way to non-Pentecostal communities.

Endnotes

[1] Douglas Jacobsen, *Thinking in the Spirit: Theologies of the Early Pentecostal Movement* (Bloomington: Indiana University Press, 2003), 2.

[2] The Christian faith is not a philosophical system. Wilson W. Chow, "Biblical Foundations for Evangelical Theologies in the Third World," in *Biblical Theology in Asia*, ed. Ken Gnanakan (Bangalore: TBT, 1995).

[3] For instance, James K.A Smith's work *Thinking in Tongues: Pentecostal Contributions to Christian Philosophy* is worth mentioning here. First part of the book elaborates general categories of Pentecostal worldview and second part on theology of speaking in tongues with philosophical base (Grandrapids, Michigan: William B. Eerdmans Publishing Company, 2010). In addition Joel Robbins already tried to locate Pentecostal philosophy plausibly between pre-modern, modern and post-modern framework. Joel Robbins writes Pentecostal culture can be termed as pre-modern since "Its frank supernaturalism and commitment to ontological preservation", postmodern since "its wide dispersal of authority and the network quality of its social organization." And the modern since the features such as individualism, gender, economy, and politics are to be considered as modern formations. Joel Robbins, "Anthropology of Religion," *Studying Global Pentecostalism: Theories and Methods*, edited by Allan Anderson, and etal., (Berkeley: University of California Press, 2010), 168.

[4] The research published by the Center for the Study of Global Christianity and the argument of a secular historian Philip Jenkins is

that "the re-location of Christianity from Global North to the Global South is with the help of pentecostal-charismatic movements." http:// www.gordonconwell.edu/ockenga/research/index.cfm; Cf. Josfin Raj S. B, "Pentecostal-Charismatic Theological Expressions in Asia," *Journal of COTR Theological Seminary* 3/1 (Feb., 2017): 71. See Philip Jenkins, *The Next Christendom: The Coming of Global Christianity* (New York: Oxford University Press, 2002), *The New Face of Christianity: Believing the Bible in the Global South* (New York: Oxford University Press, 2006). Though there are different theories prevail on the growth of Pentecostalism, Grant Wacker argues for three models such as compensation model, functional model and mobilization model for expansion of Pentecostals today. For further details see Grant Wacker, *Heaven Below: Early Pentecostals and American Culture* (Cambridge, Massachusetts: Harvard University Press, 2001), 10.

[5] "Introduction," *IDPCM* edited by Stanley M. Burgers and Edward M. Van DerMeas (Grand Rapids/Michigan: Zondervan, 2003), xvii.

[6] Grant Wacker, *Heaven Below: Early Pentecostals and American Culture*, 10.

[7] Martin E. Marly, "Forward," Paul Alexander, *Signs and Wonders: Why Pentecostalism is the World's Fastest Growing Faith* (San Francisco: Jossey-Bass, 2009), viii.

[8] Anand Amaladass, *Introduction to Philosophy* (Chennai: Satya Nilayam Publications, 2001), 1.

[9] James K.A Smith, *Thinking in Tongues*, 27.

[10] Eddie L. Hyatt, *2000 Years of Charismatic Christianity: A 21st Century Look at Church History from a Pentecostal/Charismatic Perspective* (Florida: Charisma House, 1996). The works of Vinson Synan, Allen Anderson, M. Stephen, and so on are examples for the same.

[11] Eddie L. Hyatt, *2000 Years of Charismatic Christianity*, 2-3.

[12] Eddie L. Hyatt, *2000 Years of Charismatic Christianity*, 2.

[13] Eddie L. Hyatt, *2000 Years of Charismatic Christianity*, 2-3. [Emphasis is mine]

[14] Peter Hocken, *The Challenges of the Pentecostal, Charismatic and Messianic Jewish Movements: The Tensions of the Spirit* (Farnham: Ashgate, 2009), 4.

[15] Simon Samuel, "The Charismatic and Pentecostal Movements and their Commitments to the Social Demands of the Gospel," *Doon Theological Journal* 9/2 (Sep., 2012): 214-216. Cf. Jacob Mathew, "Separated but not Sectarian': Challenges in Developing a Paradigm for Partnering Pentecostalism with Asian Christian Theology," *Doon Theological Journal* 10/1 (March, 2013):196, 108.

[16] Josfin Raj S. B, "Pentecostal-Charismatic Theological Expressions in Asia," *Journal of COTR Theological Seminary* 3/1 (Feb., 2017): 63-65.

[17] James K. A. Smith, "Thinking in Tongues," https://www.firstthings.com/article/2008/04/003-thinking-in-tongues

[18] Birgit Meyer, "Pentecostalism and Globalization," in *Studying Global Pentecostalism: Theories and Methods*, edited by Allan Anderson, and etal. (Berkeley: University of California Press, 2010), 117.

[19] Thomas J. Csordas, *Language, Charisma, and Creativity: The Ritual Life of a Religious Movement* (Berkeley: UCP, 1997). Mentioned in Joel Robbins, "Anthropology of Religion," 164.

[20] Birgit Meyer, "Pentecostalism and Globalization," 121.

[21] Joel Robbins, "Anthropology of Religion."

[22] Douglas Jacobsen, *Thinking in the Spirit: Theologies of the Early Pentecostal Movement* (Bloomington: Indiana University Press, 2003), xi.

[23] Douglas Jacobsen, *Thinking in the Spirit*, xi.

[24] Joel Robbins, "Anthropology of Religion," 156.

[25] Joel Robbins, "Anthropology of Religion," 159.

[26] Walter J. Hollenweger, "Guest Editorial: After Twenty Years' Research On Pentecostalism," *International Review of Mission* (1986): 5.

[27] Kimberley Snider, "Behavior Transformation in Filipino Christian Women," 96.

[28] Joel Robbins, "Anthropology of Religion," 167.

[29] Josfin Raj S. B, "Pentecostal-Charismatic Theological Expressions in Asia," 68-69.

[30] Birgit Meyer, "Pentecostalism and Globalization," 118.

[31] Birgit Meyer, "Pentecostalism and Globalization," 118.

[32] J. Kwabena Asamoah-Gyadu, *African Charismatics: Current Developments within Independent Indigenous Pentecostalism in Ghana* (Leiden, Boston: Brill, 2005).

[33] Birgit Meyer, "Pentecostalism and Globalization," 121-122.

[34] See Dorean A. Benavidez, "Pentecostalism and Social Responsibility," in *Prospects and Challenges for the Ecumenical Movement in the 21ˢᵗ Century: Insights from the Global Ecumenical Theological Institute*, edited by David Field and Jutta Koslowski (Geneva: Global Ethics net, 2016), 2.

[35] J. W. Shepperd, "Sociology of World Pentecostalism," *IDPCM* edited by Stanley M. Burgers and Edward M. Van DerMeas (Grand Rapids/ Michigan: Zondervan, 2003), 1086.

[36] Douglas Jacobsen, *Thinking in the Spirit*, ix.

[37] A. Cerillo Jr. and G. Wacker, "Bibliography and Historiography," *IDPCM* edited by Stanley M. Burgers and Edward M. Van DerMeas (Grand Rapids/Michigan: Zondervan, 2003), 395.

[38] Joel Robbins, "Anthropology of Religion," 163.

[39] Joel Robbins, "Anthropology of Religion," 170.

[40] Grant Wacker, *Heaven Below*, 11.

[41] Douglas Jacobsen, *Thinking in the Spirit*, xi.

[42] Philip Jenkins, *The New Faces of Christianity*.

[43] C. M. Robeck Jr., "Wisdom, Word of," *IDPCM* edited by Stanley M. Burgers and Edward M. Van DerMeas (Grand Rapids/Michigan: Zondervan, 2003), 1200.

[44] Kenneth J. Archer, "The Spirit and Theological Interpretation: A Pentecostal Strategy," *Cyber Journal For Pentecostal Charismatic Research* #16 (23/5/2017): 8/12 [online] http://www.pctii.org/cyberj/cyberj16/archer. html

[45] Kenneth J. Archer, "The Spirit and Theological Interpretation: A Pentecostal Strategy."

[46] David Wesley Myland, *The Latter Rain Covenant and Pentecostal Power with Testimony of Healings and Baptism* (Chicago: Evangel Publishing House, 1910), 15, 23–25, 55–56 cited by Douglas Jacobsen, *Thinking in the Spirit*, 2.

[47] David Wesley Myland, *The Latter Rain Covenant*, 15, 23–25, 55–56 cited by Douglas Jacobsen, *Thinking in the Spirit*, 2.

[48] James D. G. Dunn, *Baptism in the Holy Spirit: A Re-Examination of the New Testament Teaching on the Gift of the Spirit in relation to Pentecostalism Today* (Philadelphia: The Westminster Press, 1970), 225.

[49] "Introduction," *IDPCM*, xvii.

[50] Joel Robbins, "Anthropology of Religion," 164.

[51] Douglas Jacobsen, *Thinking in the Spirit*, 2.

[52] A. Cerillo Jr. and G. Wacker, "Bibliography and Historiography," 396.

[53] Douglas Jacobsen, *Thinking in the Spirit*, 7.

[54] Walter J. Hollenweger, "Guest Editorial: After Twenty Years' Research On Pentecostalism," 6.

[55] Walter J. Hollenweger, "Guest Editorial: After Twenty Years' Research On Pentecostalism," 10-11.

[56] Grant Wacker, *Heaven Below*, 11. [emphasis added]

Pentecostal Evangelism in India: A Subaltern Reading

Viju Wilson

St. Thomas, one of the disciples of Jesus Christ, is traditionally believed to have brought the Christian faith in India in 52 AD. The Catholic, Protestant and Evangelical missionaries came in different periods, and established their respective ecclesiastical systems and traditions. Many became Christians because of the work of different mission organizations throughout the centuries. Though it was numerically less, people from different socio-cultural-religious communities were attracted to Christianity. The missionaries and the native Christians established Churches, schools, colleges, hospitals etc as part of their mission work in different parts of the nation. In the beginning of 20th century, the Pentecostal missionaries came to India and began their evangelistic activities particularly revival meetings among Christians of other denominations. Many non-Christians particularly the people belong to lower caste origin became Christians. More than non-Christians, the Christians of different denominations became Pentecostals because of the work of foreign and native Pentecostal missionaries. The Pentecostal movements and Churches have qualitatively and quantitatively contributed to the growth of Indian Christian community. Many native Pentecostals propagated Christian faith in remote villages where Christianity was not heard even once, and established Churches and faith communities. Despite its denominational divide, the Pentecostal community has emerged as one of the growing faith communities within Christianity in India. Numerically Pentecostals comprise a small percentage within Christianity which constitutes 2.3% of Indian population. Majority Indian Pentecostals are drawn from Dalit/Tribal/OBC communities. Quite a lot of Pentecostals are involved in evangelism in different parts of the country. While some voluntarily work, others work as part of mission organizations. They carry out evangelistic activities to reach the 'unreached' communities with the Gospel of Jesus Christ. However, there is no visible growth in the numerical strength of Christianity as claimed by mission organizations. At the same time, still majority Pentecostals come from other Christian denominations. In that case, whom do we evangelize? Who are really unreached: non-Pentecostals or non-Christians? This article is an attempt to reflect on some issues involved in Pentecostal evangelism from subaltern perspective.

The Contemporary Religious Context

The dualistic thinking of reached and unreached is the product of Christian evangelistic mindset derived from the Great Commission. The scope of this categorization in India cannot be perceived properly without glancing through the contemporary socio-religious context of India. Discourse on unreached has to be analyzed in the light of changing social context which is religiously sensitive. Indian majority (Hindu) religious context is shaped by the thinking that all religions are one. The question raised by majority religion is "Can Christians and Muslims say all religions are one?" "A Hindu can say that."[1] This religious outlook and assertion may not be a fertile ground for the exclusive salvific claims of Christians, particularly the Pentecostals.

The number of villages or village councils which directly or indirectly opposes the entry or work of Christian missionaries is increasing day by day. The resolutions of around 50 village councils, in Bastar district in Chhattisgarh, which banned the entry of "non-Hindu missionaries" points to the changing socio-religious trends[2] which are not conducive for traditional evangelistic activities. There are many Pentecostal evangelists work in remote villages which resist the Christian mission activities.

A strong negative feeling covertly or overtly prevails against Christian mission activities in different parts of the nation. The centre of opposition is conversion. Hindu organizations and fringe groups strongly oppose any kind of Christian work: evangelistic or humanitarian. They eye everything Christian with suspicion. Dwarkapeeth Shankaracharya Swaroopanand Saraswati asks, "Why would people change their religion if the government fulfils their needs?"[3] His question not only put the Christian work of any kind under the wrap of conversion but also misjudges the intention behind conversion. Ashok Singhal, Vishwa Hindu Parishad (VHP) Convener, said "unless conversions were stopped immediately, the day would not be far off when Hindus would be reduced to a minority in this country."[4] The purpose of such unrealistic statements is to consolidate the feeling of Hindus against Christian evangelistic activities, and thereby stop conversion. The Pentecostal evangelists and organizations are mainly accused of promoting conversion. Whenever there is a debate on conversion in public domain the non-Pentecostal Churches directly or indirectly blame the Pentecostals for creating religion tension in the name of conversion.

Another religious trend in the present context is creation of 'vegetarian zone' or 'vegetarian state.' The Jains want Palitana, Gujarat their pilgrimage centre to be declared as a vegetarian zone. For them, it is the centre of their faith. It is considered as 'eternal.'[5] Society also witnesses the appearance of 'religious housing,' exclusive housing complexes or apartments based on religions.[6] Even the food habits of people are given religious color. In the name of religion, cow is protected more than human being. Majority Indian states fully or partially banned cow slaughter. It is religious feeling which legalized the ban.

The religious fundamentalists intentionally keep the discourse on Hindutva alive. They make provocative statements and incite communal feelings. Mohan Bhagavat, RSS Chief, remarked at the Golden Jubilee Celebrations of VHP in Mumbai that "Hindustan is a Hindu nation…Hindutva is the identity of our nation and it (Hinduism) can incorporate others (religions) in itself."[7] Pramod Muthalik, Sri Ram Sena chief, promised to give all Hindus Gita and Sword in Goa where Christians constitute 26% of the population.[8]

According to the Census 2011, Hindus constitute 96.63 crores (79.8%) of Indian population, Muslims- 17.22 crores (14.2%), Christians- 2.78 crores (2.3%), Sikhs- 2.08 crores (1.7%), Jains-0.45 crores (0.4%), Buddhists-0.84 crores (0.7%), Other Religions- 0.79 crores (0.7%), Religion Not Stated – 0.29 crores (0.2%).[9] Compared to Census 2001, there is no change in the proportion of Christians including Pentecostals though they are falsely accused of promoting conversion by 'fraudulent means.'

While there is no 'official' growth of Christianity in India, the number of Christians has come down globally. Many Christians in Europe and American continents have left the Church and embraced atheism, agnosticism and alternate spirituality promoted by Indian and Asian Gurus. The percentage of professed Christians in United Kingdom, a Christian country, has reduced to 59.3%. The Christian population in USA (77%) is declining compared to Hindu population (79.8%) in India.[10] It includes Pentecostals too.

Evangelization is no longer the programme of Pentecostals alone. Today, Hindu 'evangelization' promoted by Sri, Sri Ravishankar, Baba Ram Dev, Mata Amirtanandamayi etc under the garb of 'yoga,' 'art of living,' 'universal brotherhood' attract many in India and abroad.[11] Every religious group is on the path of getting organized and religiously conscientized. Religious communities including Pentecostals look at each other through the eyes of suspicion. They put up social and cultural fencing with the intention of limiting social interactions and relationships. In this religiously charged context, the Pentecostal evangelism has to be understood and evaluated.

Pentecostal Understanding of Evangelism

The Pentecostals[12] fundamentally believe that salvation is attainable only through faith in Jesus Christ. They also believe that salvation experience is individualistic and otherworldly. Though corporal and this-worldly dimensions of salvation are emphasized in the writings and speeches of Pentecostal scholars and preachers, they have not yet influenced the theological thinking of common believers and the faith statements of Pentecostal denominations in India. Pentecostals generally maintain an exclusivist theological approach towards other denominations and non-Christians. They believe and propagate that they only hold the truth of salvation in Jesus Christ. It reflects in their social relations, formal and informal fellowships. They keep social and religious distance from other religious communities except general social relations in society. This distance can be physical or mental. It does not lead to social unrest or public disorder. The exclusive theological approach creates a mind-set of 'us' and 'them' among Pentecostals. The Pentecostal life style demands withdrawal from many social customs and recreational practices. Sometimes, circumstantial compulsion determines the nature of participation in social events. Before Vatican II, Roman Catholic Church believed that there is no salvation outside the Church (Roman Catholic Church). They changed the position and recognized the possibility of the rays of salvation outside the Church. However, they upheld that Jesus Christ is the source of ultimate salvation. Like Catholics, from the very beginning, the Pentecostals continue to maintain a theological position that salvation is possible only within the Pentecostal Church/ fellowship. They believe that Jesus Christ is the only savior as Christians of other denominations believe but salvation can be ultimately achieved through Pentecostal experience: Pentecostal fellowship, worship, baptism, way of life, experience of Holy Spirit etc. Though theological education has softened the exclusive theological thinking of Pentecostals, majority of them still believe that they are already saved because of their Pentecostal faith experience in Jesus Christ.

The salvation understanding of Pentecostals defines their theology of evangelism. Pentecostals believe that all except Pentecostals are unreached and unsaved. For them, evangelism simply means reaching the unreached with Gospel of Jesus Christ. It is not limited to reaching the unreached but to make them Pentecostals in faith experience and in life style.

A Pentecostal believer is basically an evangelist. S/he is not simply a believer but an evangelist who propagate Christian faith in personal and organizational capacity. S/he cannot escape from this responsibility. The Pentecostals preach the Gospel to non-Christians and non-Pentecostal Christians equally. They encourage people from non-Pentecostal denominations and non-Christian faith traditions to join their fellowship. The salvation theology of Pentecostals places all except Pentecostals within the scope of evangelism. The evangelistic approach of Pentecostals earns them the titles such as 'sheep stealers' given by non-Pentecostal denominations and 'promoters of conversion' by non-Christian faith traditions. The Pentecostals claim that in evangelism they follow the Great Commission of Jesus Christ after his resurrection and the life and witness of Apostles after the Pentecost event.

The Unreached and Nazareth Manifesto

Propagation of faith is one of the tenets of Christian faith. It is based on the Great Commission narrated in the Gospel According to Mathew 28: 19-20. No other book in the Bible explicitly says about it. The word used in Christian parlance for 'the propagation of faith' is 'evangelism' which means 'to announce the *euangel*, the Good News.'[13] Traditionally, evangelism is understood as the propagation of the Goodnews of Jesus Christ to the people who do not know about Jesus Christ whom Christians believe as the only Savior of humanity. In evangelistic language, evangelism is reaching the 'unreached' with the Gospel of Jesus Christ. The Pentecostals also understands evangelism in this direction. According to the Lausanne Covenant "to evangelize is to spread the gospel, that Jesus Christ died for our sins, was raised from the dead, according to the Bible, and that as the reigning Lord, He now offers the forgiveness of sins and the liberating gift of the Spirit to all who repent and believe. Evangelism should result in people's obedience to Christ, incorporation into His Church and responsible service to the world."[14] The Catholics define evangelism as "proclaiming Christ to those who do not know him, of preaching of catechesis, of conferring Baptism and other Sacraments."[15] These definitions based on Great Commission provide us the hint for who are unreached? The 'unreached' are the people who do not know or experience the Lordship of Jesus Christ. But the Pentecostals consider all non-Pentecostals are unreached. It has to be tested in the light of Nazareth Manifesto, the manifesto of Jesus' ministry. The Nazareth manifesto gives another description of 'unreached.'

The life and work of Jesus Christ was centered on the Nazareth Manifesto-'The Spirit of the Lord is up on me because he has anointed me to preach good news to the poor. He has sent me to proclaim freedom for the prisoners and recovery of sight for the blind, to release the oppressed and to proclaim the year of the Lord's favor' (Luke 4:18-19) than the Great Commission. It was the crux of His ministry. The Nazareth Manifesto teaches that the Goodnews which Jesus Christ proclaimed is 'Goodnews of Life.' It is the Goodnews that empowers the people and leads them to celebrate transformed life. In line with Nazareth Manifesto, Leonardo Boff observes that evangelization in Latin America context is "saving the lives of poor."[16] Saving the lives of poor implies helping them to live as 'humans' with God-given rights and privileges. Jesus' method of evangelism reminds us that good news cannot be proclaimed without responding to the broken realities of human life. It defends the deprived and stands for the salvation/liberation of people from oppressive social-cultural-spiritual bondages. The ultimate goal of evangelism in the light of Nazareth Manifesto is humanization: enabling a person to live as authentic human as willed by God in Jesus Christ. Then who are unreached? They are not only the people who are ignorant of Jesus Christ as we traditionally interpret but also the people who need salvation/liberation from oppressive systems and structures in respective context. Reaching the people with Gospel of Jesus Christ cannot be meant to make people Christians, but empower them to celebrate the life in its fullness. Those who are disempowered are the real 'unreached' in society. The poor, the blind, the oppressed, the crippled mentioned in the Nazareth Manifesto are not simply spiritual categories, but social categories too. Unless the people experience "whole salvation"[17] they continue as 'unreached.' The Nazareth Manifesto redefines Pentecostal understanding of evangelism. The non-Pentecostal Christians are not the real 'unreached' in evangelism but the people who do not know Jesus Christ and are spiritually and physically disempowered. They are to be reached first with the Gospel of Jesus Christ.

Conversion and Reconversion: Victims and Victors

The non-Pentecostal missionaries, who recognized the place of upper castes in the caste hierarchy, initially attempted to convert the upper castes. They even discouraged the conversion of lower castes who believed that Christian faith would give them social status and spiritual satisfaction. When they failed to bring the upper castes into Church, missionaries shifted their focus on lower castes. They even interpreted mass conversion as act of Holy Spirit.[18] B.R. Ambedkar observed that Christian missionaries had opened schools and hospitals with an eye on upper castes. The caste people took full advantage of Christian schools, hospitals and colleges, and continued in their faith.[19] The mass conversion happened among lower castes even changed the image of Indian Church-numerically and socially. According to Nirad C. Chaudhuri, "the power of the caste system is such that the Hindus from the low castes who embraced Christianity did not raise themselves to a higher level, but on the contrary brought down the religion to their level."[20] Though his observation is debatable, it has some truth. Since upper caste Hindus are resistant to Christian faith, lower castes/subaltern communities have been the main targets of conversion throughout the centuries. Though the native and foreign Pentecostal evangelists shared the Gospel with upper castes they were not successful in converting the upper castes as they achieved among lower castes. The Pentecostal evangelists could not get many coverts from other communities except Syrian Christians, Nadars and different Dalit and Tribal communities in India. In fact the lower castes, particularly the Dalits continue to be the targets of Pentecostal evangelism. They are the victims of conversion because except 'spiritual contentment,' the status and life-condition of majority Dalit Pentecostals has not been enhanced. They are still 'Dalits' in the eyes of both upper caste and OBC Hindus and Pentecostal Christians. There is no concrete upward social mobility among them. If social and economic empowerment of new believers does not happen, evangelism remains as incomplete exercise.

Historically, lower castes particularly the Dalits are not only objects of conversion but also of reconversion. The practice of reconversion or *Shuddhi karan* (purification) can be traced back to the Arya Samaj in the 19th century. Though it applies to all who want to come back to Hindu faith, Dalits have been main targets of *Shuddhi karan* movements. Mahatma Gandhi and Swami Vivekananda supported voluntary reconversion.[21] Dalit Christians are forcibly asked to go through *Shuddhi karan* conducted by *Sangh Parivar* organizations. Dharam Jagran Vivad conducted *Shuddhi karan* ceremony of 72 Valmikis, who had become Christians in 1995, in Asroi, Aligarh, Uttar Pradesh, on 23rd August 2014. It was a widely reported reconversion event in the decade. It was reported that they became Hindus through *Shuddhi karan* ceremony held inside the Seventh Day Adventist Church. The leaders of the movement called it as 'successful *ghar wapasi*' (return home). Khem Chandra, Sangh pracharak and pramukh of Dharam Jagran Vivad in Aligarh, said, "This is *ghar wapasi*, not conversion."[22] He says, "They left by choice and today they have realized their mistake and want to come back. We welcome them. We can't let our Samaj scatter; we have to hold it tight. I have told them that honor comes from within the community and not from outside."[23] Many new Pentecostal believers especially Dalits in remote villages are also under the threat of reconversion. People who promote reconversion of Dalits misunderstand that Dalits are incapable of taking decisions related to their faith. Dalits have capacity to challenge and combat the dominant. Negation of one faith by Dalits is tantamount to the affirmation of their selfhood.[24] What is the outcome of religious conversion and re-conversion in India? It actually creates two categories: victims and victors. The poor converts, particularly Dalits are real victims. On the one hand, they have not been able to enhance their status in society; on the other hand they are deprived of legal protection and constitutional privileges which facilitate their social and economic empowerment. In spite of having sufficient resources, Church and mission organizations both Pentecostal and non-Pentecostal could not facilitate successful social mobility of converts, particularly the Dalits. Who are victors? They are Pentecostal and non-Pentecostal mission/ Church agencies and contemporary Hindutva brigades. The former emerge as victorious in the eyes of their sponsors

whereas latter get political mileage. The poor converts pay
the price for conversion and reconversion: physical violence
(Kandhamal, Orissa), social boycott, court cases, mental
harassment etc. Spiritualization of conversion is against the spirit
of Jesus' method of evangelism. In the process of reaching
the unreached, particularly, Dalits and other weaker sections
of society, the outlook of Pentecostals has to be changed. We
need to share the perspective of converts: 'whole salvation.'

The Constitution, Propagation and the Unreached

The Constitution of India guarantees religious freedom: freedom
to profess, practice and propagate religion. Article 25 (1) of the
Constitution says, "Subject to public order, morality and health
and to the other provisions of this Part, all persons are equally
entitled to freedom of conscience and the right freely to profess,
practice and propagate religion."[25] The word 'propagate' was
inserted in the clause mainly because of Christians in India.
It is evident in the debate on this provision in the Constituent
Assembly. K.M. Munshi, one of the leading members of the
Drafting Committee said, "I know, it was on this word that
the Indian Christian community laid the greatest emphasis,
not because they wanted to convert people aggressively, but
because the word 'propagate' was a fundamental part of their
tenant. Even if the word was not there, I am sure, under the
freedom of speech which the Constitution guarantees, it will
be open to any religious community to persuade other people
to join their faith. So long as religion is religion, conversion
by free exercise of the conscience has to be recognized."
(Constituent Assembly Debates, Vol 7, 837-8). But in the
case of Rev. Stanislaus Vs State of Madhyapradesh (1977 1
SCC 677), Chief Justice A.N. Ray, ruled that "what Article 25
(1) grants is not the right to convert another person to one's

own religion, but to transmit or spread one's religion by an exposition of its tenets." This ruling was criticized by H.M. Seevai, constitutional lawyer, "…..Successful propagation of religion would result in conversion…."[26]

A few states have passed freedom of religion bills in different names. Though it is claimed that the main purpose of these laws is to prohibit conversion by force or inducement or by fraudulent means, the main targets are Christian mission activities. Majority cases charged under the clauses of such religion freedom bills are against Christian Pastors, Mission or Social Workers. It includes Pentecostal evangelists also. The Gujarat Freedom of Religion Bill says "No person shall convert or attempt to convert either directly or otherwise, any person from one religion to another, by use of force or allurement or by fraudulent means nor shall any person abet such conversion."[27] We need to understand the propagation of faith and 'unreached' in the light of Constitution, Supreme Court ruling and Freedom of Religion Bills. The Constitution is unambiguous about the propagation of faith. In Pentecostal evangelistic language, there is no legal hurdle to 'reach the unreached.' The so-called 'unreached' has right to exercise 'freedom of conscience' to accept or reject Christian faith. The Supreme Court ruling interprets the provision 'right to propagate religion' as 'not the right to convert.' The person who propagates the faith has no right to convert another person, but the 'unreached' who exercise the 'freedom of conscience' has the right to be converted. This freedom has to be respected. The freedom of religions bills are actually anti-conversion bills. The contents of such bills not only curtail the right to propagate religion but also the freedom of conscience. Religious discrimination is not constitutional and legal. Nevertheless the Presidential

Order of 1950 which denied Scheduled Caste status to Dalit Muslims and Christians is an outright negation of 'the right freely to profess, practice and propagate religion.'[28] We need to place the unreached subaltern communities, particularly the Dalits in the framework of Constitution which guarantees the right to propagate religion and the freedom of religion bills which provide restricted freedom to change religion and propagate and the Presidential Order 1950. Our propagation of faith should result in the 'whole Salvation' of people than the 'half-salvation.'[29] In short, a Pentecostal has right to profess, practice and propagate his/her faith, but not to convert another person. Propagation of faith must be carried out within legal and constitutional provisions. It may or may not lead to conversion which is purely personal decision of one's conscience.

Religion, Social Life and Response to Christian Faith

There are many Pentecostal mission organizations and Churches actively engaged in 'reaching the unreached.' According to Census Reports, the percentage of Christians is same for last two/three decades. Of course, the mission organizations can claim otherwise. There may be truth in their claims too. Even if we believe the claims of mission organizations, the present growth does not do justice to the economic and human resources spent till the date. The geographical presence of Christianity particularly the Pentecostals-more in South India and less in North-East and North Indian States- does not support the growth stories. Apart from dual-religious membership which some Dalit Christians keep in some states, what are other reasons which prevent the growth of Christians including Pentecostals? Why numerical growth of Christianity is not visible? It is viewed that "the story of Christianity in India is a story of dismal failure, demographically speaking."[30] Frequently mentioned reasons are caste and religious fundamentalists. There is some truth in them. We need to look into some of the other factors which influence people to respond 'negatively' to Christian faith propagated by the Pentecostals.

Hindu religion does not object its adherents to observe the beliefs and practices of other religious traditions.[31] Religiously, they are Hindus as long as they are not baptized or circumcised. A moderate/liberal Hindu may not have problem to keep Jesus' photo or Christian symbols along with Hindu Gods/Goddesses in his/her *pooja* room or in vehicle. This "embrace-cum-rejection"[32] attitude is visible throughout the nation. Non-objection to other religious symbols and beliefs is the result of the influence of the outlook that all religions are same. Moreover, there is no concept of 'false gods' and 'one true God' in Hinduism. The Hindus have no theological problem to go and pray in the Church/Mosque/Synagogue. Theologically they are inclusive, and they can worship any animate or inanimate beings/things.[33] The Pentecostals are theologically exclusive and reject the approach of a moderate Hindu in terms of worship and faith. They do not have any alternative except their theological stubbornness towards the inclusive religiosity of Hindus. The traditional understanding of Pentecostal evangelism may not be successful among the people who are religiously inclusive.

Aggressive evangelistic activities in the past revived the Hindu reformers to conscientize their followers of the consequences of conversion. It not only helped them to bring some changes in the social life of Hindus but also to prevent mass conversions of lower caste people.[34] Recently, Arch Bishop Thumma Bala of Hyderabad alleged that the aggressive preaching of Pentecostals condemning other religious traditions instigated the people to attack a newly-built Catholic Church in Kundapalli village in Telangana.[35] Aggressive evangelism always brings negative results. Monier Williams in his lecture in the missionary congress held at Oxford on 2 May 1877, while mentioning the obstacles of evangelism, observed that people in India are proud of their religion and traditions. They are also self- complacent with their beliefs and practices.[36] If a person is contented with his/her religion in spiritual and material life, he/she may not be reached with the Gospel successfully. The upper castes are proud of their traditions. Ambedkar observes that high castes will not be receptive to Christian faith because it teaches brotherhood of believers which leads to social equality. [37] They will not be ready to lose their social status which revolves around caste and traditions. That is why the percentage of Christians particularly the Pentecostals among upper castes is extremely minimal. The success of 'reaching the unreached' depends on how we respond to inclusive religious attitude and self-contentment of people.

Though they are generally known as peaceful community, the internal and external witness of Pentecostals is not appealing to the large sections of people. The Pentecostal community in India is a divided house in theory and in practice. The words of Ambedkar about Indian Christianity are applicable to the present Pentecostal community. He observed that "… the Indian Christian is a disjointed-it is a better word than the word disunited-community."[38] Strong denominationalism has crept into the mind-set of Pentecostals. Spirit-filled Pentecostal fellowship is replaced by denominational fellowship. The presence of Pentecostals in service sector-health, education and social service-is very minimal. Majority Pentecostal theological and secular educational institutions are run by families. Money plays its demonic role in Pentecostal Church as it does in the larger society. Care to the poor within the community has reduced considerably. The exclusive mind-set of many Pentecostals affects the social relations with people of other faiths and denominations. The Pentecostals in government sector as high officials and administrators are not completely untouched by the culture of bribe. The Pentecostal faith identity is being replaced by caste identity. Pentecostal denominations and churches are either formed or functioned on the basis of caste or ethnic origin. Gender prejudices highly prevail in community life and in ministerial space. Political participation is still allergic to majority Pentecostals because of the influence of other worldly theological outlook. Alarmingly, the morality of Pentecostal leaders including Presidents, Pastors, and other officials is being questioned in society. Above mentioned reasons compels us to think that if our house is not in order, why we should bring the people especially Dalits and other weaker sections of society into Church. Are we theologically sound to counter the inclusive mindset and self-complacency of 'unreached?'

Prospects of Pentecostal Evangelism and the 'Unreached'

In the light of social inequality among Indian Christians, B.R. Ambedkar opines that Christianity does not inspire the Dalits to advance in life. Christianity preaches 'spiritual' Christianity which discourages engagement with material life. It 'spiritualizes' the social issues and does not go beyond exhortation. Love is preached but not reflected in the social attitude of Christians.[39] The words of Ambedkar are more apt to the Pentecostals today. The Pentecostals who teach about otherworldly life neglects the struggles of marginalized communities in this world. They spiritualize the social issues more than any other Christian communities. They may claim that they live a Spirit-filled life, but their social relations are determined by caste and ethnicity. Though the Pentecostal movement has apparently contributed to the enhancement of Dalits, their social status is not changed even after conversion. Actually they lost their legal and constitutional privileges. The Pentecostals in general neither take initiative nor identify with Dalits of other denominations to achieve the rights of Dalit Christians. Thus, reaching the subaltern 'unreached,' particularly the Dalits, completely depends on how Pentecostal evangelism facilitates their social and economic enhancement. If Pentecostalism fails in this regard, the argument of Ambedkar stands valid. Still, the question remains: Why don't Dalit Pentecostals advance as Pentecostals of non-Dalit communities do? Who is culprit-Church/Missions/Dalits/Dalit leaders/Upper Caste or OBC Christians/Governments? Do we have resources to contribute to their development? Are we willing to change our social mind? These questions must to be asked in Pentecostal evangelistic activities.

Aggressive evangelism has to be reconsidered in the context of religious revival and fundamentalism. Knowingly or unknowingly, abusing or discrediting the customs and beliefs of other religious traditions is involved in the Pentecostal propagation of faith. It can make people more offensive and violent. It can also dissuade people from respecting or accepting the faith. Gandhi shares how his dislike towards Christianity developed:

> In those days Christian missionaries used to stand in a corner near the high school and hold forth, pouring abuse on Hindus and their gods. I could not endure this. I must have stood there to hear them once only, but that was enough to dissuade me from

repeating the experiment. About the same time, I heard of a well known Hindu having been converted to Christianity. It was the talk of the town that, when he was baptized, he had to eat beef and drink liquor, that he also had to change his clothes, and that thenceforth he began to go about in European costume including a hat. These things got on my nerves. Surely, thought I, a religion that compelled one to eat beef, drink liquor, and change one's own clothes did not deserve the name. I also heard that the new convert had already begun abusing the religion of his ancestors, their customs and their country. All these things created in me a dislike for Christianity.[40]

Gandhi might have had other reasons to dislike Christianity. But there is some truth in his comments. The aggressiveness of 19th century Christian missionaries can be seen in Pentecostal evangelists. One can propagate the Gospel without condemning other religious traditions. There must be change in the approach of Pentecostal evangelical activities. Today, Pentecostals do evangelism more among subaltern people groups. Since the subalterns are genuine in their approach, they embrace the faith sincerely. They may also learn aggressiveness from evangelists. It may lead to social unrest, and dissuade people to ignore the faith propagated by Pentecostals.

The life-style and community consciousness of Pentecostals will decide the future of reaching the unreached. Gandhi writes, "The pious lives of Christians did not give me anything that the lives of men of other faiths had failed to give. I had seen in other lives just the same reformation that I had heard of among Christian disciples."[41] What Gandhi indirectly asks is what the uniqueness of Christians including Pentecostals is? He might have come to the conclusion based on his experience and observation on Christians. It directly points to the fact that Christians are not genuine imitators of Christ. As a 'New Humanity in Christ' Christians including the Pentecostals must reflect the image of Jesus Christ to convince the unreached. Nirad C. Chaudhuri predicted future of Christians in India. He observed that "The wealthy and well-placed among them will become merged in the Anglicized Hindu upper middle class, with only a difference of faith, which nobody, including themselves, will take very seriously. On the other hand the majority of Indian Christians, that is those who are poor and already depressed socially, will become something like inferior castes in Hindu society."[42] This is what exactly happening now in Pentecostal community. Wealthy Pentecostals identify more with Christians of other denominations and members of other religious traditions than their co-religionalists. They reluctantly maintain social fellowship with poor Pentecostals. It has to be noted that the lack of community consciousness cannot attract a person who looks for an alternative. The subalterns who long for social support and fellowship may be discouraged to accept Pentecostalism.

We need to have new approach to conversions. Pentecostal organizations have to leave their adamant stand on the number of conversions. Charles Trevelyan is right when he says "The evangelism of India must not be measured by annual number of declared conversions."[43] Spreading the knowledge of Gospel has to be prioritized. Some groups have tendency to 'celebrate' the conversions through print and mass media. It will only provoke the religious fundamentalists. Jesus Christ is not concerned with number, but the diffusion of Gospel knowledge and quality of believers. The words of Max Muller are relevant here, "Christianity of our nineteenth century will hardly be the Christianity of India." (*Life and Letters of Max Muller,* Vol.1, pp.357-8).[44] We cannot expect that all Indians will be converted and made them the members of the Church. Yet, all can be reached with the Gospel message through different means. In the multi-religious, social and cultural context, a visible Church going Christianity may not be the Christianity of India, but Churchless, invisible Christianity which consists of people who follow Jesus Christ in their personal life but may not publically profess the faith. In this category more subalterns, particularly the Dalits who are not able to publically acknowledge their Christian identity because of legal problems involved in scheduled caste status, may be included. Instead of being inflexible in approach and in the nature of faith community, the Pentecostal evangelism must consider the social and religious niceties in a context and design a relevant form of professing faith.

The propagation of Christian religion is still considered as conspiracy of so-called Christian nations. Hence, people approach evangelism with suspicion. They wrongly assume that once they become Christians they will be denationalized. Jawaharlal Nehru rightly pointed out that "Indian converts to some of these religions never ceased to be Indians on account of a change of their faith. They were looked upon in other countries as Indians and foreigners, even though there might have been a community of faith between them... An Indian Christian is looked upon as an Indian wherever he may go."[45] The myth of conspiracy and denationalization has to be countered in the evangelism efforts. It also directly points to the need of reducing the dependency on foreign missions and sponsors. Can't Indian Christians support Indian missions? The victims of conspiracy and denationalization theory are subalterns. Dominant political and social class alleges that foreign mission agencies fund the conversion of Dalits and other subaltern communities. They also maintain the view that Dalit Christians get foreign resources needed for their advancement in society. This view badly affects the prospects of scheduled caste status to Dalit Christians. It is a fact that many Indian Churches/ Christian organizations including Pentecostals do get foreign resources. How much is spent for the empowerment of the weaker sections within a respective community remains as a big question without answer. Though majority Indian Pentecostals are poor, there are wealthy Pentecostals who can share their resources for the advancement of poor within the community. The Pentecostal evangelistic organizations which raise money within and outside the country must prioritize the empowerment of subaltern Pentecostals. In a religiously revived social context, evangelism may not bring expected result except communal tension and more stringent rules and regulations which restrict conversion. Thus, time has come to concentrate on the advancement of Pentecostals who have not yet empowered socially and economically. The Pentecostal evangelism must give attention to the disempowered Pentecostals, the unreached (socially and economically) among the reached.

It is not uncommon in the Pentecostal propagation of faith to claim that the strong holds of other religious traditions are breaking. Such claims are to make mission leaders happy. Once Max Muller said, "And yet I do not shrink from saying that their religion (Hinduism) is dying or dead. And why? Because it cannot stand in the light of the day."[46] This language is language of arrogance. What he said is actually happening in his continent, particularly in Germany, his country. More and more Christians become irreligious in Christian dominated countries. Many have already become the followers of Hindu gurus. Which religion is actually 'dying' in number and in quality nationally and globally? It is Christianity! Reaching the unreached is not possible in the framework of arrogant language and irrational claims. Before venturing into the mission of reaching the unreached, we need to think of the condition of those who are already reached, particularly the subalterns and of the present Pentecostal Christian community.

Conclusion

Has Pentecostal Christianity failed in India? Is it 'dying' qualitatively and quantitatively? Though these questions are debatable from different perspectives, some realities/truths in terms of the growth of Pentecostal Christianity and the life conditions of subalterns within Christian community can't be ignored. Apart from a few Dalit, Tribal communities, the Pentecostal Christianity has a sizable number of its adherents only among the Syrian Christians and the Nadar community in south India. The Pentecostals are very minimal among communities in North India and in North East India. Though the Pentecostal evangelists work more among Dalit and Tribal communities in North India, number of believers are very less compared to other denominations. The Pentecostal movement could attract very few people from upper castes throughout the nation. The Pentecostal Christianity of today cannot claim that it is successful in the efforts to empower its adherents to experience 'whole salvation.' Still we are influenced by 'other worldly' theological/missional outlook which looks everything through the lens of 'life after death.' It reflects in Pentecostal evangelistic endeavors. A subaltern look on reaching the unreached informs Pentecostals that 'unreached' are not simply spiritual/otherworldly category but social/ 'this worldly' category also. The unreached has to be defined in terms of Nazareth Manifesto. The 'unreached' must be reached not only with Gospel but also with resources and initiatives of empowerment. Then, Pentecostal Christianity will not fail/die in India. Subaltern look encourages us to re-define mission methods and re-route missionary journeys. Instead of being adamant in 'converting' people, we need to focus on diffusing the knowledge of Christ among them. Biblically speaking, it is through the work of Holy Spirit, one comes to faith. We cannot bring someone to Christ unless s/he responds to the Gospel through Holy Spirit. S/he can respond positively or negatively to the work of Holy Spirit. We are entrusted with the task of communicating and living out the Gospel of Jesus Christ. In reaching the unreached, we have to be theologically sound enough to respond to the inclusive religious outlook and spiritual and material self-complacency of people. The 'unreached' becomes reached when they are empowered with Gospel in all aspects of their lives. The 'reached' with Pentecostal community remain 'unreached' if they are not spiritually and socially empowered. The Pentecostal evangelism in India must an evangelism of wholistic empowerment.

Endnotes

[1] Anuradha Raman, Interview with Yellapragada Sudershan Rao, Chairman, Indian Council of Historical Research, *Outlook* (21 July, 2014), 15.

[2] Yashwant Dhote, "Streak of Violence," *Outlook* (28 July, 2014), 12.

[3] Yashwant Dhote, "Streak of Violence," *Outlook* (28 July, 2014), 14.

[4] *Sunday Times of India* (23 February 2014, New Delhi), 26.

[5] Namrata Joshi, "Soot on the Melting Pot? *Outlook* (21 July, 2014), 51.

[6] Siddharth Varadarajan, "Why can't Mr. Zaveri live where he wants?," *Sunday Times of India* (April 12, 2015, New Delhi), 12.

[7] *The Hindu* (August 19, 2014, New Delhi (Noida), 10).

[8] Mayabhushan Nagvenkar, "After A Series of U-turns, Goa turns Right," *Hindustan Times* (Monday, August 18, 2014, Lucknow), 8.

[9] *Indian Currents* (Vol XXVII/No 36, 07-13, September, 2015): 26.

[10] Tony Joseph, "A Religion That Lost The Race," *Outlook* (13 April 2015), 31.

[11] Tony Joseph, "A Religion That Lost The Race," *Outlook* (13 April 2015), 32.

[12] As a member of a Pentecostal Church the author makes his observations on the Pentecostal evangelism and the social life of Pentecostals.

[13] Prakash Yesudian, *Fishers of Men* (Chennai: RZIM Life Focus Society, 2001), 16.

[14] Samuel Jayakumar, *Mission Reader* (Delhi: ISPCK and Oxford: Regnum International, 2002), 207.

[15] Samuel Jayakumar, *Mission Reader*, 207.

[16] Leonardo Boff, *Good News to the Poor* (New York: Orbis books, 1992), 36.

[17] James Massey, *Dalit Theology: History, Context, Text and Whole Salvation* (New Delhi: Manohar, 2014), 245. It refers to Spiritual and Material aspects of salvation/liberation.

[18] Mark Juergensmeyer, *Religion as Social Vision* (Berkeley: University of California Press, 1982), 184-185.

[19] *Dr. Babasaheb Ambedkar: Writings and Speeches* Vol 5, Compiled by Vasant Moon (Bombay: Education Department, Government of Maharashtra, 1989), 438-439.

[20] Nirad C. Chaudhuri, *The Continent of Circe* (London: Chatto & Windus, 1967), 274.

[21] Arun Shourie, *Missionaries in India Continuities, Changes, Dilemmas* (New Delhi: ASA Publications, 1994), 44-45.

[22] *The Times of India* (August 28, 2014, Bhopal), 1.

[23] *The Times of India* (August 28, 2014, Bhopal), 7.

[24] Kancha Ilaih, "Productive Labour, Consciousness and History: The Dalitbahujan Alternative," in *Subaltern Studies IX*, edited by Shahid Amin and Dipesh Chakrabarty (New Delhi: Oxford University Press, 1996), 169.

[25] *The Constitution of India* (Delhi: Ministry of Law and Justice, Government of India, 1989), 12.

[26] A. G. Noorani, "Conversion to Hindu Raj," *Frontline* (January 9, 2015), 123.

[27] Faizan Mustafa and Anurag Sharma, *Conversion: Constitutional and Legal Implications* (New Delhi: Kanishka Publishers, 2003), 113.

[28] James Massey and T.K. John, eds., *Christians of Scheduled Caste Origin in India* (New Delhi: Centre for Dalit /Subaltern Studies, 2013), 163-170 & 224-226.

[29] Spiritual Salvation directly or indirectly emphasized by Christian denominations ignoring faith praxis in social realities.

[30] Tony Joseph, "A Religion That Lost The Race," *Outlook* (13 April 2015), 30.

[31] Arun Shourie, *Missionaries in India Continuities, Changes, Dilemmas*, 187.

[32] Tony Joseph, "A Religion That Lost The Race," *Outlook* (13 April 2015), 30.

[33] Devdutt Pattanaik, "Hinduism isn't a Country Club one can Waltz in and out of," *Sunday Times* (4th January 2015, New Delhi), 12.

[34] Arun Shourie, *Missionaries in India Continuities, Changes, Dilemmas*, 4.

[35] *Indian Currents* Vol XXIX/No.22 (29 May-04 June 2017), 43.

[36] Arun Shourie, *Missionaries in India Continuities, Changes, Dilemmas*, 152-153. This point is applicable to other religious traditions also.

[37] *Dr. Babasaheb Ambedkar: Writings and Speeches* Vol 5, 444.

[38] *Dr. Babasaheb Ambedkar: Writings and Speeches* Vol 5, 476.

[39] *Dr. Babasaheb Ambedkar: Writings and Speeches* Vol 5, 471.

[40] M.K. Gandhi, *An Autobiography or The Story of My Experiments with Truth* (Ahmedabad: Navajivan Publishing House, 1927 Reprint 1996), 28-29.

[41] M.K. Gandhi, *An Autobiography or the Story of My Experiments with Truth*, 113-114.

[42] Nirad C. Chaudhuri, *The Continent of Circe*, 277.

[43] Quoted in Arun Shourie, *Missionaries in India Continuities, Changes, Dilemmas*, 89.

[44] Quoted in Arun Shourie, *Missionaries in India Continuities, Changes, Dilemmas*, 139.

[45] Jawaharlal Nehru, *The Discovery of India* (London: Meridian Books Limited, 3rd Edition, 1951), 46.

[46] Max Muller, "Westminster Lecture on Missions," December 1873, in *Chips from a German Workshop*, Vol IV, pp.238-78. Quoted in Arun Shourie, *Missionaries in India Continuities, Changes, Dilemmas*, 143.

Evolution of Pentecostal Culture in South India: A Historical Discourse

Rajeevan Mathew Thomas

M an/woman is a social animal. In fact, s/he is a cultural animal too. As per the sociological and anthropological perceptions, it is the segment of culture which distinguishes human beings from animals. Every social or religious group have their own cultural traits. In fact, it is vital to note that every culture is divergent. This cultural diversity persistently brings beauty and uniqueness of culture. The Pentecostals, one of the mainstreams of global Christianity, is also having distinct cultural traits. In this article, I would like examine the cultural moorings of Pentecostals, particularly of South Indian topography from a historical point of view.

Culture: Basic Description

The word 'culture' is a quite accustomed term to all, particularly to the students of social science. People groups can claim culture but few can own civilization which is the advanced form of culture. Culture is a community product and it is the sum total of common social systems, customs, behaviour, values, identity, thoughts, ideology, transmitted from one generation to another. In other words, culture is the social personality of a people group which is internal and hereditary in nature. The comments of A. L. Kroeber and Clyde Kluckhohn would give a consensus about the culture as,

> Culture consists patterns, explicit and implicit, of and for behaviour acquired and transmitted by symbols, constituting the distinctive achievement of human groups, including their embodiments in artefacts; the essential core of culture consists of traditional (i.e., historically derived and selected) ideas and especially their attached values; culture systems may, on the one hand, be considered as products of action, on the other as conditioning elements of further action.[1]

It is also stated that, "[w]hen a group of people behave similarly and share the same institutions and ways of life, they can be said to possess a common culture."[2] Similarly, as S. K. Sharma states "[w]hen the ideals, idea, behaviours and ways of life of a group or community are, by and large, same or similar, i.e., when they share a common way or style of living, it shows their culture."[3]

Since culture is a universal phenomenon, one needs to understand the basic formative factors of culture. The scholars like T. Walter Wallbank and others comments that there are certain human needs which facilitate the universal pattern of culture and they enumerate six such requirements as:

1. The need to make a livelihood by availing food, shelter, clothing, etc.

2. The need for maintaining law and order to keep up the peace, people's protection of property and internal and external attacks, etc.

3. The requirement of generating social organization like family, marriages, government, etc.

4. The quest for knowledge and learning.

5. The need for self-expressions like arts, music, poem, dance, painting, etc.

6. The need for religious expressions like prayer, worship systems, festivals, and so on.[4]

Culture is forming whenever and wherever, men and women working as a group to satisfy the above requirements. It may vary from place to place and one group to other and, in fact, one can perceive polyphonic cultures within one region or nation. According to S. Kappen, "Culture may be described as the organic whole of ideas, beliefs, values and goals, which condition the thinking, and acting of a community or people. Understood thus, culture finds conceptual expression in ethics, philosophy and law; symbolic expression in art, literature, myth and cult."[5]All these portents to the facts that, culture is the collective social way of behaving, thinking, and doing all basic needs in a given inhabited area. The member of this society is learning all the customs, manners and perceptions from their past generations and pursuing with essential deviations.

Role of Religion in Cultural Formulation

Religion is the fundamental need of humanity which is having vertical and horizontal dimensions with God and fellow human beings. Though religion is primarily depicted as a personal affair, it has centrifugal and centripetal functions in connection with socio-cultural and nation at large. The inferences of D. S. Sarma is significant to comprehend the substance of religion and he states,

> Religion is the response of the whole being of man to the call
> of God. It is the most comprehensive of all our activities. It is
> more comprehensive than poetry, art, science, politics etc. In fact,
> religion, properly understand is not a separate activity of all, but
> something which comprehends and transcends all our activities.
> Hence, every part of our being has a place in it.[6]

Concerning the role of religion in the formation or reformation
of culture, the observations of S. Abid Hussain is notable,

> Religion in its wider sense coincides with, and goes beyond, culture
> and in its narrower sense, forms an important part of it. Where
> religion signifies the inner experience which reveals to the mind
> the real meaning and purpose of life, it is the very soul of culture;
> but where it is used for the external form in which the inner
> experience has crystalized itself, it is only a part of it. Religion as
> the inner realization of the highest truth can never be oppose to
> culture; but positive religion, when it has degenerated into mere
> form without substance, is often in conflict with culture life.[7]

The role and application of religion in the modern scientific
world has not extraneous. The remarks of Vidhya Bhushan and
D. R. Sachdeva is factual that, "[a]s long as suffering exists in
the world, the value and essence of religion is necessary. There
is much strain in modern life.... Science cannot solve all the
problems of modern life."[8] Thus, religion is a vital requisite
for humanity to meet the needs and challenges of physical and
metaphysical spheres. Here, one can affirm that religion and
culture are contributory and complimentary, and religion is one
of the formative factors of culture too. Nevertheless, it may
change its role as per the targets of its proponents. Against
the changing scenario of India it is ironical to note that, "...
In the 1880's a religious icon had once been the means to
introduced *national* unity, from the 1980's cultural nationalism
became the strategy to induce *religious unity*-cultural allegiance
to legitimize the divide between those born of the soil and
'other' minorities."[9] Thus, religion is one of the key catalysts for

the formation of culture. As Israel Selvanayagam commented, "Indian culture can convey the message of Christ as much as, and in the Indian context, even better than Western culture. We were taught to think somehow that everything Indian is evil. We did not learn to distinguish between what is of Hindu religion and what is of Indian culture it is a difficult task, but has to be attempted."[10] Thus, religion is not merely a cluster of faith and rituals, but a galaxy of values that has a profound nexus with holistic culture of its adherents.

Pentecostalism: Fundamental Discourse

The term 'Pentecostal'/'Pentecostalism' is quiet often seemed to be a tantalizing or bamboozling on the grounds of its polyphonic (mis)understanding. The very prototype or role-model of Pentecostalism has trace back to the Apostolic Church of the first century. The book of *Acts of the Apostles* and the apostolic teachings in the Epistles are the manual of Pentecostalism though it had its prophetical moorings in the Old Testament.[11] The very nomenclature 'Pentecostal' as prefix to churches was derived from the second chapter of the *Acts of Apostles*.[12] The people from Jerusalem to South India/ Kerala should replicate it with needful inculturization to make it relevant and meaningful to their polyphonic contexts.

In both theory and praxis, Pentecostalism is a movement of the Holy Spirit. According to Daniel E. Albrecht and Evan B. Howard, "[m]ore than a collection of kindred denominations and organizations, more than breakthrough of doctrine, Pentecostalism is a spiritual movement; a movement united its experience of 'life in the Spirit'."[13] According to Douglas Jacobsen, Pentecostal (to be Pentecostals) means, "one is committed to a spirit-centred, miracle-affirming, praise-oriented version of Christian faith." [14]As per the nature and functions of

Pentecostal movement and its adherents, it is further interpreted that Pentecostal community is a restoration movement, renewal movement, protest movement, and liberative movement.[15] Based on the *Book of Acts*, Pentecostal revival leads to mission. Hence, Pentecostal movement is depicted as a missionary movement.[16] It is also regarded as a global religious movement.[17] Pentecostals can be regarded as the eschatological people (Christians) who are ultimately anticipating for the Second Coming of their Lord Jesus Christ and subsequent events.

Pentecostal Culture: Basic Features

A skim survey of the basic features of Pentecostalism is vital to decipher its cultural value system. Steve Durasoff enumerates the basic features of Pentecostals as follows: (i) The Pentecostals always believe in supernatural experiences phenomena. (ii) The Pentecostals are always trying to do holy or right living. (iii) The Pentecostals are always praying and worshipping in an unknown language (other tongues). (iv) The Pentecostals are always zealous for public witnessing for Christ. (v) The Pentecostals are always challenging the traditional churches such as Lutherans, Presbyterians, Methodists and others on the issue of exercising the spiritual gifts.[18]

Similarly, Pentecostal scholars like Allan Anderson and others are deliberated Pentecostalism as an emerging religious phenomenon of modern age and they could trace out its five classical traits by analyzing its history as,

> First, there is the new form it has given to the Christian message, emphasizing the role of the Holy Spirit and creating an environment in which the gifts of the Spirit can be practiced. Second, there is its surprising numerical growth, an achievement by itself that contradicts all predictions on the supposedly secularizing effect of modernization process. Third, it is flexible: throughout its expansion this form of Christianity has shown itself to be gifted

with the capacity to adapt to the world's cultural heterogeneity while remaining loyal to its identity. It thereby represents a laboratory in which globalization process can be observed in concrete practice. It also illustrates what a religious approach to the body and to the material side of life can do. Accordingly, it has produced a rich variety of manifestations, not only in its organization, but also in its strategies and uses of communication technology. Fourth, it has been capable of attracting a wide verity of audience, each of which has selected from the rich Pentecostal repertoire and made its own adaptations. The presence of a majority of female adherents is an important characteristic of Pentecostal audience. Fifth and finally, that most Pentecostals live in Southern Hemisphere, in the heart of Christianity's new center of gravity, has contributed to its fame as a special case in the religious field.[19]

From the Kerala Pentecostal context, it is obvious that women are holding the highest membership ratio in the various local churches. They became a catalyst to bring the rest of their family members to Christian faith. The comments of Elizabeth Brusco is interesting that,

> When a man gets sick he must withdraw from his usual activities and return home so that his wife (or other female relative) can nurse him, he becomes dependant on his wife and family in a way that would be unthinkable if he were well. He is also physically suffering, and his fear of what is going to happen to him and his dependence on his wife and family combine to render him uncharacteristically receptive to their counsel. If his wife has already converted she is armed with the logic of the church to argue that his illness is the result of his *vicious* (vices) and that only by giving them up will be well again. The spectacular aspects of evangelical worship (e.g., speaking in lounges and other displays of ecstatic worship) provide further fuel to convince him of the power of the new religion.[20]

Though the modern Pentecostalism started as movement in the last century, it became a global movement with an amazing enhancement. In fact, the students of history must raise a query that what is the causation behind this growth and why people are embracing it in the midst of traditional non-Pentecostal denominations and other faiths? Almost certainly it may due to the simplicity, liberty, equality, user-friendly nature, physical and spiritual catharsis and so on. The inferences of Paul Alexander is noteworthy that,

> Emotional freedom, hopefulness, and joy seem to be as significant as any other factors in explaining why Pentecostalism is such fast- growing faith. Pentecostals see themselves as people of the Spirit, and as the song says, 'Where there is Spirit of the Lord is there is freedom', freedom to weep, freedom to dance, freedom to hope for and experience a better life. No wonder it's contagious.[21]

Thus, Pentecostalism is quite distinctive in its nature and functions predominantly guided by the Holy Spirit. In one sense, the holistic execution of the gifts and fruit of the Holy Spirit (I Cor. 12: 4-31; Gal. 5:22) and its benefits to the people is the prime stimulating factor of the propagation of Pentecostal faith and culture in South India and elsewhere.

Pentecostal Moorings in India: A Historical Synopsis

Though Christianity/Pentecostalism (Pentecostal experience?) had manifested in the first century (Acts.2), the modern Pentecostal movement had started in the 20th century. It is quite euphoria to note that India was prettily blessed to had both events hardly within the dawn of one or two decades of its emanation.[22] We can say it was a hazardous mission voyages from Jerusalem to Kerala (from God's own City to 'god's own Country'!). Here we need to scan some methodological issues (i) the enigmas of the nexus between the Azusa Street Revival and Indian Pentecostal revivals (ii) the historical starting of Pentecostal revival India (iii) Modern Pentecostal Movement: American or Global endeavour? A.C. George has pointed out two misconceptions with regards to the historical base of Pentecostal movement in India,

One incorrect notion is that Pentecostalism in India is directly linked with Azusa Street Revival of 1907[sic]. The fact that Pentecostal or Pentecostal like movements began in India nearly fifty years before the Topeka revival or the Los Angeles revival. Another false notion that needs to be rectified is that the revival that broke out in the girls Home of Mukti Mission marked the beginning of Pentecostalism in India. There are probably two reasons for this thinking. Firstly, Western historians paid very little attention to early Pentecostalism in India. This was partly because of the lack of documented history or lack of knowledge on the part of the historians. Secondly, more people have heard about "Pentecostal fire" that fell upon the girls of Pandita Ramabai's Mukti Mission because of the international publicity given to this mission.[23]

Concerning to the real historical starting of modern Pentecostals is an enigmatic issue among the emerging contemporary scholars. Until recent past, it is commonly pursuing a theory that modern Pentecostalism was 'made in' America and later extended to other nations. Nevertheless, modern scholars are refuting this theory. According to Peter Hocken, "Today an increasing number of scholars, often from other parts of the world, are insisting that the Pentecostal movement broke out in several widely disparate places at around the same, of which Azusa Street was but one".[24] As Douglas Jaccobsen comments, "It is impossible to trace the modern Pentecostal movement to any one individual or event. Instead Pentecostalism began like a rain shower with a drop of Spirit-filled faith here and a dribble of Holy Ghost fervor there scattered around the world".[25] Similarly, it is also reported that "...Pentecostal movement can be seen as acephalous (without leaders) or polycepalous (with any leaders) but not as possessing strong central leaders. Segmentation refers to the existence of many similar local group, each responsible for itself, while the idea of reticulation points to the diverse connections between segments".[26]

Pentecostalism has emerged as an antidote to the multiple socio-economic problems of the 19th and 20th centuries of India such as caste system, untouchability, feudalism, illiteracy, diseases, and so on.[27]

Pentecostal Cultural Traits in South India: Various Dimensions

The Pentecostal or any other cultural phenomena is the sum total of the amalgamation of vertical and horizontal interactions in their given context. It can be interpreted as human and divine or physical and metaphysical forces. The scholars like Andre Droogers have suggest that one can understand the diagram of culture politics of a church (Pentecostal community/ church) by applying a repertoire model based on transcendental, internal and external segments. According to him, the transcendental repertoire of believers consist their relation with God, Jesus, Spirit and Satan; the internal repertoire comprise their nexus with leadership and fellow-believers within their community; and the external repertoire constitutes their relation with outside society, culture, the people of other faith, religious and secular authorities, etc. These main repertoires are inseparable but distinguishable and reciprocal influencing collectively to formulate a corporate community culture.[28]Andrew M. Lord, argues that Pentecostal and charismatic movements have contributed for the contextualization process with their knowledge and experience with the Holy Spirit. He stated that, "The task of contextualization involves spanning the gap between church and culture... Pentecostal/Charismatic missiology can particularly contribute to the contextualization debates through its understanding in three areas: the work of the Holy Spirit, eschatology, and experience."[29]

As an insider or participant observer, the writer is intentionally giving more credentials to Kerala whenever and wherever the term South India is mentioned. The writer is subjectively argues that Kerala can be designated as the 'Capital' of South Indian classical Pentecostalism/Christianity. It is also significant to note that 'Kerala Pentecostal model' is quiet distinctive or divergent with regards doctrine of separation and its cultural moorings while comparing with other parts of India or abroad. Hence, this model is known with a nomenclature- *'Malayali Pentecostals'*!

Social Life

As stated earlier, culture is the common social way of life, one must examine the main aspects of social life of Pentecostals to decode their cultural elements. Social life of Pentecostals is typical in nature and function, which is rooted in their principle of holiness as envisaged in the scripture. Though their social perception is private and anomalous, it is not contrary to the general ethical value systems of the society or nation. The Pentecostal social or cultural life is not anti-social or anti-national but always complimentary to it. They are always tried to keep up the principles of holiness, simplicity, separation, justice, etc. in the social life.

Food and Drinks

Pentecostals have an exclusive diet culture. The quest of holiness is exercising its rheostat in it. They are always trying to avoid food and drinks offered to or by any idolatry obsession either Christian or non-Christian religious groups. Similarly, they are strictly evading food and drinks encompassing intoxications both in overtly and covertly. In fact, they are avoiding or strictly advised to avoid use of opium, ganja, tobacco, betel chewing, cigarette smoking, toddy/alcohol consumption, and so on based on the scriptural parameters.[30] Billy Graham, the world famous evangelist, responds to the issue of alcohol consumption. According to him, it destroys the relations, bring sickness, sorrow, sufferings, financial bankruptcy, etc., and strongly recommending the total abstinence on the ground of the scriptural base and also state that it is not an urgent thing to have for a healthy or gracious living of any person.[31] Similarly, the Pentecostal ethical value system rooted in their spirituality gives more importance to spiritual than of physical gratification. The use of intoxicated substances is injurious to the health of body and spirit. The inferences of Marlin D. Miller is noteworthy that,

> For the Christians, there are spiritual values that are more important than the physical satisfaction of using tobacco. When we satisfy physical appetites to harm of the body, we are sinning against God who created our body. We are spiritual beings, not physical animals. When we do something that hurts us physically, it becomes a spiritual sin.[32]

The violation of such diet and beverage rules would seriously affect their relationship with God and membership in the congregations.

During the initial years of the sprouting and spreading of Pentecostal faith in India, especially in Kerala, majority of its leaders and adherents had ate inexpensive food items due to the general economic scenario as well as the personal financial deprivation. The tapioca, jackfruits, and similar menial items were their staple foods. Even non-Pentecostal people used to mortify them by calling these food items as either prefix or suffix to address them! Nevertheless, they have no discriminations of vegetarian or non-vegetarian food items.

Common prayer before and after the common meals/table fellowships is mandatory.

Pentecostal diet and beverage systems are quiet complimentary with the canons of Indian Constitution, the corner stone of Indian nation.[33] The Pentecostal culture is respecting the rules and regulations of government with regards to the public health. The Pentecostals are not a problematic people to police and excise department. Pentecostal culture nourishes non-violence and peace-loving culture. They are peace promoting people due to the self-denial of intoxicating drinks and ingredients even at the times of religious festivals or family events including marriage, birthday parties, etc.

Comparatively Pentecostal food culture is also contributing for the sparing of foodstuffs of society up to certain extent on the ground of their fasting systems. An average believer is taking two or more times fasting per weeks.[34] Though fasting is a common Christian endeavor, Pentecostals have more profound concerns and convictions. The interpretations of Daniel E. Albrecht and Evan Howard is noteworthy,

> Even though fasting is not limited to the Pentecostal community, Pentecostals have preserved a particular use of fasting that is rare these days, although it was common among Puritans and other Protestants from the seventeenth through the nineteenth centuries. Whereas fasting often has functioned, especially among the Catholics and Orthodox Christians, as an ascetical practical practice oriented towards the purification of desire, Pentecostals see the restriction of food, following the lead of Old Testament portraits of fasting (with a nod to Acts 13:1), as a way of expressing an intensity of the pursuit of God. When Pentecostals get serious about desiring something from God, they fast, often for days at a time. This is true with regards to their personal devotions, and it is especially true of seasons of united prayer for a Holy Spirit revival.[35]

Dress and Cosmetics

The Pentecostals have their own inimitable dress codes. Generally, they are expected to wear simple and light colour dress codes. Nevertheless, they had/have been preferred to be in white cloths in the church meetings, especially on Sundays. They are envisaging white colour as holy and divine. From past to present, the pastors/ mothers are strictly advised to be in white dress in church meetings. The pastors are always appearing in white full sleeve shirt and *dhoti*. It was Pentecostals who made the white dress culture more popular in Kerala though this culture is facing a considerable eclipse within its original abode. Though this is not the integral part of the Pentecostal dogmatic or pragmatic spirituality, it gives a uniformity and external identity to them up to certain extent in the yester years. On the other hand, the traditional/classical Pentecostals are counting this as the part of their 'doctrine of separation' from the rest of the Christians or non-Christians. As Glen L. Schultz comments, "Dress is a reflection of the attitude of the heart… If a Christian is to dress in accordance to God's design he or she must first make the heart right."[36]

The Pentecostal adherents, particularly in Kerala, are noted for their elimination of gold and silver ornaments as the part of their ethical doctrine of separation. The traditional / classical Pentecostals are deliberately purging of visiting beauty parlor, using cosmetics like lipstick, coloring, nail polishing, and so on. They are also not using golden lockets like rings, chains, bangles, etc. at the important times like marriage. This is one of the external marks which distinguish Pentecostal and non-Christians in South India, especially in Kerala.

The Pentecostal believers are furnishing multiple reasons behind the self-denial of ornaments. It is depicted as the part of simplicity, to avoid the disparity between haves and have not, as the token of holiness, spirituality and so on.[37] Some even claims that they are pursuing the non- ornamental culture to make a distinction with the non-Pentecostal church believers and also to make a brake with idol worshiping systems. Yet others avoid on the grounds of economic and social causes such as using gold as dead money or causative factor for the robbery and murder and so on.

Housing and Hospitality Systems

The Pentecostal faith and practices have played an important role in the (re)formation of housing and hospitality concerns. The Pentecostal pastors are giving more importance to pastoral care to their believers usually by doing two or times house visits per months besides irregular visits in times of sickness or similar other emergencies by 'on call'. Besides these, the believers should arrange their house for prayer meetings probably two or more times in a year. As a result of it, believers are deliberately cultivating a domestic culture of creating big rooms ('prayer room'/hall) facility in each house and also keeping the visiting room/hall neat and tidy with needful furniture and other utensils to entertain their spiritual guests as the part of the hospitality. Thus, the frequent visits of pastors and the reciprocal visits of believers for family prayers and other fellowships is greatly influencing the advancement of housing and hospitality culture of Pentecostals particularly in Kerala settings.[38]

Community Organization and Festivals

The Church is the prime community institution of the Christians as well as Pentecostals. It can be regarded as the 'warehouse' and 'powerhouse' of Pentecostal community fellowship and spirituality. In Kerala it is traditionally known as 'the Faith

Home.' It denotes both the worship place and parsonage, and as this name designates, the early Pentecostal pastors led a faith life in all of their activities. Though Pentecostal church members are a healthy community, there was no serious community festivals and celebrations either Christian or non-Christian except their church gatherings both local and state levels.[39]

Economical Life

The recipients of the beginning stage of the Pentecostalism in India/Kerala were predominantly poor and mediocre families. They had been enduring economical sinking stage with the vicious circle of poverty and unemployment. It is reported that, "Pentecostalism has been a religion of the poor from its very inception whether it was in the United States or India".[40] The Dalits/low castes within and out of Christianity were embraced Pentecostalism to certain extent to have an escalation even in the socio-economical levels. Later, it pawed the way for the intruding of prosperity theology which came to the Pentecostal churches in the last decades of the 20th century and is spreading present days. Prosperity theology generally rests on following biblical beliefs and theological arguments that function like *meta-principles* in the movement. These core beliefs resonate to varying degrees with most prosperity proponents. First of all, prosperity teachers claim that the curse on creation that resulted from Adam's disobedience as well as the curse of the law that results from human disobedience has been eradicated through the death and resurrection of Jesus Christ (Gen 3:1ff; Deut. 28:1ff; Rom 5:1-11; Gal 3:10-11, 13-14).The curse has been reversed and now the children of God live under the original blessing of creation. Secondly, it is believed that the material and spiritual blessings of Abraham are now available to those who are in Christ (Gen 12:1-3; Gal 3:16, 26-29). The blessing of Abraham is holistic in that it provides both the spiritual and material needs. Thirdly, according to Jesus the heavenly Father cares for His children about earthly needs and desires. His children can ask God to meet their needs so long as certain criteria are met and it is reasonable to expect God to meet these needs (Matt 6:25-33; Luke 11:9-13; John 15:7-8). Thus, prosperity teachers believe God does not receive glory from the physical and material suffering or poverty of His children. If earthly fathers and mothers bless their children, why should one's heavenly Father continually allow His covenant children to suffer and lack materials things? Instead, God is understood to receive glory as a result of the children's health and prosperity.[41]

Traditionally, the Pentecostals of Kerala are economical in income and expenditure. They are not profligates due to their special spiritual and ethical life principles. The absence or alienation from social festivals, non-purchasing of cosmetics and ornaments of gold and silver, self-denial of intoxicative drinks, court cases, luxuries, gambling, etc., are contributing behind this economical life of Pentecostals. They perceive that money or similar items are the gifts of God, and in fact, they are saving and spending it with the fear of God. Thus, the spirituality of Pentecostals are envisioning and empowering themselves to personal/family saving.

Moral Life

The Pentecostals are particular about their moral principles. Their doctrine of holiness or doctrine of separation demands staunch moral efforts from its aficionadas both in their public and private life. M. Stephen narrates it as follows,

> Pentecostals feel that they are separated people. Betel-chewing, smoking and consuming intoxicants are prohibited among them. Homosexuality, lesbianism, premarital sex, extramarital sex and

incest are serious moral problems for them. Divorce and remarriage
are not permitted unless there are adequate reasons....Remarriage
are permitted only if the partner is dead. Pentecostals recognize
the sacramental aspect of marriage and emphasis the indissolubility
of marriage. Abortion, sterilization, contraception, euthanasia
and the use of artificial means of overcome childlessness are not
generally promoted.[42]

There is a close nexus between spirituality and morality, and
it would continuously shape or reshape the cultural standards
and values. According to Konard Raiser, "Churches and their
members are seen as the 'moral agents' who participate in
and influence the discourse on public policy."[43] The doctrine
of separation should not be a separation or animosity with
other denominations to be a scandal to the unity of the body
of Christ. Alike, it should not be a farewell to the secular or
the people of other faith to dismantle the cultural identity and
unity. It is acting as a fencing to keep up the moral standard
of the Pentecostals. It can be regarded as the fulcrum of their
unique existence.

Social Inclusion of the People at the Margin

Pentecostalism develops a culture of social inclusion of the
excluded people groups in the society such as Dalits, tribals,
women and others. Pentecostal Church is the fulcrum of their
inclusion theory and praxis. The observations of M. Stephen,
one of the emerging Pentecostal theologian from Kerala, is
vital to decode this fact as,

> Pentecostalism advocates an open church. It entertains people from
> all classes, castes and races if they accept Jesus Christ as Lord and
> believe in the exercise spiritual gifts. The Pentecostal movement
> affirms the fact that the church is not meant for a particular
> group or class. It is meant for all, including the marginalized. It
> is interesting to note that the Pentecostal churches in India have
> been very keen on giving membership to those who belong to

the so-called lower castes, the Dalits. Pentecostals have accorded them honour and dignity…Pentecostalism does emphasize human dignity, equality and fraternity. Brotherhood is an important factor among its followers. They uphold the feeling of oneness, and caring and sharing. Pentecostalism promotes the understanding of 'Koinonia.' It is important to mention that Pentecostalism has contributed much to reduce caste feeling in our society… Pentecostalism promotes women's participation in all spheres. Women have the freedom to share their testimony, to preach, to sing and to exercise their spiritual gifts such as the gift of prophecy.[44]

Therefore, one can infer that Pentecostalism is an open ended community with ample message of egalitarianism. Similarly, the inference of V. V. Thomas, one of the emerging Pentecostal historian, is also portents the Dalits inclusion to Pentecostalism that, "Although conversion to Christianity gave the Dalits an outlet to break out the caste oppression that they had been experiencing, their hopes of a total transformation was shattered even in the mainline churches. In fact the Dalits Christians from other mainline churches embraced Pentecostalism in the context of marginalization within their own churches."[45]Thus, the moral or ethical concerns of Pentecostalism are escalating its public utility and desirability.

Aesthetic Life

Different art forms, literature etc., are the basic ingredients of aesthetic life and culture of the people around globe. According to S. Kappen,

Aesthetic creation consists in letting truth unveil itself in sensuous forms or, more correctly, in letting sensuous forms reveal themselves as truth. The form may of tone (music), word (literature), colour (painting), or gestures (dance, drama). In works of art the deeper meaning of reality assumes tangible, visible, audible shapes. Where the meaning has found an adequate form it shines forth and the shining forth of meaning or truth is what we call beauty.[46]

As per our study, it is vital to examine how far Pentecostals contributed towards the development of various art forms and literature and what is their identity or perception on it? The comments of Mathew Daniel, one who studied the topic of Kerala Christian culture, argues that the Kerala Christian community in modern times were showed almost a negative attitude towards art forms and the church leadership were busy with the founding of institutions and similar concern. In fact, they did not distillate on the field of arts and we can claim only individual contributions in this field.[47] In one sense, it is appropriate to argue that the Pentecostals are discriminatory with regards to the reception of art forms and the genres of literature towards their religious/spiritual aspects.

Arts and Sports

The Pentecostal contributions to different art forms like sculpture, architecture, paintings, icons, drama, dance and other martial arts are quite desolate on the ground of their doctrine of separation and holiness principles. Every religion is envisaging the art forms in and around their worship centres: temples, Mosques, Churches, etc. Usually all these are adorned with fabulous monuments of art works including divine or human icons from ancient times to the present.[48] Nevertheless, the church buildings of Pentecostals are not swayed with any aesthetic touch just like of the other Christian denominations like Syrians or Catholics of Kerala. It is more or less similar to a conference hall or house. According to their perception, human heart is the temple of God and the worship centre/ Church is not His abode and in fact, the Pentecostals are not giving any special sanctity to their church building like the Christians of traditional churches. Similarly, the Pentecostals are keeping quite antipathy to the veneration of any icons due to their ardent dogmatic and pragmatic principles resolved from scripture. Meanwhile, the traditional churches are very fervently venerating the phantasmagorias and pictographs of Jesus, Mary and other saints. The Pentecostals are not only contesting these practices but also not even keeping the Cross in or out of their churches. Thus, Pentecostal culture is not artistic but pietistic in colour and flavour. Hence, the role and contributions of Pentecostals to the promotion of art forms are hardly to showcase in the annals of the South India or beyond. Watching the films, circus, dance, etc., are also regarded as social sins by Pentecostals as per the 'doctrine of Separation'.[49]

Music

Music is one of the important art forms in every culture. Paul Poovanthingal is right when he asserts the efficacy of the music towards the culture that "The culture of any country is intrinsically related to its religion, art and literature. Therefore Indian music is an essential part of Indian culture".[50] Among the various art forms, the music has received a special momentum from the heart and hands of Pentecostals. It is obvious that the Pentecostals have no proper written or unified liturgical songs or chanting. Nevertheless, Pentecostal people are largely using songs, especially worship songs. In the Pentecostal worship, believers are singing congregational songs as well as personal songs in connection with their sharing of testimonies. As Apostle Paul instructs, "... with psalms and hymns and spiritual songs, singing and with all your hearts making music unto the Lord; and at all times for all things give thanks to God."(Ephesians 5:19-20; *cf.*, Psalms. 40:3; 108: 3). Thus, the Pentecostals songs are popularly known as 'spiritual songs'. Majority of these songs are revival songs.[51] The traditional Pentecostals always tried to bifurcate/ scrutinize the songs into secular or worldly and sacred or spiritual ones. For instance, Pentecostals are strictly prohibited to sing film songs and it is counted as a sign of perversion of their faith traditions. Bible is not against music. As Dennis W. Mills comments, "Music is more than lyrics, rhythm, melody, and harmony. It includes the listener's personality and perception of the attitudes and lifestyle of the performer…as Christians; we are warned not to participate in evil. If some music or performers are identified with nihilism, violence, sexual promiscuity, and drugs, we are to avoid them."[52] Thus the 'baptised music' is the prime art form nurtured by the Pentecostals in Kerala. It is not appreciated on the ground of their aesthetic or self-expressions but only on the efficacy of spiritual endeavour.

The perception of Pentecostals towards the sports, games and martial arts is quite lethargic or abhorrence in nature. The traditional Pentecostals are courting these as a syndrome of spiritual eclipse or the falling into worldly love. They are preventing their children/youths from participating in these programmes of their local or cities even at the time of national festivals of Kerala like *Onam* and subsequent programmes. Some of the orthodox Pentecostal parents/leaders are even discouraging their students/youths from joining in local arts and sports clubs out of their fear of spiritual dismantling. Nevertheless, the Pentecostal contemporary children/ youths are daring to express their disruptions and aversions towards the 'holy restrictions' to keep aloof from their peer groups.[53] Thus, they are in between their own traditional culture and the emerging culture of the society.

Literature

The quality and quantity of the creation of literature is the legacy of cultural development of a community or nation.

It includes both secular and sacred segments and it is the brainchild of community. As we know Christianity is religion of the scripture, in one sense, the overall literary contributions of Pentecostals are motivated by and focused towards scripture with special emphasis to the doctrine of Holy Spirit. They have produced hagiographical literature, auto biography, biography, commentaries, homilies, dogmatic books, historical books, song books etc. are the main literature of traditional Pentecostals. Journals and magazines/news letters of various mission organizations, churches, seminaries of Pentecostals are mushrooming day by day.

The Pentecostals are keeping a bifurcation of literature into secular and sacred ones. They are practicing some sort of repulsion towards the diverse branches of secular literature like novels, fictions, poems, etc. Comparatively, they are neither composing nor reading them in a respectable scale. They did not produce any serious such literary pieces or men/women of letters to be acknowledged or even criticized by secular literary experts. Though there are highly educated professionals and academicians among the Pentecostals, they did not resume to these literary public sphere by keeping them as a 'spiritual islands' due to the lack of visionary encouragements from the church leaderships. Hence we have only few handful people to quote sporadically in this trajectory.[54] Thus, it is one of the failures of Pentecostals who did not excel themselves in these areas to enhance their cultural legacies.

Education

Like literature, learning is also an integral part of culture of a community. The culture itself is the sum total of the customs and manners of a community learned from their predecessors. Just like the non-Pentecostal churches, the Pentecostals are giving compulsory religious education on Sundays (Sunday school) with a syllabus covering Bible and basic Christian doctrines. As Zenas J. Bicket states, "Christian education begins in the home, continues in the church and church school, and is advanced in the halls of Christian higher education."[55] It is compulsory to all children of the Pentecostal families to lay the moorings of basic Christian/Pentecostal faith. It is quite euphoria to record that the emerging Pentecostal theological scholars are attempting to bring out lot of theological treaties and research reports.[56] As Miguel Alvarez states, "...Pentecostal education is not interested in offering purely academic programs. It aims to prepare students mentally, emotionally, spiritually, and practically."[57]

Pentecostals are giving importance to secular education besides the spiritual/religious education. Comparing with the people of other faiths, Christians particularly the Pentecostals are very fervent to give maximum education to their children irrespective of their economic or social status. They do strongly believe in the divine blessings and education is counted as a means for it. The reading/studying of the Bible at home and Sunday school has greatly influencing and motivating the Pentecostals to impart education to their offspring.

In one sense, the Pentecostals have been focussing on starting of Bible schools/colleges/seminaries in Kerala. They are investing their focus and finance in it. Though there are ample opportunities under the provision of Minority Rights of Indian Constitutions, their contributions to the establishing of public education schools/ colleges/medical and technical institutions are comparatively almost barren except few numbers. Lack of visionary leaderships and guidance, the negligence or ignorance of social obligations, the rigid bifurcations of secular/worldly and sacred sectors, imminent eschatological anticipations, financial shortages, etc., can be regarded as the causative factors behind this paucity. Thus Pentecostals are delimitated to the consumers rather than of producers of educational endeavours.

Historical Appraisal: Select Issues

From the above historical discourse, one should examine whether Pentecostal/ Christian culture is contributory or contradictory to national culture. Is it promotes local or indigenous culture or foreign or global culture? Are they exclusive or inclusive? Is it flexible or rigid? The present Pentecostal Christians are the hybridity of traditional and modern cultural trajectories. The hidden tensions between the traditional orthodoxy and modern cultural influences are ultimately causing for the emergences 'New Generation' Pentecostal movements. Culture is always mutable. Any institutions, movements, systems and people groups are ought to amicable with the changing cultural traits to be relevant to the time. Change and continuity is a natural principal that all must pursue.

Pentecostal Culture in the Age of Globalization: Degenerating or Regenerating?

Present era is depicted as the era of Globalization. It is directly or indirectly affecting the cultural systems of the religious and other spheres of human life in the global scale. According to Konard Raiser,

> In its most generalized form, globalization reinforces interdependence between people and societies, including their culture and religions. Hither to self-contained and more or less homogenous cultural and religious spaces are being opened up, leading to increased interaction. As consequence, truth claims are relativized and new religious movements emerge together with more fluid contours of religious identities. Globalization in this

sense is a direct cause of the increase in the religious plurality that has begun to manifest itself in all parts of the world.[58]

The history of Pentecostal culture is influencing more or less similar in the above trajectories. The globalization offers ample avenues to sprout and spread lot of new movements within Pentecostal spectrum including the new generation churches. Nevertheless, Pentecostalism offers a global culture. Under this scenario, globalization is contributing slightly towards the degeneration of the classical or traditional Pentecostal cultural legacies. Globalization demonstrates a global market culture. It is always longing to transform the traditional forms of work, family, society and community life. Certain extent it dismantled the traditional belief systems and moral parameters particularly in the Pentecostal cultural milieu. Some people count it as a the demonstration of the progress. But others cry that it is the erosion of traditional values.[59]

The Question of Denominational Plurality: Division or Diversity?

As per the Trinitarian economy of God as well as the creation account of Genesis, one can straightforwardly imbibe that division is anti-divine, anti-human and, even a 'sin' from Christian perception. Nevertheless, the history of global Christianity is the history of unity and disunity; union and disunion; divergences and convergences. But it is the obligation of Christians to withstand unity in diversity or even uniformity to keep up the meaning of 'church as the body of Christ'. The churches should keep on exercise the inter-confessional and ecumenical praxis or more beyond until reaching to the optimum consensus of organic unity model by asphyxiating the theological and non-theological factors including pugnacious denominational plurality. The diversity is the minimum ratio of the maximum target of unity. It can be called as the 'lesser evil' or the 'baptized form' of division. Traditionally, the global Christianity has been divided by the historians into three main segments (i) the Roman Catholic Church (ii) the Eastern Orthodox churches (iii) the protestant churches. The scholars like Timothy Tennent counts that the Pentecostals and Charismatic groups constitute the fourth branch of Christianity.[60] But even the Pentecostals are also divided into several denominations. However, they possess certain uniformity. Their life styles are more or less similar. In fact one can see that denominational plurality within and outside of the Pentecostal orbit is a 'necessary evil'!

Question of Conversion and National Culture

Does conversion in Christianity as well as in Pentecostal streams an impediment or sabotage to the sustenance of national culture? According to Bruce Nicholls, "The gospel must penetrate and transform every level of culture... If conversion to Christ does not lead to change at every level of one's culture, it is not true conversion."[61] It is observed that conversion leads to brotherhood and also minimize the caste discriminations.[62] In fact, genuine and volunteer conversion under the provision of the Indian constitution and the Scripture would not hinder the uniqueness of the Indian culture.

When we are doing an analytical study of Indian culture, one can identify that many of the essential elements of Pentecostals are quite similar to Indian culture. Indian culture is not a material culture alone. The spirituality is regarded as the essence of Indian culture. The Indian nation and her culture are entrenched in religion and spirituality. The quest for Non-violence and peace / *shanty*, the quest for *satayam, shivam* and *sundaram* , the spirit of toleration, etc., are the cardinal features of Indian culture.

From past to present, India (or the actual Hinduism) is noted for the spirit of religious/spiritual toleration and communal harmony. The advent of various foreign religions like Judaism, Zoroastrianism, Christianity, Islam to India from the period of B.C. to A.D., the sprouting and spreading of native religions including the Protest religions like Jainism and Buddhism, the peaceful co-existence of various religious people and their worship centres like Temples, Synagogues, Churches, and Mosques etc. are corroborating this fact. India is not a theocratic State but secular State. Similarly, Pentecostals are also noted for their toleration which is an inbuilt quality envisioned by Jesus and apostles.[63] Even in the midst of severe persecutions and anti-Christian violent assaults in the different parts of our nation, the Pentecostals are enduring all these without any revulsion and revenge from past to present.[64] In fact, the Pentecostals through their life and mission proved that optimum tolerance is possible to enhance India's hallmark of the tolerance culture.

Whether Pentecostal culture promote Western Culture is an another question to be addressed. According to Paul Poovanthingal, "It is a fact that native Christians in India have been sandwiched between the western and Indian culture".[65] Similarly, L. Anthony Savariraj has also commented that, "It may not be an overstatement that Christianity in India has exhibited more of an institutional identity than a religious or cultural identity. More often than not, Christians are considered to be outsiders, having an allegiance to a foreign institution."[66] Pentecostal identity is both complementary and contributory to Indian culture. Cornelis Bennema states three basic features of Christian identity:

> First, the Christian identity is a religious identity that is not attached to a particular geopolitical entity (a nation), ethnicity or culture. Second, it is an inclusive transformational identity that transcends, absorbs, affirms, relativizes, pervades, rather than abrogates, existing identities. Third, it is a unifying identity that directs the various identities towards Christ.[67]

Cultural indifference is a danger. No religion or movement can be surviving long without being linked with native culture. Francis Vincent Antony suggests the need of inculturation and interculturation to avoid the danger of cultural isolation, and also to attain a mature identity of 'fully Indian and fully Christian'. He states, "The growth of Indian Church is not just of a question of increasing the number of baptized or of the church building, but is a matter of forming mature Christians capable of integrating their faith and their indigenous culture in their day to day life, thus offering credible and relevant witness to the Gospel message in the changing context of India".[68]According to Bruce Nicholls, "Christianity is a prophetic faith which judges all of culture, rejecting in every facet of culture what is contrary to its understanding of God and His law and transforming what is not contradictory to His general and special revelation."[69] And he further states, "Our task is to work towards truly Christian cultures which manifest both the universality of the gospel and the fruit of the Holy Spirit and the same time reflect the particularity of the national cultures refined by the Word of God."[70] Here, we need to understand that Christian or Pentecostal culture is not anti-national culture but a counter-culture or a corrective culture working without harming the national culture. It is not against the contextualization or indigenization.

Concluding Remarks

Let me sum-up the discourse on the culture of south Indian Pentecostals with following observations:

(i) The Pentecostals are the exclusive Christians among the total Christians on the ground of the antiquity and continuity of apostolic faith and practices of the first century.

(ii) They claim that they are pious Christians who are giving actual importance to the Holy Trinity both in theory and in praxis.

(iii) The Pentecostalism with their unique doctrine of pneumatology is the 'software' or 'operating system' of the hardware of Christianity.

(iv) The configuration and ramification of the parameters of Pentecostal culture is rooted in and around the gifts and fruit of the Holy Spirit. It distinguish them from other Christian streams.

(v) It is the life blood/the spirit/ personality of proper Christianity (body of Christ) envisaged by Jesus and the apostles.

(vi) Pentecostalism is the inherent culture of Christianity. Nevertheless, Pentecostals are often misunderstood and misinterpreted due to the lack of the first-hand knowledge and experience of Pentecostalism by their opponents.

(vii) Pentecostals are the exclusive Christian people and 'Pentecostalism' is their culture.

(viii) Pentecostalism is a private culture or the sub-culture which is not a harmful to the national culture.

(ix) South Indian Pentecostal culture is distinct on the ground of the theory and praxis of their 'non-scriptural' doctrine of separation particularly the issue of white dress code, mustache and so on.

(x) South Indian Pentecostal cultural attributes are proliferating the common culture of India – 'unity in diversity'.

In short, Pentecostalism is primarily an experience of true Christians beyond the denominationalism. It is true that Pentecostal culture is distinctive than the general culture of the Christians on the ground of the due emphasis of Holy Spirit: its fruit and gifts. Pentecostalism promotes a global culture/ trans-national culture. Pentecostalism has never promotes a religious or communal nationalism too. Nevertheless, there is no pan-India /Asia/West Pentecostal culture on the ground of the adoption and adaption of local or native culture. Thus, one can observe a 'unity in diversity 'and 'diversity in unity' in the trajectory of Pentecostal culture. The South Indian, especially Kerala Pentecostals are giving emphasis to the doctrine of separation with or without scriptural basis. Hence, it should be re-defined in the changing world without losing the scriptural moorings to be relevant in the cotemporary scenario. Meanwhile, all Christian denominations ought to do a critical re-examination to decipher how far they are devoted to, or deviated from Apostolic/New Testament Church before mortifying or gratifying Pentecostals/Pentecostalism.

Endnotes

[1] A. L. Kroeber and Clyde Kluckhohn, *Culture: A: Critical Review of Concepts and Definitions* (Cambridge: M. Museum, 1952), 181.

[2] T. Walter Wallbank, Alastar M. Taylor and Nels M Bailkay, *Civilization: Past and Present* (Glenview, Illinois: ScothForesman and Company, 1967), 5.

[3] S. K. Sharma, *Society and Culture: An Indian Perspective* (Gurgaon: Shubhi Publications, 2003), 76.

[4] T. Walter Wallbank, Alastar M.Taylor and Nels M Bailkay, *Civilization: Past and Present*, 5.

[5] S. Kappen, *Towards a Holistic Cultural Paradigm* (Tiruvalla: CSS, 2003), 79.

[6] D. S. Sarma, *Essence of Hinduism* (Bombay: Bharatiya Vidya Bhavan, 1971), 5.

[7] S. Abid Hussain, *National Culture of India* (Delhi: National Book Trust, 1987), 3.

[8] Vidhya Bhushan and D.R.Sachdeva, *An Introduction to Sociology* (Allahabad: KitabMahal, 1995), 675.

[9] Geethi Sen, "National Culture and Cultural Nationalism," in *India: A National Culture?*, edited by Geethi Sen (New Delhi: Sage Publications, 2003), IV. Emphasis original

[10] Israel Selvanayagam, *Samuel Amritham's Living Theology* (Bangalore: BTESSC/SATHRI, 2007), 699.

[11] In one sense, Pentecostalism or Pentecostal experience based on the work of the Holy Spirit is the fulfillment of Old Testament Prophesies: Dream of Mosses,(Numbers 11: 29); Prophecy of Joel 2:28-29) and also promise of Jesus (Lk. 24:49;Acts 1:8)

[12] See, Henri Gooren, "Conversion Narratives," in *Studying Global Pentecostalism: Theories and Methods*, edited by Allan Anderson, Michael Bergunder, Andre Droogers and Cornelis Van der Lann (London: University of California Press, 2010), 99.

[13] Daniel E. Albrecht and Evan B. Howard, "Pentecostal Spirituality," in *The Cambridge Companion to Pentecostalism*, edited by Cecil M. Robeck, Jr. and Amos Young (New York: Cambridge University Press), 235.

[14] Douglas Jacobsen, *Thinking in Spirit: Theologies of Early Pentecostal Movement* (Bloomington: Indiana University Press, 2003), 12.

[15] See, M. Stephen, *Towards A Pentecostal Theology and Ethics* (Kottayam: Chraisthava Bodhi, 1999), 3-4.

[16] Roger E. Hedlund, "Critique of Pentecostal Mission by a Friendly Evangelical," *AJPS* 08/01(2005):68ff.

[17] Birgit Meyar, "Pentecostals and Globalization," in *Studying Global Pentecostalism: Theories and Methods...*, 116ff.

[18] See the details, Steve Durasoff, *Bright Wind of the Spirit: Pentecostalism Today* (London: Holder &Stoughton, 972), 1-12.

[19] Allan Anderson, Michael Bergunder, Andre Droogers and Cornelis Van der Lann, "Introduction," in *Studying Global Pentecostalism: Theories and Methods*, 3.

[20] Elizabeth Brusco, "Gender and Power," in *Studying Global Pentecostalism: Theories and Methods*, 89-90.

[21] Paul Alexander, *Signs & Wonders: Why Pentecostalism is the World's Fastest Growing Faith* (San Francisco: J.B.A.W. Imprints, 2009), 149.

[22] Both these peaceful infiltrations were manifested under the 'Pax-Romano' (Roman peace under Roman Rule) and 'Pax-Britanica' (British peace under British colonial rule). See, A.M .Mundadan, *History of Christianity in India: From the Beginning up to the Middle of the Sixteenth Century.* Vol.-I (Bangalore: TPI, 1989), 1ff. *cf*, C.B. Firth, *An Introduction to Indian Church History* (Delhi: ISPCK, 2000), 1-17; Saju Mathew, *Kerala Pnecostu Charitram(Malayalam)[Kerala Pentecostal History]*, (Kottayam: Good News Publications,1994),1ff.

[23] A.C. George, *Trailblazers for God: A History of the Assemblies of God of India*(Bangalore: SABC, 2004), 29-30.

[24] Peter Hocken, *The Challenges of the Pentecostal, Charismatic and Messianic Movements: The Tensions of the Spirit* (Farnham: Ashgate Publishing Limited, 2009), 12.

[25] Douglas Jaccobsen, *Thinking in Spirit: Theologies of Early Pentecostal Movement...*, 16.

[26] See, Joel Robbins, "Anthropology of Religion," in *Studying Global Pentecostalism: Theories and Methods...*, 162.

[27] Se the details, V.V. Thomas, *Dalit Pentecostalism: Spirituality of the Empowered Poor* (Bangalore: ATC, 2008), 79ff.

[28] See the details, Andre Droogers, "Cultural Dimension of Pentecostalism," in *Cambridge Companion to Pentecostalism...* 208-211.

[29] Andrew M. Lord, "Holy Spirit and Contextualization", *AJPS* O4/02(2001):209.

[30] See, Leviticus 10:9; Proverbs 20:1; Ephasians 5:18; I Timothy 3:3.

[31] See the details, Billy Graham, *Answers to Life's Problems* (Waco, Texas: World Books, 1970), 70.

[32] It is reported that the cigarette smoking holding around 4,000 chemicals among them, 40 are causing for Cancer and others are poisonous. See, Marlin D. Miller, "Should Christians or Anyone Smoke Tobacco?," in *Handbook for Christian Living...*, 286.

[33] See the provision from Articles 136 of the Indian Constitution.

[34] Select people used to take one week/one moth complete fasting as per their personal decisions. It is not fallacious to claim that it is Pentecostals who made the 'fasting prayer' as a common Christian experience in Kerala and rest of the world at large. It is one of the brand traits of Pentecostal spirituality.

[35] Daniel E. Albrecht and Evan Howard, "Pentecostal Spirituality," in *Cambridge Companion to Pentecostalism*, 240.

[36] Glen L. Schultz, "What Biblical Standards Should Christians Follow Concerning Clothing?," in *Handbook for Christian Living…*,62.

[37]Interview with Chenkulam Podiyachan, Prophet and Pastor, Chenkulam, Kottarakkara, 15th October,2017.

[38] 1Timothy, Hebrew 6.

[39] It is significant to note that the traditional Pentecostals are neither celebrates national festivals like *Onam,* etc. nor celebrates the Christian festivals like Good Friday, Easter, Christmas and so on. Their conventions are their spiritual celebrations. Each Pentecostal denomination has its own conventions: Kumband Conventions-IPC, Punalur AG. Conventions, Tirvalla Sharon Fellowship, and so on.

[40] See, V.V. Thomas, *Dalit Pentecostalism: Spirituality of the Empowered Poor*, 282.

[41] Lewis Brogdon, *The New Pentecostal Message?: An Introduction to the Prosperity Movement* (Bangalore: SAIACS, 2016),36.

[42] M. Stephen, "Pentecostalism and Christian Ethics," *SATHRI Journal* ix/2 (Oct, 2015): 106.

[43] Konard Raiser, *For a Culture of Life: Transforming Globalization and Violence* (Tiruvalla: CSS/ISPCK/WCC, 2003), 151.

[44] M. Stephen, "Pentecostalism and Christian Ethics", *SATHRI Journal* ix/2(October, 2015):105.

[45] V. V. Thomas, *Dalit Pentecostalism: Spirituality of the Empowered Poor*, 391.

[46] S. Kappen, *Towards a Holistic Cultural Paradigm* (Tiruvalla: CSS, 2003), 82.

[47] The Christians in South India, particularly in Kerala, during the ancient Persians and Portuguese colonial period (1498-1947) had produced lot of church buildings, images, Christianised dances, music, martial arts, and so on. It has received an eclipse in the modern age. See, Mathew Daniel, *Kerala Christava Samskaram (Malayalam) [Kerala Christian Culture]*, 153-154.

[48] See, Mathew Daniel, *Kerala ChristavaSamskaram (Malayalam)* [*Kerala Christian Culture*], 140-145.

[49] See, Sharon R. Jerry, " Should Christians Dance?," in *Handbook for Christian Living...*,74-76.

[50] Paul Poovanthingal, "Christian Music with Reference to India," in *History of Science, Philosophy and Culture in Indian Civilization*, volume-VII, Part-6,515.

[51] The Pentecostals are learning charismatic and congregational songs. They are mainly focusing on topics of Christian hope, second coming of Christ, Holy Spirit, etc. When we analyse the Malayalam songs of Pentecostals, one can understand their theology, anticipations, etc. They are not only learning the traditional songs but also new songs. The different Pentecostal denominations are availing their freedom to publish new song books. See, EBC, *Zion Gheethavali*, revised 18th editions (Kadumthurunthe: EBC, 20030), 1ff.

[52] Dennis W. Mills, "What Biblical Criteria Should Christians Follow when Listening To, or Performing Music?," in *Handbook for Christian Living...*, 221.

[53] The present writer could grasp certain problems of Pentecostal children and youths through group discussions. They argue that they are facing some sort of discriminations and mortifications from their classmates for not mingling with them. The Pentecostals are not advised to imitate thehairstyle, trendy dress models and so on. Hence, many are prefer to attend the new generation churches than their own old churches.

[54] *Palamthettiyathivanti*, by Pfo.Ezhamklam Samkutty.

[55] Zenas J. Bicket, "What is the Biblical Basis for Christian Colleges and Universities?," in *Handbook for Christian Living: A Resource Manual for Applying God's Truth in a Mixed-up World*, edited by Paul A. Kienel (Nashville: Thomas Nelson Publishers, 1991), 53.

[56] For the details of the Pentecostal authors and books, check the catalogues of major publishing companies like ISPCK, and similar others. One can also check the list of gradates of Senate of Serampore College (University).

[57] Miguel Alvarez, "Distinctive of Pentecostal Education," *AJPS* 3/2 (2000): 286.

[58] Konard Raiser, *For a Culture of Life: Transforming Globalization and Violence*, 151.

[59] See Harvey G. Fox, "Pentecostalism and Global Culture: A Response to Issues Facing Pentecostalism in a Post modern world," in *The Globalization of Pentecostalism: A Religion Made to Travel*, edited by Murray W. Dempster, Byron D. Klaus and Douglas Petersen (Oxford: Regnum Books, 1999), 389.

[60] Timothy Tennent, *Invitation to World Missions: A Trinitarian Missiology for the Twenty-first Century* (Grand Rapids: Kernel, 2010), n.p.,cited in Simon Samuel, "Pentecost/al Charismatism: '... What This Would Come To?" *SATHRI Journal*, ix/02 (October, 2015):18.

[61] Bruce Nicholls, "A Living Theology for Asian Churches: Some Reflections on the Contextualization Syncretism Debate," in *Biblical Theology in Asia*, edited by Ken Gnanakan (Bangalore: TBT, 1995), 22.

[62] Samuel Jayakumar, "Dalits and the Mission of the Church" in *Mission Agenda-II*, edited by Ezra Sargunam (Chennai: Mission Education Books, 2006), 65.

[63] Jesus' teachings on the obligations of His followers to pursue forgiveness, peace building, loving opponents, meekness, etc. in the Sermon on the Mount motivate to keep up the toleration towards others. See, Mathew chapter 5; Romans 13:1-2.

[64] See, Anto Akkara, *Early Christians in the 21stCenturies: Stories of Incredible Christian Witnessed from Kandhamal Jungles* (Bangalore: Veritas India Books, 2013.), 1ff.

[65] Paul Poovanthingal, "Christian Music with Reference to India", in *History of Science, Philosophy and Culture in Indian Civilization*, volume-VII, Part-6, edited by A.V.Afonso (New Delhi: Centre for Studies in Civilizations,2009), 514.

[66] L. Anthony Savariraj, "The Intercultural Journey of Contemporary Indian Christianity," in *History of Science, Philosophy and Culture in Indian Civilization*, volume-VII, Part-6,400.

[67] Cornelis Bennema, "Early Christian Identity Formation and Its Relevance for Modern India," in *Indian and Christian Changing Identities in Modern India* (Bangalore: SAIACS Press, 2011), 72.)

[68] Francis Vincent Antony, "Identity, Culture and Faith: Challenges and Tasks", *KristuJyoti*, 22/1 (2006):21-22.

[69] Bruce Nicholls, "A Living Theology for Asian Churches: Some Reflections ....., 34-35.

[70] Bruce Nicholls, "A Living Theology for Asian Churches: Some Reflections ....., 34-35.

Contributors

Dr. David Shibley, M.Div., D.D. is founder and world representative of Global Advance, a ministry that has equipped more than 800,000 leaders in 100 nations to help fulfill the Great Commission. He is the author of over 20 books and writes the column, "On Their Shoulders" for *Ministry Today*. He is a graduate of John Brown University and Southwestern Baptist Theological Seminary and received an honorary doctorate from Oral Roberts University. Shibley and his wife, Naomi, have been married since 1972. They have two married sons and five grandchildren.

Dr. John Thannickal is the Founder Director of Nava Jeeva Ashram and New Life College, Bangalore. He served various institutions and became a catalyst for the National Association for Theological Accreditation (NATA). He held leadership within the Pentecostal movement in India, served on the Advisory Committee of World Pentecostal Conference for about 20 years.

Dr. M. Stephen M.A., BD., M.Th., D.Th. (Christian Theology and Ethics) is the Principal of Faith Theological Seminary, Manakala, Adoor. He has authored around 30 books in Malayalam and English. The famous publishers such as

'Concept', 'Serials' and ISPCK have published his books including *A Liberated Vision: A New Mission Agenda, Introducing Christian Ethics, A Christian Theology in Indian Context, Human Rights and Ethics of Love in Human Context,* and *Introducing Post-Modernism and Post-Colonialism.*

Dr. Rajeevan Mathew Thomas, M.A., M.Phil, PGDES, M.Th., D.Th. is the Principal and HoD of History of Christianity department at New Life Biblical Seminary, Cheruvakkal, Kollam. He frequently contributes articles to academic books and journals. He is married to Blessymole K. J and blessed with two children – Febin and Feba. Reach him at dmrt2020@ gmail.com.

Dr. Raju M. Thomas, M.Th., Ph.D. is the Post Graduate Dean and HoD of New Testament department at New Life Biblical Seminary. He is a notable Pentecostal orator and biblical expositor.

Dr. Shaibu Abraham holds a PhD in Theology from the University of Birmingham, the United Kingdom and now is on the faculty of the India Bible College & Seminary, Kerala. He is also the author of the books, *Pentecostal Theology of Liberation: Holy Spirit & Holiness in Society, The History of the Pentecostal Movements in North India* and other articles in various books and journals. He is married to Sheena and now lives in Kumbanad, Kerala.

Dr. V. V. Thomas, Professor of History of Christianity, Union Theological College, Bangalore. He served as the faculty member of several other eminent theological institutions including UBS, Pune. He is expertise in the area of Dalit Pentecostalism and published many books including *Dalit Pentecostalism: Spirituality of the Empowered Poor.*

Dr. Viju Wilson, M.Th., D.Th., Professor of Christian Theology at Union Biblical Seminary, Pune. He formerly served in different eminent theological institutions including Bethel Bible College, Guntur, Andhra Pradesh. He penned many articles and edited few academic works.

Rev. Josfin Raj S. B, M.A (English Litt. & Christian Studies) and M.Th. currently serves as the Academic Dean at New Life Biblical Seminary, Kerala, India. He authored *Inclusive Christ and Broken People: Towards a Dalit Christology in the Light of the Early Church Faith Confession* (CWI, 2018) and *Pauline Corpus: A Paradigm for the Effective Christian Journalism in Contemporary India* (ISPCK, 2013). He has contributed several articles for various theological journals and magazines presented papers in international forums like ATA Theological Consultation Manila, Philippians. He is married to Ross and has two-year-old son Jeevan. Reach him at josfinraj@gmail.com.

www.ingramcontent.com/pod-product-compliance
Lightning Source LLC
Chambersburg PA
CBHW031121030726
47496CB00002BA/630